MORE THAN MEETS THE EYE

ASTON FALLS BOOK 3

SARA JANE WOODLEY

Cover Design by
CANVAPRO

JJ & Christian art by
ARISTARH VIA DEPOSIT PHOTOS

Copyright © 2021 by Eleventh Avenue Publishing Inc.

All rights reserved.

No part of this book may be reproduced in any form or by any electronic or mechanical means, including information storage and retrieval systems, without written permission from the author, except for the use of brief quotations in a book review.

This is a work of fiction. Names, characters, business, events and incidents are the products of the author's imagination. Any resemblance to actual persons, living or dead, or actual events is purely coincidental.

www.eleventhavenuepublishing.com

A THANK YOU TO MY READERS

In August 2020, I released my first book in the Legacy Inn series. I was passionate about this project, and I was hopeful that people would like my stories as much as I loved writing them. But, I never could have imagined that I would be blessed with the most amazing community of readers!

I can't begin to tell you how thankful I am for each and every one of you. I've loved every message, email, and review, and always appreciate hearing from you. Your support and kind words have been some of the *best* parts of this journey.

To my Advance Reader Team, thank you for your incredibly valuable and consistent feedback. It means so much to me to have such a wonderful group of dedicated readers.

If you'd like to connect further, drop by my Facebook Page, Instagram or Tik Tok! I like to engage with my readers and share my book inspo, new releases, and photos of my cat's antics.

Thank you again for everything you do.

Love always,

Sara Jane

1

CHRISTIAN

If I've learned anything in life, it's that there's often more to people than meets the eye.

And as I watched Josh's round, baby-cheeked face get progressively redder, it occurred to me that he was no exception.

"I can't believe you walked out!" Josh exploded. "You left an awards ceremony honoring YOUR biggest hit. What were you thinking?!"

I wiped my face with a towel. My heartbeat was still thundering in my ears from my run on the treadmill. "Hold up, man. You *know* that's not what happened."

"It might as well have." Josh crossed his arms. "You made a fool out of me... out of Crown House Records."

He stared down his nose at me, which was difficult given his height of 5'9" compared to my 6'2". Not for the first time, I wondered how we'd gotten here. I met Josh while playing guitar on the streets of LA before my first single made it big. Back then, he was a scrawny, scraggly kid with dreams of being a music manager.

Fast forward eight years and here we were. Josh was now

working as my tour manager through the record label I'd signed with. He wore thousand-dollar suits to match his similarly-priced watch. He'd filled out thanks to a number of supplements and personal training sessions, and his teeth were alarmingly white.

Plus, those hair plugs couldn't have been cheap.

Bit by bit, the guy I'd known—the person I'd considered my friend—had been replaced with someone who cared mostly about schmoozing other artists and rising in the industry. Not that there was anything wrong with that... It just wasn't what I saw for myself.

"Josh, I didn't walk out," I said reasonably. And, it was true—I stayed longer than I intended so that I could sign autographs, talk with fans, and do that Q&A with the radio contest winners. Not that I'd tell Josh any of that—he wasn't interested in the time and energy I put into the people who supported me. "I left when the party was winding down."

He crossed his arms. "That's not the party I'm talking about."

"The after party? I'm sorry, man, I didn't think you needed me for that. I've had promo events for *I'll Be Waiting For You* every night for months. And with Christmas coming up, I know it's going to be full-on again soon. I needed a break." I slapped Josh on the back good-naturedly. "Besides, I figured you were taking the night off too. Don't you want time with the Mrs?"

"No." Josh's scowl told me that he didn't appreciate me trying to make light of the situation. "And you have no idea what you missed."

I sighed and walked towards the mini-fridge at the back of the gym. My condo was in a prestigious, luxury apartment complex in West Hollywood that catered specifically to celebrities, politicians, and other high-profile people.

The building prided itself on keeping things as quiet and low-key as possible—including being able to book one of the state-of-the-art gyms for yourself and your fitness trainer.

And, apparently, your angry tour manager.

I grabbed a cold water bottle and downed the whole thing. "Alright, tell me. What did I miss?"

Josh raised an eyebrow. "You missed Vermouth."

"Excuse me?"

"Vermouth," he said impatiently. "It's THE hottest club right now."

"I'm not really into clubbing."

"It isn't about that. There's a person you *should* have met there..."

He trailed off, eyes almost bugging out of his head. In the corner of my eye, I noticed my fitness trainer, Louie, pick up his phone. Anyone working with or around me had to sign an NDA, but I had a distinct feeling that tomorrow's tabloid headlines would read "Christian West DIDN'T Attend an All-Star Afterparty?!"

"Okay, I give. Who should I have met?"

"Annabel Burnwood." Josh waited a moment for dramatic effect. "THE Annabel Burnwood."

I frowned. I'd met Annabel a few times. Nice girl, always smiling. She was only a couple of years younger than me, but she reminded me of a hyped-up, overdramatic kid sister. In the past few months, her popularity had exploded thanks to her sweet, down-to-earth country melodies. Going viral on YouTube didn't hurt either. "What about her?"

"Her world tour! She's basically sold out of pre-sale tickets. Have you forgotten that our one and only focus right now is to get you as a featured guest on her tour?"

I refrained from rolling my eyes. It was tough to keep up

with Josh's "one and only focus" when it changed on the daily.

"Last night was *supposed* to be the next step in your career," Josh huffed. "Getting in with Annabel is our way to move forward. Don't you want to be successful?"

I snorted, couldn't help myself. "Depends how you define success. I didn't come from much. My mom worked hard to make sure we had everything we needed growing up, and I spent a lot of my teens scrimping and saving and working odd jobs around school hours." My fingers clasped the silver chain I always wore around my neck. The one Mom gave me right before she passed. "I never dreamed I'd have a life like this. So I'd say I was pretty darn successful already."

"It's not enough."

I suddenly felt totally and completely bone-tired. I sagged against the wall. "It's never enough," I muttered.

"What was that?"

"Nothin'."

Josh's nostrils flared and he threw his hands in the air. "Whatever. If I didn't know better, I'd say that you don't care about making music anymore."

At this, I stood straight. Set Josh with a firm stare. "That's out of line and you know it."

Josh knew almost better than anyone how much I loved being a musician. Writing words and melodies that came straight from my heart. Strumming on my guitar and letting songs flow out of me like rivers to the ocean. Music had been the backbone of my life, my first memory, the thing that had carried me through every major life event. From the best, to the very, very worst...

But, as of right now, it had been months since I'd written a song. Ironically, the more well-known I became, the less time I had for writing. In the last year, Josh had booked me on tour after tour after tour. I had music videos, award ceremonies, talk shows and even the occasional TV cameo.

Don't get me wrong, I loved it. Loved connecting with the wonderful people who supported me. There was nothing better than hearing that your music helped someone through a tough time or a breakup. Whenever I played, my fans were at the forefront of my mind, and hearing from them warmed my heart.

Well, it used to. Things were different now.

These days, I didn't feel much of anything.

Josh's expression softened and he perched on the edge of a weight machine so he could throw an arm around me. "I know it's been crazy lately. It won't be like this forever. But last night, when I was chatting with Annabel's manager—awful lady, by the way—I had a thought. Something to get the press hyped up that you two are touring together."

I held back a sigh. "What's that?"

"You two should date."

"Date." I furrowed my brow. "You want me to *date* Annabel Burnwood."

"Yes." He noted my expression and hurriedly added, "Don't worry, it doesn't have to go long-term. Annabel's just broken up with that Calvin Klein model—you know, the one on all those jean billboards. It's a good time to move in. The press will go nuts for it."

I could hardly believe what I was hearing. Sure, Josh sometimes entered questionable territory, blurred lines I'd rather he didn't. But this was too far. "You're saying you want me to take advantage of Annabel's broken heart... for a press opportunity."

Josh scoffed. "Like getting a date with her will be a problem for you."

I ignored him. I might've felt like I was in a blurry haze these days, but I knew when something was plain wrong. "Look, I can put up with the niceties and shallow conversations at these promo events. I can even put up with everyone's fake smiles and even more fake personas. But pretending to date Annabel just to advance my career is not okay."

Josh smiled slowly. "Oh, Christian. Don't you get it? *Everyone's* goal is to get ahead. To go for what they want, no matter the consequences. To progress is to be human." He shrugged as he took out his phone. "Is it a little cutthroat sometimes? Sure. But, is it worth it? Absolutely."

He turned his attention to his phone, ending the discussion. And for some reason, my best friend's odd little hometown popped into my head. Austin and his now-wife Ella did the whole fake dating thing last year, but their situation was very, very different.

In Aston Falls, "cutthroat" wasn't even on the radar. Every time I'd visited in the past few years, it was like a breath of fresh air, a much-needed break from reality. Time moved slowly there, everyone was genuinely kind. Genuinely good.

They didn't use people at their lowest for their own personal gain.

"You know what, Josh?"

"Hmm?"

"I quit."

Josh continued fiddling on his phone. "Yeah, yeah."

"I'm serious. I don't want to work with you anymore."

Now, Josh froze, while a few feet away, Louie typed even more furiously. "What did you just say?"

"You heard me." My voice was calm and sure. "I don't

want to do this anymore. I don't want to work in LA, I don't want to do any more tours. I'm taking a break."

Josh guffawed. "You can't do that. You can't just 'take a break.'"

It occurred to me that I should've been surprised by my own statement. Maybe even tried to backpedal out of it. I hadn't thought this through in the least, and I wasn't known to quit anything. I was Christian West—I reached for the stars and dreamed big. I always went for what I wanted.

But, not like this.

Josh's face, once again, turned beet red. "You're making a big mistake."

I shrugged. "Doubt it."

Josh's mouth was wide open as I slung my towel over my shoulder. I nodded at him once before turning on my heel and walking out of the gym. Louie hadn't looked up from his phone once.

I could only imagine tomorrow's headlines.

"Christian West quits music?!"

2

JJ

The gravel road was a familiar if not unwelcome sight. I knew the twists and turns, the potholes and narrow bridge crossings, like the back of my hand. There was only one house at the end of this road—my parents' dairy farm.

Flickers of dust swirled around the cab of my truck, coming in from the open driver's side window. The air was crisp and cool, though the sun was out. It was an unseasonably nice day for the beginning of November. The trees had all lost their golden leaves and the grass was getting progressively more brown. I had a feeling we'd have our first snowflakes in no time, and I was already excited for winter.

There was nothing like Christmas in Aston Falls.

Though maybe "excited" was stretching it.

I reflexively peeked into the rearview mirror. Boxes littered the trunk and the backseat. Boxes full of what I'd imagined I'd use to build my life. OUR life.

Instead, it was all coming back with me.

Me, alone.

It'd been six months since Ted and I split up. I didn't want to go into the details, didn't like to talk about it. The most I'd told my parents before moving back to their farm was that things just hadn't worked out. We decided to go our separate ways.

I'd spent half my life with the man, but apparently, we weren't meant to be.

Today was the final nail in the coffin that held our broken relationship—the apartment I'd bought for us years ago had sold. The new owners took possession this morning.

Which meant that, as of this moment, I was single, alone, and basically homeless.

As if she could sense my thoughts, George barked. I looked at my Aussie shepherd, her tongue wagging, and petted her.

"Alone except for you, Georgie," I murmured.

She whined and curled back up on the passenger seat, emitting a desperate sigh. I usually took her for long walks by the river in the morning, but because the new owners were moving in, we didn't go today. By the time we left the empty, desolate apartment, she was practically bouncing off the walls with pent-up energy.

Leaving the keys to the apartment was a more emotional process than I'd expected. It was a sweet little place with a big, open living room and two bedrooms. When we got the apartment, Ted had just gotten his CPA license and didn't have a job yet, so I paid the deposit out of my savings. I made the best of the space, made myself at home there. I moved easily around the pile of boxes that Ted had unceremoniously dumped in the living room while he was living in his parents' basement.

He was meant to move in after we tied the knot, but we

never even made it to setting a date. After a five year engagement.

My heart squeezed as I considered, once again, how different things were now. It was like I was teetering on the edge of a cliff, looking into the unknown. I hadn't been single since before high school, had no idea who I was without Ted.

What was I going to do? How was I supposed to move forward when I had no idea which direction was up?

The only bright spot in the chaotic tornado I called my life was that I was moving back into the Barn—a small, red standalone barn adjacent to my parent's house. It used to be a storage shed for our horse tack, but after months of begging and grovelling and doing extra chores around the farm when I was a teen, Daddy finally agreed to renovate it to become my little suite.

It still looked as it did all those years ago. It was still my safe space, my haven, the place I felt most at home. In high school, I'd have my best friends—Grace and Ella—over for sleepovers. As I got older, the Barn became my second home whenever things with Ted weren't going well and the thought of being in *our* apartment was too much.

If I was going to start healing from this mess of a broken engagement, the Barn was the perfect place to do it.

Another gust of cool air blew through the window and I shivered. Darn thing broke a couple of days ago and I hadn't been by the mechanic yet to get it fixed. If anyone asked, I said that I liked having the window down, liked smelling the fall breeze and having the wind on my face.

It was true. Most of the time.

For good measure, I tried to wind up the window one more time.

No dice.

I shivered again and hunkered into my seat.

"What about some music?" I asked George. "What do you feel like?"

She stared at me and tilted her head towards the radio. I smiled. Call me crazy, but I could've sworn that she understood me sometimes.

"Have it your way." I turned on the radio and used the dial to find the right station. Soon enough, I landed on Bozeman Vibes—the station my cousin, Bowie, ran. He usually played a good mix of country and rock.

The truck cab filled with the sounds of a song I knew well—*I'll Be Waiting For You* by Christian West. I hesitated for a moment and a grimace flitted across my face.

Then, I turned up the volume and started belting along.

Here it was, my guilty little secret. The one I'd take to the grave.

I was unfortunate enough to have met Christian West more than a few times, and I could fill entire books with lists of his terrible qualities. He was arrogant, condescending, the type of guy who'd never worked a day in his life. Who got exactly what he wanted, all the time, and lorded it over you.

Maybe what I hated most, though, was just how catchy his songs were. How could such a toad of a human create something so heart-wrenching, so beautiful?

I chalked it up to him hiring ghost songwriters. It was the only explanation. Guys like him weren't known for their sincerity.

I could only hope that I'd never have to see him again.

I turned down the volume on the radio, hushing his annoyingly mesmerizing gravel voice. I was turning the dial to find another station when a hulking black SUV sped past me, kicking up a mess of dirt and debris.

"Hey!" I squealed, though, of course, the driver was too far gone to hear me.

I coughed and sputtered against the brown cloud showering in through the window. Within seconds, the crisp smell of fall was replaced by a thick veil of dust. I let out a string of curse words while George barked. The idiot scared her as well.

I scratched the sweet spot behind George's ears and sang to her softly until she settled back in the seat. Then, I glared at the retreating haze as it crested over a small hill and disappeared.

"Who on God's green earth could that be?" I grumbled as I shook the dirt off my flannel shirt. I didn't know anyone in Aston Falls who would drive like *that*, let alone drive an SUV. Most people had small cars or pickups, nothing like that fancy, jacked-up car. "Absolutely no respect."

And where were they going anyway? They couldn't be going to my parents' place. They must've been lost, or...

"Teenagers," I decided, rolling my eyes. Probably just a couple troublemaker teens from Aston Falls High, out for a joyride. Which meant that they'd probably come back this way soon, assailing me and George with another wave of dust.

I pressed down on the gas pedal.

3

JJ

By the time I parked my truck in front of my parents' house, George was standing on the passenger seat, yapping away. I killed the engine, reached over and opened the door to let her out.

"Yeah, yeah," I muttered as she shot towards the house. "Let the entire world know that we've arrived."

I assessed the two-storey log house that my parents called home. It was refined but understated, with shuttered windows and an iconic red slanted roof. The wraparound porch had several couches and chairs—my favorite place to read when I was a kid—and hanging flower pots filled with colorful blooms in the summer.

With a sigh, I got out of my truck, wrestled the keys out of the ignition, and reached for my bag. I'd bring my boxes to the Barn later. Right now, I wanted to say hi to Ma and Daddy. And round up my hyper little canine.

I walked up the porch steps, avoiding the creaky one—Grandma dropped a frozen turkey on it one year—and tried the handle. The door was unlocked so I walked inside.

"Ma?" I called. "Daddy?"

No answer.

I walked through the house and found it empty, but the smell of the blueberry pancakes keeping warm in the oven and the fresh pot of coffee indicated that my parents would be back soon. Probably checking on the cows and horses out back.

Still, George was nowhere to be seen or heard, and that was unusual.

I walked towards the back of the house and peeked out the window, hoping to see her by the stable.

Instead, I froze, uncomprehending. Because that awful, noisy, annoying black SUV?

It was parked in our back lot.

I stepped away from the window. There was only one explanation—the driver was lost, and my parents were giving them directions.

Which would give me a chance to kindly inform them that they shouldn't drive like an idiot on a gravel road. Especially when an antsy Aussie shepherd was involved.

I walked outside and heard voices to the left, towards the Barn. Then I spotted a familiar figure, crouched and petting George while she lolled on her back.

"Daddy." I ran over to give him a hug, and was instantly soothed by his familiar scent of cigar smoke and leather.

"Hey, sweet pea." He patted my back. "You're home early."

I didn't miss the question in his tone. I pulled back to look at him. "Yeah. Change of plans. The new owners wanted to move in today instead of next week. I hope it's okay."

"Okay?" he asked with a fixed smile. "Of course that's okay. You know you're always welcome."

"Thanks, Daddy." I smiled and only then did I realize

that something was off. Earl Sutton was a relatively stoic and quiet man, known for his direct, confident gaze. Now, he was looking everywhere but at me.

In fact, his eyes kept glancing towards the Barn. As if he was waiting for something.

"What's going on?" I frowned. "I noticed an SUV in the back lot. And where's Ma?"

Dad shifted on his feet and cleared his throat gruffly. "Well, you see, sweet pea... me and your Ma, we weren't expecting you until next week. We have something to tell—"

At that moment, the door to the Barn wrenched open and Ma stepped out.

"And we can remove the posters if you want—"

Her eyes met mine and her wide, bright smile disappeared. She froze, mouth open.

But her shock was nothing compared to mine. Because the person who stepped out after Ma was the very last person I ever expected to see here, at my parents' farm. The man that everyone always said looked like a god, with his chiseled cheekbones, dark, wavy hair, and eyes you could lose yourself in.

Me? I saw the devil in disguise.

My fists clenched by my sides and my voice was a growl. "What are *you* doing here?"

4

CHRISTIAN

I'd never forget the first time I saw JJ Sutton.

She was stomping around in the shallows of the Aston Falls river at sunset, her long black dress hiked to her knees. Her strawberry blonde hair was wild and unkempt, and with the golden light playing off the strands, she seemed almost ethereal. She wore a jean jacket a size too big and a plaid scarf to ward off the early spring air.

I couldn't help but wonder why such a beautiful woman was splashing around in the freezing water.

I knew I had to talk to her.

When I did, she gave me a look I'd remember forever. Pure frustration radiated from the depths of those wide, honey-colored eyes.

I must've done something, said the wrong thing. Because suddenly, she was directing her irritation right at me, and the fire behind her words was unlike anything I'd ever experienced. This was around the time my life got so hectic, around the time that I found myself too busy and stressed to care about much of anything.

But her? She cared.

Loudly. And a lot.

And now, here she was again, glaring at me outside of the cozy barn I'd rented for the next couple months. Her ruby red lips were curled and her brows were drawn in. A raging storm traveled across her features.

"So? Why are you here?" she demanded again.

It was a valid question. I came across this farm the last time I was in Aston Falls, and when I decided to take a break from my LA life, it was all I could think about. My gut told me to come back here, and I always followed my gut.

I knew it was a long shot when I messaged Mr. and Mrs. S—as they called themselves—asking if they ever rented their house. They didn't, but they mentioned a renovated barn that I could stay in. They seemed gracious and kind, and didn't make a fuss when I told them my name. Their farm seemed like the perfect place to get away.

Not that I'd tell JJ any of that.

Instead, I fell into our familiar pattern and a slew of smart, biting retorts came to mind. I didn't want to bicker in front of this lovely couple though, so I bit back my harsh words. "I could ask you the same thing."

"Don't play dumb with me."

"JJ!" the older woman exclaimed. "Mind your manners."

JJ backed down. Her features softened as she turned to Mrs. S. "Sorry, Ma."

My eyebrows shot up. This sweet, elderly couple were JJ's parents?

She turned her gaze back to me and when she spoke, her voice was nearly angelic. "Don't you have a pretentious party you should be attending? Or a million dollar boat to float around on?"

I couldn't help but smile. This was one of her favorite topics, and it was fun to play into her (often incorrect) assumptions about my life. "The jet's on standby for the next party. And the yacht is currently docked in St Tropez."

Her nostrils flared and a light flutter of gratification flew through my chest. "I should've known."

"You do know that celebrities don't just sit around all day getting fanned by palm fronds and eating grapes."

"Why not? Are grapes *beneath* you?"

I bit back a smile and gestured towards Mr. and Mrs. S. "Your parents were showing me around their beautiful property."

"No. They're showing you around *my* barn."

"*Your* barn?"

"Did I stutter?"

At this point, JJ's mom stepped in. "Sweet pea, let me explain. Your dad and I should've told you earlier, but this all happened so quickly. Christian," she shot me a smile, "sent us an email asking to stay. We have plenty of space, and you know it wouldn't be right for us to say no."

JJ's mouth twisted. "So you offered the Barn?"

"That's right, sweet pea," her dad cut in. He was tall and regal, with bright eyes and a salt and pepper beard. He had the kind of presence that demanded respect. "We figured you wouldn't mind staying in your room in the main house."

"My childhood bedroom, you mean. With the princess bed."

I snorted. Covered it with a cough.

JJ shot me a glare. Then she squeezed her eyes shut. When she opened them again, she offered her mom a smile. A strange, small, placid smile. "Okay. If that's what you want."

Mrs. S patted her daughter's hand. "Thank you, sweetie, that's generous of you." She turned to me, beaming. "Now,

Christian. Why don't we bring in your things so you can get settled?"

"Thanks for the offer, Mrs. S, but I didn't bring much with me today. I'm getting most of my things shipped out."

"On the Aston Falls Express?" JJ's dad asked.

"Yessir."

Mrs. S tutted. "Well, let's hope the snow stays away. The train has the most horrendous delays around the first blizzard of the season. Why don't you come in for a fresh cup of coffee and pancakes when you're settled?"

"Thanks, Mrs. S." I smiled and cast a sideways glance towards JJ. "I'd love to."

JJ's honey eyes narrowed to slits.

"Oh, for the last time." Mrs. S giggled, oblivious to her daughter's withering stare. "Call me Mary."

JJ's parents said their goodbyes and went back to the main house. I shot JJ a final smirk before turning to go inside the Barn.

"Don't get too comfortable," she warned. "You won't be here long."

I knew I shouldn't, but I took the bait. Arguing with JJ was as much a part of my Aston Falls experience as anything else. I faced her, still smirking. "Why do you say that, Jessica?"

She set her jaw at my use of her given name. She always hated when I did that. *Jessica Jade Sutton.* "Because this is my home, and I'd do anything to protect it from people like you."

"What kind of person am I?"

"The kind who wouldn't understand hard work if it hit him right in the face."

I gave an unaffected shrug. "Sounds painful."

"You still haven't answered my question—why are you

here? Aston Falls isn't exactly a vacation hotspot for celebs," she sneered. Then, before I could answer, her lips stretched into a smile. "Or... is this not a vacation at all? I thought I saw a couple of headlines about you leaving the music industry. That you're giving up and quitting. Is it possible that the infamous Christian West is *running away* to Aston Falls to lick his wounds?"

Something in her words hit wrong and I pressed my lips together, no longer in a joking mood. "Not that I owe you an explanation, but I'm here to get my music back on track. Not quitting, just refocusing."

"And you can't 'refocus' somewhere else?"

"After I've had such a warm welcome here?"

JJ crossed her arms, planted her feet firmly. She wasn't going anywhere.

I leaned my back against the Barn, stuck my hands deep in the pockets of my leather jacket. "Alright, you want the truth? I thought going away would give me some privacy. Peace and quiet. Why do you care if I stay here anyway? Don't you have a place with that fiancé of yours?"

I could've sworn I saw a shadow cross her features, but the next moment, it was gone. "Consider yourself warned, Starboy. If you don't leave soon, I'll find a way to make you leave."

I took her challenge, squared up to her. "Try me."

Her eyes flashed, and I remembered the first time I saw her in that river. How different she was from anyone I'd ever encountered.

With a final glare, JJ turned on her heel and marched towards the house. I watched her go with a bemused smile.

As she approached the stupid flashy SUV I'd rented—as luck would have it, the only car they had available with winter tires—I felt the words rise up. I couldn't help myself. Couldn't resist.

"And Jessica, make sure you don't scratch the SUV with that truck of yours. The steering wheel is probably worth more than your entire car."

JJ stopped mid-step. Detoured towards the SUV.

Then, she licked her thumb and walked slowly along the body of the vehicle, thumb pressed into the metal, leaving her mark on the sleek black frame.

5

JJ

I placed the tub of M&Ms on the counter and began to scoop the sweets into a smaller glass container. There was a whole set of glass jars I had to refill with crushed Oreos, maraschino cherries, nuts and more. Mr. and Mrs. Applebaum were anything but stingy when it came to sundae toppings.

I glanced around before sneaking an M&M or two (or five). It had been a busy afternoon in Sweets n' Sundaes, and the Applebaums were in the office doing inventory while I refilled the candy station.

I picked up the tub of black licorice bites next. Of all the toppings we offered, black licorice would always serve as the biggest mystery to me. Things tasted like sweet rubber and nightmares.

But customers seemed to love them. Maybe I was wrong in hating black licorice. Ted hated them—maybe there was a part of me that hated them because of him?

I cleared my mind of all judgments about black licorice and gingerly picked up one of the bites. Popped it into my mouth.

Almost gagged. Spat it back out.

Nope, black licorice was not for me.

I finished filling the jars, then put out more of the delicious Belgian chocolates that Mrs. Applebaum imported directly. They were by far my favorite treats, and I helped myself to one before moving on to grinding up peanuts. As I worked, my mind wandered to Ted, to the breakup, to the aftermath. My heart twisted, as it always did, and I forced my thoughts to move away from that day.

I hummed mindlessly along with the song on the radio and it soothed my sadness. The beautiful guitar, the soulful melody, the gorgeous gravel voice—

I froze, mid-chop.

I knew that voice. Knew it too well.

Knew it because its owner was the one person who never failed to drive me up the wall.

I darted over to the small, retro radio in the corner and changed the station to something more rock and roll. I'd have to talk to Bowie about the amount of Christian West on his playlist.

"Not a fan of country music, dear?" Mrs. Applebaum asked as she whizzed around the corner. She was wearing the same flannel shirt she always wore on Toppings Tuesdays—the one with the tiny ice cream cone emblems. Now that we were getting closer to December, she'd be swapping out for her Christmas tree shirt any day now.

Mrs. Applebaum and her husband owned Sweets n' Sundaes, and they treated the shop like it was their child seeing as they didn't have any of their own. Just like any parents, they were extremely picky about who they chose to take care of their baby. To this day, I counted myself lucky that I got a job here.

Even if there were times when I wasn't sure this was the job I wanted.

"Country music's fine, Mrs. A. I'd just rather not listen to Christian West."

Mrs. Applebaum approached the counter and set down the box of napkins she was carrying. She exhaled loudly. "Yes, I've heard all about the little war between you and Christian West. But you have to admit, the boy does make incredible music. Not to mention those dimples. Bah! Like a young Brando. Let me tell you, if I was young and unattached—"

She cut herself off, one hand hovering over the napkin box.

Oh man, here we go...

Sure enough, Mrs. Applebaum threw a sympathetic arm around me. "Oh, I'm so sorry, dear. How insensitive of me. Of *course* you don't want to listen to me going on about love right now. Not after... everything that happened."

I forced a smile, eager to divert what I already knew would quickly become a mildly intrusive line of questioning. "It's fine, Mrs. A. I just want to listen to something else."

"I know, dear. I know." She tutted. "We've all been there. Lord knows I've had a broken heart or two in my lifetime."

Fantastic. Mrs. Applebaum rehashing her past would surely steer us away from her questions. "Haven't you been with Mr. A since you were teens?"

"Of course, dear. Gerald was my high school sweetheart." She sighed wistfully. "But before him, there was Donnie Haynes."

"Who?"

Her eyes turned glassy as she strolled down memory lane. "We were so young then. I was just six and he was seven when I scraped my knee outside his house and he gave me a pack of bubble gum. He stole my heart that day..." She trailed off, then shook herself off and smiled. "But I fell in love with Gerald in high school, and all's well that ends well, as they say."

I put the nuts away, hiding my smile. Mission accomplished.

"You and Ted reminded me a lot of myself and Mr. A. It really is a shame about your broken engagement." She placed a hand on mine.

Drat. So close.

"We were all *so* surprised when you two mysteriously called off the wedding. It was a shock. You were our hometown love story, after all. Whenever you're ready to talk about it—you know, about who broke it off and why—I'm here for you, dear."

Mrs. Applebaum's eyes were kind and genuine, and I appreciated the thought behind her words.

But I also knew who ran the town rumor mill.

I patted her hand back and smiled. "Thanks, Mrs. A. I'll let you know."

She squeezed my arm, then picked up the small calendar we kept behind the register. "Wonderful. In the meantime, you should know that, because of the Aston Falls Christmas Carol, I may not be around much over the next couple of months. We're just a few weeks away from Christmas, can you believe it?"

The first Christmas I'll be spending without Ted. "Barely."

"Well, as you already know, Alicia Rodriguez and I are heading up the planning committee for the Carol. Now, as usual, we will be having the performance and the party afterwards at the Aston Glow Inn on Christmas Eve, but we're having a hard time finding a variety of performers for the Carol. Pastor McLean and his church choir have already signed up, of course, along with the kindergarten class and the school band from Aston Falls High."

"Of course," I said, nodding along gravely with Mrs. Applebaum.

"However, we were hoping to have something a little different this year. Maybe a surprise guest. A surprise guest who hasn't performed in years..."

She trailed off suggestively and the puzzle piece fell into place. My eyes widened slightly. "Oh, no. I don't think that's a good idea, Mrs. A. I don't sing anymore."

"Oh, please, JJ?" She clasped her chest dramatically. "It would mean the world to Alicia and I. Just say you'll think about it?"

I clenched my jaw but forced a smile. "Sure. I'll think about it."

"Fantastic." Mrs. Applebaum clapped her hands once, with a smile so satisfied we might as well have discovered how to fly a horse to the moon. "I'll get you the details as soon as I have them."

With that, Mrs. Applebaum disappeared around the corner towards the office, her rose perfume lingering in the air. I pasted a neutral expression on my face as I busied myself behind the counter, but I felt a strange sense of unease.

No, I didn't sing anymore. *This* was my job—I was an ice cream server. It was a good job. I made a decent salary and had nice bosses who didn't mind if I snuck the odd M&M. The only thing I'd change were the uniforms. The candy striper look, while cute on some people, was *very* much not my style. The short, pink flared skirt always sat funny on my curvier hips.

Aside from that, I could be happy working here for the rest of my life. Content.

Sure, maybe it wasn't exactly what I originally wanted or dreamed for myself, but now wasn't the time to start chasing my dreams.

"Sorry we're late!" a familiar voice exclaimed as the bell above the door tinkled.

I turned to see Grace Bell-King—one of my best friends—standing the doorway of Sweets n' Sundaes with her little boy, Dallas. Behind her, our other best friend, Ella Bell, was shimmying backwards through the door, attempting to force her double stroller into the shop.

I ran over and took Grace's place holding the door open.

"Thanks, J." She shot me a grateful smile while Dallas fixed his gaze on me. Then, he reached his arms out.

"I can take him, Gracie," I said, smiling at the sweet little boy.

"You sure? He's getting pretty heavy."

"I can handle it."

"You're a Godsend. My arms are *aching*." Grace tenderly kissed Dallas's head, then passed him onto me. I held him close, rocked him gently. Maybe sniffed his light blond hair a little bit. He was such a well-behaved one year old. But Grace wasn't kidding about the weight—he was growing fast. Likely got that from his ex-pro quarterback dad.

Between Grace, Ella and I, we finally managed to maneuver the stroller into the ice cream parlor. By now, Dallas was wriggling around, so Grace took him to our favorite corner booth.

"Need to get used to driving this thing." Ella grunted as she tried to turn the stroller around. Unfortunately, she curved a little too wide and knocked into a table, sending a couple of metal napkin holders clanging to the floor. She squeezed her eyes shut, waited a beat. But there was silence from the stroller. She smiled at me apologetically. "Whoops!"

"Don't worry about it." I scrambled to pick up the holders, then threw my arms around my friend. "How are you? And how are Kali and Gia?"

"Good." Ella dropped her voice. "Sleeping. These little... miracles have been up all hours of the night. But the good news is that they sleep all day."

"That's very European of them."

"Don't tell them that. I'm trying to get them on a North American schedule ASAP."

I took the handle of the stroller and pushed it to the corner booth, where Grace and Dal were playing peek-a-boo.

After telling Mrs. Applebaum that I was taking my afternoon break, I collapsed onto the seat with my two best friends. It'd been a long time since we'd caught up, and even longer since we'd all sat down together.

Things were moving so quickly in their lives. Dallas was over a year old, and between being a full-time mom and running Morning Bell Cafe, Grace was crazy busy. As for Ella, her twin girls were a few months old, and aside from their bizarre sleep schedule, they were little angels. It helped that Ella was Lead Editor for *The Weekly Best*, an online magazine that strove to make a difference. She worked whenever the girls slept.

And, of course, they both had supportive, engaged husbands who would move the earth and sky to make sure their wives and children were happy.

It was the sort of life I thought I was moving towards. Despite the fact that I was in what appeared to be a never-ending engagement, I thought I was happy. I thought Ted and I were happy...

Weeknight dinners at "our" apartment, weekends spent watching documentaries—Ted loved World War II historical movies. And any film about trains. We'd follow that with dinner at the country club his parents loved. The food was great... even if the dress code wasn't. I'd always felt most comfortable in cozy jeans and flannel shirts, but I was ready to wear those stiff and uncomfortable dresses to fit in.

Sure, it might not have always been the most thrilling life. But I figured that wouldn't matter as long as we were happy.

"So you're back home, JJ." Grace's voice brought me back to the moment. She gave Dal a little lick of her Rocky Road ice cream, then took a big lick for herself. "How was it moving out of the apartment?"

"A little sad, but it went smoothly."

Ella raised an eyebrow. "Have you talked to Ted?"

The chocolate chip cookie I'd been chewing dried in my mouth. No, Ted and I hadn't talked. Not in person, at least. Though he had messaged me the other day to see about giving me a box of my things. I shouldn't have been surprised that the message was six months late.

I didn't particularly want to get into all of this with my girls though. Don't get me wrong, I loved them to the moon and back, and they were there for me when I had to disentangle my life from Ted's. But I hadn't even told *them* what had really happened.

The moments we had together were few and far between—I didn't see the point in dampening our time with my sob story. So I shrugged. "Nope, didn't need to. Everything's good."

Ella raised an eyebrow as she lightly pushed the stroller

back and forth. Kali had woken up and started fussing, but she quieted down the moment Ella moved the stroller. I had a feeling she'd be a feisty, energetic little one. "*That* was convincing."

"No, really guys," I said, more firmly this time. "I'm good. All good here."

"Are you?" Grace asked. "Because it's okay if you're not. You can talk to us, JJ."

Ella nodded. "We just want to make sure that you're facing facts with Ted. Not sweeping it all under the rug."

I opened my mouth, but nothing came out. Their kind words meant the world to me, but where would I even start? The story was messy and complicated and full of stupidity and regret. What was done was done, so what was the point in fixating on it?

"You know what?" I blurted out. "There is one *big* problem I'm having right now."

Grace and Ella both leaned forward, curiosity etched in their faces.

I sighed dramatically. "There's a pest at the farm."

Ella blinked. "A pest?"

"Yes. An awful, disgusting, ugly pest."

"Oh, JJ." Grace looked horrified. "Are the mice back? I can send Nicholas over to help."

"Worse than mice." I paused again. I wasn't planning on telling the girls this news, but it served as the perfect distraction. Both Ella and Grace were bent over the table, their eyes huge. Even Dal and the twins were perfectly quiet.

"It's Christian West."

Grace exhaled through her teeth. "Christian West... is living at the farm?"

"Yes. In the Barn."

"The *Barn* is still standing?" Ella asked out the side of her mouth.

"It is, for now. I might have to burn the place down whenever he moves out. Anything to get rid of that big-city-music-star stink." I grimaced, remembering when he called me "Jessica" in that stupid, smug tone of his. He *knew* how much I hated being called by my first name.

"What are you talking about?" Grace laughed. "You have a real-life celebrity living at your house. Teenage girls literally dream about this exact situation."

"Well, I dreamed about—" I cut myself off. Shook my head. No use in pointing the conversation in another useless direction. "Anyway, it sucks. He moved into the Barn, which means that I've had to move back into my bedroom in the house. Remember? With the tiny twin bed and the princess covers? The amount of pink and frilly things in there makes me nauseous. I don't even remember liking pink that much. No wonder I moved to the Barn as a teen."

"JJ Sutton doesn't exactly scream 'girly girl,'" Ella said. Gia let out a cry and Ella murmured to her softly.

"It's just not my thing. And now, Christian West is invading my personal space. Probably tearing down my posters in the loft, using my favorite mug, clogging up the sink with his stupid facial hair…" I trailed off, my blood pressure rising by the second. "Meanwhile, I'm cramped into my princess bedroom with all of my boxes."

Grace pulled a stuffed animal from her purse and waggled it in front of a now-bored Dallas. "Come on, JJ, you're being dramatic. It can't be THAT bad."

"But it is."

"Living with a musician who happens to have the loveliest, most toe-curling voice in the entire world sounds great to me. It's not a bad view to look at everyday either."

Ugh. Why was everyone so insistent on Christian's good looks? "Aren't you married, Gracie?"

"Yes," Grace said with a smile. "But I'm sure even Nicholas would agree—Christian's easy on the eyes."

"Plus," Ella piped up. "Think of how easy you'll sleep when he's serenading you from next door."

She shivered with glee and I rolled my eyes. "You guys are too much."

Suddenly, from behind my left shoulder, someone cleared their throat.

Grace's eyes lifted to a point behind me and she pressed her lips together before wiping at an invisible blob of ice cream on Dallas' cheek. Meanwhile, Ella busied herself peeking under the blanket covering the stroller.

I half-turned in the booth to find Mrs. Applebaum peering at me from beyond the edge of the wall.

"I couldn't help but overhear," she said sweetly. "Is Christian West—country star heartthrob Christian West—staying at the Sutton farm?"

My gut reaction was to say no. Shut down any rumors before they could start. I was never one to feed into the rumor mill, I preferred to steer clear of gossip.

But before I could say a word, I had an idea. A brilliant idea.

"Yes. Yes, he is," I said. "And you should probably let everyone know that we have a celebrity in our midst."

Mrs. Applebaum's eyes literally lit up and she clapped her hands. "Ooh! This *is* good news, I have to tell Alicia right away. She's been on a streak lately, always phoning me first with the latest news."

She was about to bustle away when she froze mid-step. I could almost see the gears in her mind working.

"Wait a minute," she said. "How long is Christian West staying with us?"

I grimaced. "Hopefully a day or two."

"Well. If he's staying for a while, wouldn't he be just the most *perfect* surprise guest for the Christmas Carol?" Mrs. Applebaum clapped her hands, her cheeks turning pink. "Ooh! This is amazing. Can you put a good word in for me, JJ?"

"Why don't you and Ms. Rodriguez come by the farm yourselves?" I said easily. "Tomorrow morning? Christian is an early bird, so just drop by whenever."

"Amazing! I'll call Alicia right away. Maybe tell Pastor McLean and Mayor Davis too. They were both *so* curious as to who would be performing at the Carol this year." Mrs. Applebaum skittered down the hallway towards the office.

I sat back in the leather booth, a satisfied smile on my face.

"What was that about?" Grace asked.

Ella shook her head. "I doubt Christian wants the entire town to know his whereabouts. They'll be hounding him for days."

"Exactly."

Grace and Ella continued frowning at me, confusion in their eyes.

"Don't you see? All I want is to get the Barn back. Once I have my own space, I can get my life on track. Which means that I need Christian to leave. And, if I can't drive him out of town, maybe the rumor mill will."

Grace and Ella pursed their lips, not saying anything. I knew they probably weren't on board with my plan, and an annoying little niggle of morality was telling me that I shouldn't have done that.

I hushed the whisper. Christian West represented everything that was wrong with the world. He was the kind of person who got everything he wanted at the drop of a hat, who didn't understand what it meant to put in real effort. To make sacrifices.

On top of being a pest of a human, he'd gone ahead and taken my home. He could've gone anywhere, stayed in the Aston Glow Inn or a fancy hotel. Instead, he took my safe haven.

Which meant the game was on.

Get ready for this curveball, Starboy.

6

CHRISTIAN

I wrapped a towel around my waist and shook out my damp hair as I stepped out of the shower. It'd been a long time since I'd been shocked with spurts of cold water during a shower, but I shouldn't have been surprised.

The Barn was rustic. Bare bones. It was part of its charm.

I made a mental note to take a look at the pressure-balanced valve tomorrow morning when it was light out. The thought made me smile. In LA, there were maintenance teams on hand to deal with stuff like this, but I liked the idea of getting back to my roots. Being handy came easy to me, and before I made it big, I used to do all sorts of odd jobs around the city.

I whistled as I sifted through the clothes strewn around the loft. My PA, Antonia, was sending me the bare necessities from LA on the Aston Falls Express. I could've chartered a private jet, but I didn't see the point in using a jet purely to ship out my things—it wasn't exactly fuel efficient. Plus, as far as I knew, there was only one "airport" in the area—a tiny regional one with one landing strip.

I'd been living out of my duffel for days now. Despite its

name, the train was anything but express. Not that I was complaining. There was something comforting about being *that* far away from my real life.

After changing into dark wash jeans and a black henley, I lazily scanned the loft. It doubled as a bedroom, with a huge skylight above the bed.

Hard to believe that *this* was the childhood lair of the founder of the Christian West Haters club. It was not what I expected—less demons and fiery pits; more fluffy pillows, moody mountain photos, and an odd but kind of endearing Disney mug. Posters lined the walls and I remembered Mrs. Sutton saying that I could take them down if I wanted.

Part of me was tempted, just to get a rise out of JJ. But I knew I'd probably end up feeling bad and putting them back up again. Besides, the fact that I was staying here seemed to bother her enough. Which made absolutely no sense given that she had an apartment of her own.

Still, I was drawn towards the posters. What kind of music did the girl listen to? Was she a pop princess? Into metal and screamo? Maybe the Disney mug hinted at her love of musicals.

As I got closer, my eyebrows shot up.

"Bon Jovi," I murmured. "Tim McGraw."

I perused every poster, and with each one, I was more surprised.

JJ and I had the same taste in music. She even had posters of Johnny Cash and Hank Williams, who served as my biggest sources of inspiration.

I stepped away, feeling like I'd gotten a weirdly intimate peek into JJ's soul. I resolved to put her and her eerily similar music taste to the back of my mind as I thundered down the rickety wooden stairs to the kitchenette.

I grabbed an iced tea from the fridge—another welcome

delivery from Antonia—and wandered into the living room, where my guitar case was leaning against the wall. I took out the instrument and ran my fingers over the frets and strings, the discolorations and depressions. My decades-old guitar was the one thing I made sure I had with me when I left LA. It sounded crazy, but a part of me firmly, stubbornly believed that it was my good luck charm.

Now that I was independent, I needed all the luck I could get.

Since quitting working with Josh, I had a huge task ahead of me. Music was my career, my life, and there was no question that I would continue writing songs. But I had to re-establish myself in the industry, which meant that I had to go above and beyond what I was doing before. My old style wouldn't cut it, and if I was being completely honest, that style just didn't feel *right* anymore.

Though what was so off about it, I couldn't tell you.

It had been a long time—too long—since I sat down with my guitar. But I'd been procrastinating since I got here and creating new music was, after all, the main reason I came to Aston Falls.

I strummed the strings once, twice. Waited for inspiration to flow through my fingers.

Nothing.

I tried again. Began to hum aimlessly.

Still nothing.

I felt... blocked. Like my mind was in a haze.

I strummed once more, closing my eyes as I tried to touch base what I was feeling. All I got was the blurry funk that had followed me around for months.

I thought about the other songs I'd written in my life, what fueled those. I was never one for writing love songs—you know the type, the sort of love song you'd sing to someone. In truth, I had no idea what I'd say. I'd never experienced that true, once-in-a-lifetime kind of love. The kind of love that other country singers crooned on about but that I never really understood.

Don't get me wrong, I used to date a lot, especially when I was rising in the music industry. Had a few relationships that ended just as quickly as they started. I owed a lot of my songs to that time of my life—dating, fleeting attractions... and inevitable break ups. Because when I started touring and everything got busy, I didn't want to commit time and energy to someone I didn't feel strongly about.

In the end, I pretty much stopped dating altogether.

Maybe that was why I felt stuck.

After several more attempts, I placed the guitar on the sofa. I frowned as I fingered the silver chain around my neck.

A walk. Maybe a walk would clear my head. It wasn't late, but the sun had set awhile ago. Maybe the evening air would help.

I crossed the Barn, a bad feeling twisting my stomach into a knot. How was I supposed to write music if I couldn't even figure out what I was feeling?

As I passed the window, I could've sworn I saw something. Was that a flashlight?

I bolted to the window, looked outside. But there was nothing. Only trees and the long gravel road.

Maybe I should lay off the iced tea, I thought as I threw on my jacket and walked out the door.

It was dreary and cold as I set off across the Suttons' farm. I made my way towards a set of lights just beyond the house, my mind spinning and distracted.

Until I stepped in something that squished.

The smell was almost immediate.

"Great." I grimaced as I shook the fresh cow patty off my boot. Definitely didn't see *that* in LA. Other disgusting things? Sure. Cow dung? Nope.

I tried to ignore the stench as I strode through a small patch of trees and popped out by the lights just on the other side. The stable.

At that moment, Mrs. Sutton marched around the corner carrying a couple of large bags. She dropped the bags by her feet, stood straight and stretched her arms.

"Hey, Mrs. S," I called.

She whirled around. "Christian! Hello! I wasn't expecting you." She gestured to her outfit—dirty blue jeans and a torn flannel shirt under a vest. "Sorry about this. It's been a busy day."

"Don't worry about it." I chuckled, then nodded at the bags by her feet. "What's that?"

"Horse feed. Just needed a break from carrying them, my back's been acting up lately."

"I'll give you a hand."

"You?" Mrs. S looked horrified. "Don't be silly, you're our guest."

I stifled a smile at her reaction. "It's really no trouble. I'm out here anyway."

Plus, a distraction like this will keep away me from the Barn and my guitar for at least a half hour. I hushed the whisper. I wasn't procrastinating, just lending a helping hand.

Mrs. S hesitated, looked between me and the bags. "Well, if you insist. It's been a long day and Earl's checking on the cows. I'd ask JJ for help, of course, but she isn't home."

Too busy with the fiancé and the apartment, I supposed.

Though Mr. S had mentioned that JJ was staying here the other night. Maybe she did that occasionally?

"So, Mrs. S, it's been pretty busy at the farm, huh?" I picked up the bags of horse feed.

Almost fell over.

No wonder her back was hurting. The fitness trainers in LA could bring in a bag or two of this stuff for their training circuits. I was good friends with a few of them—over the last few months, working out had my only outlet seeing as I'd had no time or ability for songwriting.

My muscles strained as I followed Mrs. S into the stable, but I couldn't get a word in over her chatter. I was hoping to dig a little deeper into what was happening with JJ, but Mrs. S had diverted the conversation to the horses and animals at the farm.

She showed me where to drop the bags of horse feed and we were walking out of the stable when she suddenly went serious. "How's your stay in the Barn so far, Christian?"

"It's been great. Very comfortable."

"Good, good." She cleared her throat. "Hopefully not comfortable enough to throw any big parties, hm?"

Her question took me off guard. "No... That's not really what I'm about these days. Besides, I'm trying to keep a low profile. Keep to myself."

"Wonderful." Mrs. Sutton nodded once, clearly relieved. "That's settled, then. Because I'd hate for my husband and I to have to break up any 'ragers.' We're not into the party scene anymore, aside from Aston Falls' fabulous Christmas party, of course. But that's all caroling performances, Santa visits for the children, and mulled apple cider. Nothing like what you kids have in the city."

A smile tugged at my lips. "I wouldn't dream of throwing any ragers, Mrs. S. Especially without your permission."

"I figured you wouldn't. When I dropped by Sweets n' Sundaes earlier, JJ lightly mentioned a party you were thinking of having here, I just wasn't sure what to think—"

I stopped walking. "Hang on. JJ said what?"

"Well, I believe her exact words were that you intended to 'throw the party to end all parties.'" Mrs. Sutton frowned.

I bit my lip to hide a smile. That little minx. Of course JJ would plant a seed that could lead to me being kicked out of the Barn. *Point, Jessica.*

"I would never disrespect you and your husband like that," I said sincerely. "JJ must be mistaken."

"That's exactly what I said to her. And as soon as she's finished her shift, I will tell her so." Mrs. Sutton patted my arm. "I've got a feeling about you, Christian, you're a good type. My JJ is stubborn as they come, she likes things her way. But you give her a run for her money."

As Mrs. S and I went our separate ways outside of the stable, I couldn't help but smirk. "Stubborn" was one word I'd use to describe JJ… along with bossy, headstrong, determined. The girl gave twice as good as she got.

It occurred to me that, though most of our interactions had been negative, JJ *definitely* made me feel something. Even if that something was somewhere between baffled amusement, curiosity, and plain annoyance.

What would she come up with next?

Give it your best shot, Jessica Jade.

7
JJ

I blinked my eyes open against the dim light coming in through the window. For a moment, I could almost believe that I was back in the apartment.

Until I saw the pink.

So, so much pink.

I squeezed my eyes shut again, grunting. Then, something warm and wet slurped along my hand and I jerked in surprise.

"Morning, Georgie," I murmured as I gave my dog a pat. Of course, she insisted on jumping onto the bed with me. There was already barely enough space for me alone, but I squished myself against the wall so she could curl up next to me.

It wasn't long before she started whining and licking my face.

"Time for breakfast?" I asked and she barked in response.

It was early—just after dawn—but I rolled out of bed and danced around the boxes piled around my room. Sure, I couldn't say I was a fan of my childhood bedroom, but I was making do. Even made a little maze for myself. Like I was a child again.

I definitely hadn't spent time creating the maze in an effort to avoid running into Christian West. Between working at Sweets n' Sundaes, helping my parents with farmwork out in the fields, and lying low maze-building, I hadn't seen Christian at all.

Assuming my sneakiness paid off, he still believed that I lived in my apartment in town, blissfully engaged to Ted Bigby.

Which was exactly as it should be.

I skittered to my laundry chair in the corner and threw on my favorite oversized maroon hoodie. Lots of girls stole hoodies from their boyfriends. Me? I bought mine from the Bozeman Rodeo—Ted wasn't a hoodie kind of guy, he preferred polo shirts and crisp knit sweaters.

I debated changing out of my polar bear pajama shorts, but I was only going to zip downstairs to put on a pot of coffee. Mrs. Applebaum and Ms. Rodriguez likely wouldn't be here for a while, so I had plenty of time to get dressed and position myself (with popcorn) to watch the fireworks go down with Christian.

As far as I could tell, the guy never actually left the Barn. He was surprisingly quiet for being a big-time music star, kept to himself and had no visitors. It made my lie to Ma about the "huge party" he was planning a little less believable.

What was he working on in there, anyway? I'd walked by a couple times and heard him strumming the guitar, but the melodies didn't seem to go anywhere.

Not that I was listening. Or cared at all.

After whipping my hair into a messy bun, I bounced down the stairs to the kitchen, George hot on my heels. I filled her food and water bowls, then switched on the coffee machine.

I glanced out the window and saw the light in the stable—Ma and Daddy were already out working, I'd join them just as soon as I got dressed. Before my eyes, the fields behind the house were gaining color with the rising sun. The ground was covered with a thin layer of frost, signaling that snow was coming. I smiled briefly as I considered the Christmas decorations that would soon pepper Aston Falls.

I found myself absentmindedly rubbed the spot on my finger where my engagement ring once sat.

Giving it back to Ted was a... surreal experience. In more ways than one. That ring was a symbol of a bond that was meant to last forever, a life-long commitment. It represented everything our relationship had been, what we'd meant to each other.

It also represented who I had been. The JJ who was Ted's JJ. Now, that was all in the past.

In the five years that we were engaged, there was only one time that the thing didn't sit on my finger. It was the day I met Christian West... not that I knew who he was at the time. I just thought he was some handsome stranger who offered to help me find my ring in the Aston Falls river.

I'd never forget what he said in that first conversation.

"Aren't you a little young to be engaged?"

His words set me off. Put a very, very bad taste in my mouth. How *dare* he say that. I loved Ted. Loved him with all my heart.

When I found out last year that the rude man from the river was actually the same country music star I listened to on repeat, the puzzle pieces fell horribly into place. Which was a shame given how much I loved his music before I knew the truth.

At that moment, I'd resolved to hate everything about Christian West. The problem was that he still had a way of getting under my skin. Riling me up with just the smallest statement, showing up at the worst possible moments—

"JJ?"

I shrieked, whirled around.

I should've known better than to speak of the devil. Because the devil had appeared in my kitchen in the form of Christian West.

And why did he have to look so good this early in the morning? His dark hair was all tousled and mussed up, and his deep chocolate eyes were sleepy. His scruff was slightly long, which meant that he hadn't shaved yet today. As much as I loved to give him a hard time for it, I actually kind of liked how it emphasized the curves of his jawline. All he wore was a leather jacket over a white henley and blue jeans, but he might as well have been on a red carpet somewhere.

"What do you think you're doing?!" I demanded, heart racing. I tried to pull my hoodie down, cover my shorts. "Don't you know how to knock?!"

To my utter annoyance, he just smiled that trademark smirk of his that all the women loved. His eyes traveled slowly up my body before meeting mine. "Sorry. Didn't think you'd be here."

"And why not? This is *my* house."

"Last I checked, it was your parents' house."

Ugh, he made me *mad*. I had to play it cool.

"Whatever." I waved a hand. "We're not all rich prettyboys with our own huge mansions."

Too late, I realized what I'd said. I watched Christian's face change—his smirk growing and his eyes dancing. Why on earth did God give the guy such gorgeous long eyelashes?

"You think I'm pretty?" he murmured.

My face burned hot. "I didn't say that."

"But you meant it."

I pretended to gag. "Not even in your wildest dreams, Starboy."

He chuckled, unaffected, which just made me more upset. Then, he pointed at the coffee machine. "Mind if I have some? The machine in the Barn's broken. I'll fix it later, but I need my caffeine fix first."

It looked like he wanted to come forward, grab a mug. Unfortunately for him, I was standing in the way. I was a coffee mug warden, holding them hostage.

And yes, maybe it was petty as could be. I just couldn't control myself around him.

I raised an eyebrow, cool as a cucumber. "You expecting me to get that for you?"

Christian bit his lip, lighting a fire of anger in my belly. "No."

"Good." I turned away and kept an eye on the machine as the roasted, smoky aroma filled the kitchen. There was a weird sort of energy swirling around the room. I didn't know what to make of it.

"So..." he eventually said, jangling his keys in his hand. "You also like coffee?"

"What gave it away?"

"You seem like that kind of girl."

I rolled my eyes. "A coffee girl?"

He shook his head. "The kind of girl who sleeps deeply."

Then, he pointed at his cheek and raised his eyebrows. I pressed a hand to my face, then, horrified, I checked my reflection in the mirror by the fridge.

No.

Please, God, no.

Faint red lines from the creases in my pillowcase crisscrossed across my cheek.

I faced Christian, hand pressed to my face. "How I sleep is none of your business."

He laughed. "What about *where* you sleep? Don't you have an apartment with your fiancé? What's his name, Thad?"

I pressed my lips together and turned away to grab a hostage mug. Anything not to look at him.

"Ted," I said shortly. "And that is *also* none of your business."

Christian took a breath in. He was going to ask another question. Something about Ted or our engagement? Was he going to ask why I was here? I refused to talk to anyone about my breakup, but the last person in the universe I'd talk about it with was Christian West.

My desperate gaze locked onto the keys he was playing with. "Still have that stupid keychain?"

Yes, it was a pointless subject change, but I would've grasped onto anything. Christian bought the yellow music note keychain last year from Sweets n' Sundaes, insisting that he was going to give it to a friend. At the time, I firmly believed that he only bought it because he wanted to waste my time, spending literally forty-five minutes going through each option.

Given that he still had said keychain, it seemed that I was right.

Christian glanced at the keys and his expression softened a touch. I suddenly wondered whether the person he wanted to give the keychain to wasn't a friend at all, but a woman. Someone he was dating. Maybe he was still dating her now.

Not that I cared.

When he looked up, the soft smile was replaced by a smirk. "I'm pretty sure that's none of *your* business."

I popped a hip, smirked. "Or is it that you have no friends to give it to?"

"Anyone ever tell you that you're hilarious, Jessica Jade?"

"Don't call me that."

The coffee machine wound down and Christian took a step forward.

Unfortunately, my body reacted before my brain could.

I leapt away from him like his proximity had burned me. *Keep it together!*

More unfortunately, Christian noticed my reaction and his smile grew. "Why not? 'Jessica Jade' is just so *you*. It's a name for a princess. You know, from far far away and all that. Pretty fitting seeing as you have a princess bed, apparently."

He took another step forward and I took a huge step back. I was now pressed against the counter, there was nowhere else to go. I grit my teeth. "Well, if I'm a princess in your little fairytale, you'd be the lowly peasant."

"And here I was, thinking that you'd make me the handsome prince."

"Maybe the prince who was really a toad."

Christian chuckled, and took a final step. Electric shocks buzzed through my veins, and I wished I could take another step away. I tilted my chin up defiantly as he stood in front of me. Close enough that I could feel the heat from his body, see the sparkles in those chocolate eyes, smell his warm, spicy scent.

"I'll be whoever you want me to be, princess."

My heart nearly pumped out of my chest, and I realized I wasn't breathing. The moment was heavy and charged, the air magnetic. I had a feeling that Christian knew exactly what he was doing, knew exactly the reaction he was getting out of me. But I couldn't escape his stare, couldn't move if I wanted to.

Then, he blinked and the spell was broken.

He reached behind me, snatched the coffee pot and a mug. He stepped away, twirled the mug in his hand, and then poured the steaming liquid, smiling at me all the while.

My cheeks burned and a fresh wave of anger flowed through my body. I jabbed his (inconveniently muscular) chest with my finger. "Listen, Starboy. You might be used to getting what you want when you want it. But someday soon, you're going to leave and—"

"You'll never have to see my face again?" He finished my sentence as he grabbed another mug. "Sounds great to me. Cheers to that."

I sputtered as he filled the mug with coffee and placed it in my hand. Knocked it gently with his. He took a long sip, playful gaze locked on mine.

There was a knock at the front door, and all at once, my body came to life.

I knew exactly who that was, and while they were early, it felt like the most impeccable timing.

I placed my mug on the counter, smiled innocently. "Whoever could *that* be?"

8

CHRISTIAN

J disappeared down the hall and I couldn't help but smile at her back. Bickering with her—as ridiculous as it sounded—was just what I needed this morning.

I was up way too late last night with my guitar, trying and failing to find a melody that clicked. I hoped to reach some sliver of emotion, channel my feelings into words, but I couldn't. Even after listening to Johnny Cash on repeat. My senses felt muted, dulled like the edge of an old knife.

Finally, after hours spent trying to summon *something* meaningful, I gave up and went to bed. And woke up three hours later to the sound of someone chopping wood.

Farm life.

When I found that the coffee machine in the Barn wasn't working, I came to the main house. I'd been meaning to kick my caffeine addiction, and given how much I loved ice tea, I briefly considered becoming a tea guy. You know the type—with the beanie and the beard and the constant arguing about the flavor notes of peppermint or rooibos.

But I wasn't big on beards. I had enough negative press

about my facial hair (all from JJ. She used to call me "Scruffer". I couldn't decide if "Starboy" was better or worse).

In the end, I decided that now was not the time to quit coffee. Not when so much was riding on my next single.

Now, I took a long sip of the sweet, smoky liquid, happy with my decision for a number of reasons. One being that, this morning, JJ offered the perfect, completely unexpected distraction. Even more so because she was wearing hilarious animal-print pajama shorts and a hoodie I assumed had to be Ted's, though I'd noticed how the maroon color perfectly set off the tones of her strawberry-blonde hair. I gave her a hard time about the marks on her cheek, but they were actually kind of cute.

Not that "cute" and "JJ" belonged in the same sentence.

There was just something about her. Something that made me want to know what was going on beneath her layers of sarcasm and biting humor.

"Mrs. Applebaum, Ms. Rodriguez!" JJ's voice trilled from down the hall. "So good to see you."

The coffee went bitter in my mouth.

No... Not today. Not this early.

"Good morning!" the ladies chorused.

I placed my mug on the counter quietly, looked for an exit.

The only way out was the back door, and it was directly in line with the hallway. I braced myself against the counter where JJ had stood moments before. The irony was not lost on me that now I was the one who was trapped.

"I know we're early, dear. I hope you don't mind." Mrs. Applebaum's voice boomed as she entered the house. "We just didn't want to miss him."

Him?

Footsteps clamored down the hall.

I had nowhere to go but the living room.

I picked up my mug and went anyway. My final, last-ditch attempt.

"Is it true that—" Ms. Rodriguez's question was drowned out by a rocketing shriek that echoed around the house.

"It *IS* you!"

Mrs. Applebaum fanned her face from across the living room, eyes wide.

I forced a smile even as my heart sank. "Hi, Mrs. Applebaum. It's been a whi—"

"Alicia!" she bellowed. "Get in here!"

Within seconds, Ms. Rodriguez—the sweet but nosy lady who owned the Aston Glow Inn—appeared at Mrs. Applebaum's side. The two stared at me, mouths open and cheeks red with excitement. They lunged across the room, patted at my arms and shoulders like I was their pet. Broke into a waterfall of chatter, their words overlapping and getting louder.

Then, JJ appeared, a smug smile on her face. Her eyes locked with mine as she leaned against the side of the couch, happily sipping the coffee I'd poured her.

Nope. She's not even going to try and help me out of this.

"I can't believe you're back in town! Here I was, thinking that you'd stay at the Aston Glow when you next came into town." Ms. Rodriguez tutted. "Now, I know that things weren't perfect last time. I can't imagine how those darned tabloid reporters heard—"

"Oh, psh." Mrs. Applebaum sat on the couch, clawing my arm to bring me down with her. "Did you consider that maybe he doesn't *want* people following him around? Maybe he wants privacy..."

They bickered around me and about me, and I couldn't get a word in edgewise even if I tried. When I opened my mouth to interject, the two women spoke louder.

Finally, after what felt like an age, JJ seemed to take pity on me. She took a step forward. "Ladies. Can I get you something to drink? Maybe a coffee or tea?"

This was the magic word. Both women turned to JJ. "Tea, please!"

Mrs. Applebaum reached out to grab JJ's arm. "And JJ, my girl, you did good. Imagine if we hadn't been able to give Christian West a proper Aston Falls 'Welcome Back'! Thank goodness you mentioned that he was staying at your parents' or we might never have known."

The room tilted sideways and I snapped my head up.

What did she say?

The sheepish, slightly guilty expression on JJ's face was all the answer I needed.

Unbelievable... She'd orchestrated this. It had to be JJ. It was probably also the reason I saw a flashlight outside my window last night. I guess my secret was out—everyone in town had to know that I was back in Aston Falls.

Another point, Jessica. It was a good one too. I was surprised I didn't see it coming.

Now, a small smile played at my lips as I stared at JJ, who was doing everything she possibly could to avoid my gaze. Keep her expression as neutral as possible. "Tea, it is! I'll be right back."

I stood from the couch, breaking the ladies' grip on my arm. "I'll help you."

"It's just tea, Christian." Was I imagining the squeaky note in her voice? "I've got it."

"I insist."

"We'll just be watching water boil."

"Sounds *fascinating* to me."

"Christian," Mrs. Applebaum cut in, her vice grip returning to my arm. "I was actually hoping to speak with you about something. Please stay for a moment. JJ, too."

JJ, who had been scurrying towards the kitchen, froze. I kept my eyes on her as she stood in the doorway, looking everywhere but at me.

"So as you've undoubtedly heard, the Aston Falls annual Christmas Carol is coming up on Christmas Eve and it's a very, *very* big deal around town. It's practically the Met Gala of Montana." Mrs. Applebaum said this so gravely, she might as well have been giving me serious news in a doctor's office. "Every year the party kicks off with a showcase of festive musical numbers, followed by copious amounts of delicious food, of course. Alicia and I are heading up the planning committee and we have a proposition for you."

My eyes didn't leave JJ, who was now staring at her cuticles like her life depended on it. "What kind of proposition?"

"We want you to perform for us!" Ms. Rodriguez burst out. "We have a list of acts lined up for the Carol, but we would be so happy to feature you in the lineup."

This got my attention. I looked at the older ladies. "You want me to headline the Christmas Carol?"

"Exactly." The ladies nodded their heads.

Then, Mrs. Applebaum quickly added, "assuming that JJ is willing to give up her spot as surprise guest."

My eyebrows shot up in surprise and my gaze shifted to JJ again. A glowing pink blush was making its way up her neck and to her cheeks. "Oh, yeah. That's fine with me."

I thought fast. "I'd hate to take JJ's featured spot at the Christmas Carol. She has a lovely voice," then, under my breath, "I assume."

Sure, I'd never heard the girl sing before, but given how

uncomfortable she seemed, this was the perfect way to get her back for spilling my secret around town. As expected, she shot me a simmering glare. *Point, Christian.*

"I know!" Mrs. Applebaum suddenly shot to a stand. "Why don't the two of you perform together?"

There was a brief silence before both JJ and I burst out with a resounding, "No thanks."

"Sue, that is brilliant." Ms. Rodriguez ignored us. "Having both of you perform would make the Christmas Carol all the better! Just think: our lovely JJ singing with the famous Christian West. Aston Falls and LA coming together." She practically swooned and I saw JJ suppress a gag.

I hid my smile. "I don't think that's a good idea. JJ and I have never sung together, and I usually do my sets alone—"

"Nonsense." Mrs. Applebaum waved a hand. "You kids will figure it out. I personally think this will be a stunning show." Then, she clapped excitedly. "Just think, we'll bring you on at the end of the show, and you can sing a couple Christmas classics. That should get the party started!"

"Or," Ms. Rodriguez pitched in. "What if they were to, you know, MC the Carol, as the kids say? Like, perform a song at the start to get everyone jazzed up for the rest of the acts, present them all, and finish off the show with a bang?!"

"We could easily get a bigger stage set up..."

As Mrs. Applebaum and Ms. Rodriguez threw ideas back and forth like verbal ping-pong, I realized that this was entirely out of mine and JJ's hands. We might as well have been watching a snowball roll down a hill, getting bigger and more destructive with every turn.

But where would the snowball crash and burn? I wasn't sure I wanted to find out.

Apparently, neither did JJ. She held out her hands. "Ladies! Before we get ahead of ourselves, maybe we should nail down the basics. Who knows if Christian will even still *be* here at Christmas."

I shrugged. "I've got the Barn rented until mid-January."

JJ shot me the dirtiest glare. "You do?!"

I nodded once. Guess she wasn't expecting that one. *Another point, Christian.*

But JJ recovered quickly, looked back at the ladies with a placid expression. "Well that's great news for the Christmas Carol, I suppose. Christian can perform. Alone."

"My dear, you should perform too," Mrs. Applebaum cooed. "Pastor McLean was overjoyed to hear that you might be singing this year. You don't want to let the entire town down do you?"

A shadow crossed her expression. "No."

"Come on, Jessica. It'll be great," I goaded her. I couldn't *not* challenge her with this. "Just you, me, and all kinds of Christmas music."

"I'll take an order of Christmas music *without* the arrogant celebrity, thank you," she shot back. Then, out of nowhere, she seemed to relax. Untense her shoulders. She smiled easily at the ladies. "I'll get the tea."

What was going through her mind right now? I had to find out.

I nodded at Mrs. Applebaum and Ms. Rodriguez, stepped away before they could grab me again. "Excuse me. I'd best go talk to my... uh, co-performer."

When I walked into the kitchen, JJ was standing by the kettle, staring out the window.

I leaned against the doorframe. "So, you happy with this?"

JJ half-turned to look at me. "What do you think?"

"I'm not sure what you're thinking, actually." My eyes

scanned her profile. She turned away before I could see anything.

"This is pretty much the last thing I expected, I'll tell you that much."

I smirked. "I have to hand it to you, getting the word out that I'm here was a smart move."

She blinked innocently, her golden eyes absolutely huge. "I don't know what you're talking about. It is a shame that everyone knows you're here though, I sure hope that you can find that 'peace and quiet' you're looking for."

JJ could barely hide her self-satisfied smile. Two can play at this game.

I forced myself to play it cool. If I'd learned anything about JJ, it was that nothing wound her up more than when I seemed unaffected. I cocked an eyebrow. "Pretty proud of yourself, huh?"

"Generally? Yes." She grinned. "In this situation? Well, I'm not admitting anything... but, also yes." She shrugged. "And, who knows. Maybe there'll be so much excitement around town, you won't be able to stay until January."

I shook my head. "When are you going to face facts, Jessica?"

"Like the fact that you can't grow a beard?"

I ignored her. "You can tell your mom that I'm planning 'ragers', you can send the town after me and encourage them to visit me unannounced, you can try to distract me with this Christmas Carol thing. But I made a commitment to myself to stay here until I've written my next single, so that's what I'm going to do."

I expected JJ's full upper lip to curl. For her already amber irises to turn into balls of flames like they do in cartoons. Something. Instead, she blinked, almost like she was taken off guard. She muttered something under her breath as she fiddled with the kettle.

I frowned. "Sorry, didn't catch that."

"Nothing." She crossed her arms. "I guess that's it, then. You're staying in the Barn. I'm staying upstairs. And it's looking like we might be doing this Christmas thing together... Assuming I can't get out of it." She muttered this last past quietly. "How about we just call a truce and agree to avoid each other as much as possible, k?"

My mind caught on one thing—so she *was* staying here at the farm. But why? What happened to her apartment?

I opened my mouth to ask, but she held up a hand. "As point one of this truce, you are not allowed to ask what I'm doing here. Just accept it. Capiche?"

At that moment, the kettle whistled. Without another word, JJ poured two mugs of tea, then strode into the living room, leaving me alone in the kitchen and more confused than ever.

What was JJ's deal? What happened to her beloved apartment?

And why on earth did I care so much?

9

JJ

One of my strongest-held beliefs was that there was nothing so adorable in the entire world as a baby's laugh. And, a few days later, when Ella and I were in the henhouse with Kali and Gia, that opinion was even more confirmed.

"Ooooh, I could just explode," I murmured as Kali squealed. She squirmed in my arms as she reached forward, wanting to pet the little yellow puffballs that scurried around the brooder.

"Babies do that to you." Ella murmured sweet words to Gia as she rocked her slowly back and forth. Gia blinked heavily, moments away from being fast asleep.

Kali, on the other hand, could not be more awake. She was completely taken with the eight baby chicks, her deep blue eyes wide and curious.

"Well, if you ever need a babysitter for these two, you have my number," I said for what was probably the million-and-first time since Ella first announced her pregnancy.

"I appreciate that, J. You're a natural with the babies, you'll make a good mom."

I wound to a stop, stunned. Kali began to fuss and I rocked her while Ella's words ricocheted through my brain.

I wanted to be a mom someday, no question. But oddly enough, I'd never actually seen kids in my immediate future. When I was with Ted, we rarely spoke about "our children", and when we did, they were a sort of faraway, abstract thing.

Now that I was alone, what would happen? Would I ever have kids?

My heart squeezed and I shook myself off. There was no point in bringing myself down with such big questions. Not here, not now. I wanted to enjoy this moment.

"Maybe." I forced a smile as I moved around the brooder so Kali could get closer to the chicks. "Speaking of babies... Christian West."

Ella froze, looked at me in surprise. "Excuse me?!"

My eyes went wide. "No! No, I did *not* mean having babies with Christian. I meant that Christian is, himself, a baby."

She pursed her lips as she bounced Gia. "Just checking."

"And nowhere near as cute as Kali and Gia. Nooo." I wasn't normally into the whole baby voice thing, but it truly couldn't be helped.

Ella chuckled. "So, you and Christian still aren't getting along? *There's* a surprise."

"Ugh, that's not even the half of it." I squeezed my eyes shut. "Mrs. Applebaum and Ms. Rodriguez have officially commissioned us to *perform* together for the Christmas Carol."

"I'm sorry, what?" Ella's jaw dropped.

"They want us to sing. Together."

"JJ." Ella's voice was low. "That's... incredible! You singing with Christian West? Amazing!" Then, seeing the skepticism and doubt on my face, she backtracked. "Wait, are you not going to do it?"

I bit my lip. When the ladies had first pitched this absurd plan, I resolved to find a way to drop out of the performance. There was no way I would sing with Christian.

But, the more I'd thought about it over the past couple days, the more unsure I became. The last thing I needed right now, on top of everything else, was to lose face in front of Christian West. I couldn't think of a way to drop out of the performance without him bothering me about it.

Plus, Mrs. Applebaum and Ms. Rodriguez were counting on me now. I didn't want to let them down. Not when they were clearly both so excited.

"I'm conflicted," I eventually said. "Part of me feels like I can't *not* do it."

"Do you want to do it?"

I shrugged. "Who knows. All I know is that, as of now, I'm signed up for the Christmas Carol."

Ella's brow crinkled for a moment, like a serious thought crossed her mind, but a moment later, she smiled. Elbowed me gently. "So this means you and Christian will be spending more time together, hm?"

"Ugh. No. Why do you say that?"

"There'll be, like, rehearsals and stuff for the Carol, won't there?"

Drat. I hadn't even considered that. But of course, knowing the dedication of the Christmas Carol's planning committee, there would be rehearsals. A few of them.

I grimaced. "Maybe I really should say no. Singing is a pretty vulnerable thing for me. It's bad enough that he saw me in my pajama shorts, but—"

"Hold up." Ella stared at me. "When did he see you in your pajamas?"

"Yesterday. He was lurking in the kitchen like a creep."

"You know, for someone who hates having him around, you sure do notice when he's in the vicinity."

"It's not my fault he's a class A stalker. Remember last year? When he was filming that music video and kept coming into Sweets n' Sundaes? I don't know how he keeps so fit eating all that ice cream."

"So, you *do* find him attractive."

I turned away under the guise of burping Kali. "I didn't say that. At all."

Ella shrugged. "Well, given that he might be here awhile *and* you might be doing the Christmas thing together, have you guys thought about laying down some ground rules?"

"We called a truce," I offered lamely.

"What does that entail?"

"I don't know... he stays out of my way and I won't throw his precious leather jacket into the washing machine?"

Ella snorted. "Look, when Austin and I were doing the whole fake dating thing for my sister's wedding, we had a list of things that weren't allowed. Like, no kissing."

"Didn't he end up kissing you anyway?"

She blushed. "Okay, so we broke that particular rule. But the point still stands."

"I don't know what kind of rules I could possibly set with him, and who knows if he'd even abide by them? The guy is stubborn as the grass is green on the Aston Falls golf course in the summertime."

"Reminds me of someone I know," Ella muttered.

I blinked at her innocently. "Who?"

"Come on, J. You're just as stubborn. Even when you *know* you'd be better off."

At this, I frowned, truly confused. "What are you talking about?"

Ella looked at me pointedly. "Sweets n' Sundaes."

"What about it?"

She sighed, like she had to spell out something extremely obvious. Which, clearly, she did. "Why are you still working there? When things ended with Ted, I thought you might take the opportunity to do something else. Figure out what you *really* wanted. You can't tell me that working as an ice cream server is your dream job."

I put on a blank expression. "What if it is?"

"Then all the power to you! You're an awesome server, and the Applebaums are lucky to have you. But it sure doesn't seem to spark a lot of passion in you. Maybe you should find something that does."

"Like what?" I asked.

"I don't know," Ella said. Unfortunately, she spoke a little too loudly and Gia let out a squawk of protest. Ella held her close and rocked slowly. "When you were little, didn't you have any hopes and dreams for when you grew up?"

"Like that I'd be a princess?"

Ella chuckled. "Sure."

"I'm not like you, Els. I didn't settle on a career when I was in high school."

"I didn't pursue writing because I was looking for a career, JJ. I became a writer because I loved doing it, it meant something to me. Haven't you ever felt passionate about something? Like... What about singing?"

At that moment, Gia's sporadic screeches turned into a full-blown cry.

I was happy for the interruption. Until her cries got Kali started.

Ella and I escaped the small, cozy, warm hen house and

ran outside. It was a cool day, but at least the sun was out. I pulled Kali's little beanie further over her ears and tucked her close to my body while Ella cooed at Gia.

My mind skipped. Ella's words struck a chord with me, and memories I'd buried long, long ago resurfaced. Obviously, I had a dream when I was in high school. Back when everything seemed possible and life was a journey waiting to be taken.

It was ridiculous, but I did dream of being a singer. The thought occupied my mind and I used to fantasize about getting up on stage, performing for a sea of eager fans. I hoped one day to hear my voice on the radio, singing a song that meant the world to me. I couldn't fathom what it must feel like to be shopping at a grocery store or something and hearing your own voice come through the speakers.

Imagine the joy of making a difference, of speaking the truth with just a melody. Magic.

Once upon a time, a once-in-a-lifetime opportunity did spring up for me. But I had to turn it down. At the time, I thought it was the right thing to do, the thing I was *supposed* to do. My home and future were in Aston Falls. I had the man, the job, the perfect plan. My life was laid out.

Or so I thought.

Now, the only places I sang were in the shower, at Sweets n' Sundaes, and when I was at my apartment. Alone.

As lovely and wonderful as Ella's words were, I knew that my dreams of being a singer were not remotely achievable. Which was why people like Christian West drove me up the wall. Life was easy for him, he couldn't possibly understand what it was like to make sacrifices, to give things up for his dream... Or, to give up his dream to do what was expected of him.

If I was going to pursue anything, it was going to be

something relatively safe. Like teaching or massage therapy. Finding success as a singer was about as likely as seeing two shooting stars collide.

I just wasn't that lucky.

"Don't look now," Ella muttered out the side of her mouth. "It's your favorite person."

Of course, my head shot up. Ella and I were back at the house, putting the babies down in their double stroller. Through the kitchen window, we watched Christian come out of the Barn and stride towards his SUV.

She wiggled her eyebrows at me. "I know he's your sworn enemy and everything, but man, does he look good in that leather jacket."

I rolled my eyes, knowing that Ella was just trying to get a reaction out of me. I supposed the leather jacket wasn't the worst item of clothing I'd ever seen.

At that moment, he spotted us and waved. He smiled his usual lopsided grin and he even went so far as to wink at me.

The cheek of him.

I crossed my arms and pointedly turned away, refusing to acknowledge the warmth in my cheeks. Ella waved back, and then returned to tending to the babies.

"You know, JJ," she said casually. Too casually. Almost like she was carefully choosing her words. "It's been six months since you and Ted broke up."

"Just about."

"Have you thought about dating at all?"

I looked at her in surprise. "What?"

Ella forced a light chuckle. "You know what, forget it."

"No, Els. What are you trying to say?"

She stood straight, shrugged. "Nothing. Just that we've been wondering when you might want to get out there again."

I blinked. "We? Who's *we*?"

"Me and Gracie."

"You've been talking about whether I should be dating?"

"Just about whether you might want to, at some point. But forget I said anything."

I narrowed my eyes at her quizzically. "What made you bring this up now?"

"No reason." Ella's voice was a little too high-pitched.

"Spit it out, Els."

"Well, it's just that... if I didn't know better, I'd say that maybe this whole 'nemesis to the death' thing you have going on with Christian is actually hiding another type of feeling..."

I raised an eyebrow. "Being?"

"Maybe you've got a little crush?"

My entire body stiffened and my mouth dropped open. Then, before I could stop it, a blaring loud guffaw of laughter escaped my body. I laughed and laughed for what must have been five minutes straight, while Ella stared at me, hands on her hips.

"There's no need to laugh," she said, face pinched. "Gracie and I both agree he's got a thing for you, too."

I laughed harder. Doubled over and grasped my knees. Waved my hand seeing as I couldn't get a word out.

"You're delusional." I hiccuped when I could finally speak. "What I feel for Christian is the opposite of a crush and exactly what it looks like. I loathe the guy. Look at him! With his SUV and his stupid, perfectly groomed scruff—"

"What exactly do you have against the poor guy's scruff?"

I ignored her. "He's arrogant and pompous and holier-than-thou. Even if I WAS thinking about dating—which I'm not—he'd be at the very bottom of my list. Right next to a Disney villain, or one of the people in the teletubby costumes."

Ella rolled her eyes and I took a huge gulp of air, finally calming down.

"A guy like Christian has 'stone cold player' written all over him. He probably goes around breaking hearts without thinking about it. The answer is no. No way. I would never date Christian West."

"The lady doth protest too much, methinks."

"Don't be quoting Shakespeare at me."

Ella chuckled and I laughed with her.

What a ridiculous proposition. Christian West was your garden variety country star heartbreaker, and as I considered his swoonworthy vocals and soulful songs, it occurred to me that a guy like that couldn't possibly know the first thing about heartbreak himself.

I washed the mugs Ella and I had used while she got the twins ready for the journey home. I had to hurry—my shift at Sweets n' Sundaes would be starting soon and I couldn't be late.

As I turned away, I glanced out the window, where Christian was pulling out of the lot in his SUV. It was the first time I'd seen him leave my parents' farm since he'd arrived. Did it have something to do with the fact that the entire town now knew he was around?

As expected, Mrs. A and Ms. Rodriguez made fast work of spreading the gossip. Yesterday afternoon, a gaggle of people showed up at the farm, clamoring to take photos and speak with Christian. They were here for hours and, in a pretty good-natured move, Christian didn't make any attempts to brush them off, return inside.

Instead, he sat out on the small porch of the Barn, speaking with everyone who'd shown up.

To be fair, I supposed, he'd always gone out of his way to spend time with his fans whenever he'd visited Aston Falls in the past. Several of the people in the crowd likely knew him well at this point.

So really, he brought that on himself, didn't he?

I had to admit I did feel a little bad when the last visitor eventually left, way past dinnertime and when the sun had long since set. As he blew warm air into his bare hands and returned to the Barn, I wondered if he wished he'd had a night of "peace and quiet" instead.

I pushed the nagging guilty voice away.

No sympathy for the devil.

10

CHRISTIAN

"Take it easy, man." I held up a fist to the toothy, gawky teen and he bumped it with a smile.

"Thanks, Christian. Becca is going to love these." He wielded the white canvas shoes I'd signed for him. "Dr. Bell, please don't tell her. I want it to be a surprise."

Beside me, Austin chuckled. "My lips are sealed. Becca won't know a thing."

The teen threw us a peace sign before walking away, whistling. The kid reminded me of myself at that age—a little too tall and a little too gangly. But he seemed like a good kid, where I'd been a troublemaker and put my mom through the wringer (I still felt bad about that).

I'd never forget the day I came home with studs in my ears. "Upset" was an understatement.

Looking back, my little rebellious streak might've been the very reason my mom asked—okay, forced—me to sing with her. Finding passion in music definitely calmed me down a little.

"Busy day for you." Austin chuckled as we continued walking down Center Street towards the river... as we'd been attempting to do for the past forty-five minutes. People had been coming up to us every couple of steps.

"Yeah, sorry, man." I rubbed my face. "I should've warned you."

"I'm just glad we're finally hanging out. Sorry I haven't been around. Things are hectic at the Medical Center. Plus with Els and the twins..."

"I get it. Besides, I've been trying to keep a low profile."

"Walking through town in the middle of the day is a *great* way to do that."

I smiled ruefully. "It was time I showed my face. Thanks to JJ, the entire town knows I'm staying here, and a group of people showed up at the farm last night. I figured I might as well save them a trip. The Suttons probably haven't loved having people sneaking around their property either." I shrugged. "Besides, if I strike out with this song one more time, I'm going to go insane."

"So, you've written a song?"

"I have..." I trailed off. I remembered how I felt when I finally completed the song—the satisfaction that burst through my veins. I kissed the chain around my neck, thanking Mom and saying a prayer in her memory.

Writing it had been a slower, more painful slog than anything I'd ever written—I still clearly had trouble accessing my deepest emotions. And in the end, I was surprised to see that the song I'd written actually read more a love song than any other song I'd ever penned. It was about the process of falling. Definitely something new for me.

"You don't sound convinced," Austin joked, picking up on my hesitation.

I ran my fingers through my hair. "Something's just... off with it."

"What's the problem?"

"I'm not sure. It's like it's missing something. I'm pretty happy with the lyrics, but every time I sing them, I get stuck. And I know I can't leave Aston Falls until I've got it figured out. If I've learned anything, it's that I can actually think here. Breathe here. If I can't put together my next single here, I'm screwed."

"Sorry, bro. That's rough. I'm sure you'll figure it out soon."

"I hope so." I smirked as the memory of JJ in her ridiculous pajama shorts sparked in my mind. "In the meantime, I'll have the pleasure of seeing JJ. Which, as you know, is always entertaining."

Austin cocked an eyebrow. "You two have finally patched things up?"

"Far from it. The girl hates me with a fiery passion."

"Why?" Austin asked. "I've known JJ since high school, not to mention she's one of Ella's best friends. She's always been stubborn and kinda blunt, but I've never seen her treat anyone like she does you."

"You tell me what brought this on. She's hated me since the moment we met."

"Maybe you did something that offended her."

I frowned, thinking back to that first meeting, crystal clear in my memory for some reason. My emotions might be faded like a pair of old jeans, but I remember every single detail of that evening. Seeing JJ splashing in the river, the cool shock of water on my legs as I waded over to help her, her Aussie shepherd barking on the shore.

I found her ring sitting in a surprisingly calm pool of water. I gave it back to her, hoping the anger in her eyes might fade.

And it did, for a second.

We started talking, meaningless conversation. Despite how beautiful I thought she was, the girl was engaged and I'd never cross that line. If anything, I was jealous—she looked to be about my age, but she'd already found her place in the world, knew right where she belonged. In comparison, my life seemed unanchored, chaotic. For a shadow of a moment, I wondered what it would be like to have a forever home...

At that point, she stomped away, smoke basically spewing from her ears. I still had no idea what happened or what I'd said, but something bothered her.

I went back to LA, but she lingered on my mind. Whenever I spoke with Austin, I wanted to ask about the mystery girl from the river, but I always held back. She was engaged, it wasn't right for me to be thinking about her.

Over the years, whenever life brought me back to Aston Falls, I always kind of looked out for her, wondering who and where she was. Eventually, I found her working at Sweets n' Sundaes. Our rivalry only amped up from there.

"I don't know how I could've offended her," I answered Austin. "But it must've been something big, because next time I saw her, she was yelling at me."

Austin raised an eyebrow. "Gotta love that small-town hospitality."

I chuckled. "I actually didn't mind her yelling at me. It was kind of a nice break from people fawning all over me. With JJ, I know where I stand. She's not putting up any sort of front."

"Wait a minute. Did I just hear you say one minorly positive thing about JJ?"

"Absolutely not." I smiled. "She's the most annoying person I've ever met. Which is going to make this caroling thing all the more fun."

Austin shot me a look. "Caroling thing?"

"Yeah, the Aston Falls Christmas Carol or whatever. Apparently, JJ and I are singing together."

"How'd that happen?"

"Mrs. Applebaum and Ms. Rodriguez," I said, shaking my head.

Austin chuckled. "Say no more."

The older ladies were definitely forces to be reckoned with when they had their minds on something. I'd briefly considered dropping out of the Christmas Carol, but there was no real reason to. In truth, I was happy to do it given how welcoming and warm the Aston Falls townspeople were, and I insisted I'd do it for free.

What I hadn't expected was for JJ to stay signed up too. I saw the expression on her face when the ladies asked her to sing, and I assumed that she had a plan to get out of the performance. But no dice. As far as I knew, we were going to "MC the Carol" together.

"It's kind of surprising though," Austin suddenly said.

"What's surprising?"

"JJ. Singing again. She used to do open mics and shows around town, but she hasn't in years."

My eyebrows shot up. "Really."

"Yeah, she was good too. Talented. Everyone was kinda shocked when she stopped."

I nodded slowly, my curiosity officially peaked. I definitely didn't peg JJ for a singer—that was a huge surprise. But what on earth would make her stop?

"Speaking of..."

Austin pointed down the street and I followed his finger to where JJ was standing in her hilarious candy striper work uniform. Across from her was a tall man with a beige jacket and combed over brown hair.

"Is that Ted?" Austin asked, sounding concerned. "What's he doing talking to JJ?"

I tilted my head. "Why wouldn't he be? They're engaged."

"Not anymore. She and Ted broke up."

For the second time in minutes, I froze in surprise. "What?!"

"They broke off their engagement, like, six months ago." Austin shook his head. "Imagine, after five years."

I blinked, my mouth dry. It felt like the world was turned on its head. "I can't believe it."

"Yeah. Last I heard, she's still pretty torn up about it. You didn't know?"

"Nope."

He pressed his lips together. "Whoops. Maybe there was a reason for that."

Austin and I watched JJ and Ted for a moment, my mind swirling with questions and confusion. Hot waves of guilt soared through me—I'd been a complete and total jerk to her. I should never have joked about her apartment and her wedding, should never have given her a hard time about staying at her parents' when I didn't know the full story.

Maybe she wanted the Barn so badly because of her breakup.

What a tool I'd been.

For the first time in what felt like forever, my heart actually ached a little. For JJ, of all people. A breakup was one thing, but a broken engagement was another. It had seemed like JJ and Ted were happy, seemed like they were in love. Not that I knew what that looked like.

Now, watching her speak with Ted, I couldn't help but notice her posture—arms crossed tight over her chest, shoulders caved in, body half tuned away. She was fidgeting with her fingers and seemed desperately uncomfortable.

All of a sudden, this bizarre, unexpected instinct soared through me. I wanted to go over there, get her out of that situation. But before I could, they went their separate ways. I exhaled loudly, and something like relief washed through me.

As much as I liked to give JJ a hard time—just as she did me—there was a line. I didn't like the idea of her, or anyone, struggling. I resolved to take it easy on her, give the girl a break. Lie low around the farm, like she'd asked (read: demanded), and drop out of the Christmas Carol thing if that would make her more comfortable.

JJ and I would never be friends—she'd made that abundantly clear over the years. And one day, when her heart was mended and she came back to me with all guns blazing, I'd be ready to pick up the fight again.

11

JJ

My next day off from Sweets n' Sundaes, I only had one thing in mind: tons and tons of…

Research.

What a joy.

Since my conversation with Ella last week, her words had been bouncing around my head. Despite all of the (very incorrect) statements she made with regards to Christian, she was right about one thing—it was time I explored other job options. Saw what else was out there.

There had to be a world of opportunities for me sitting between "ice cream server" and "world-famous singer."

I bundled into my gray sweatpants and maroon hoodie, grabbed a huge, steaming thermos of coffee, and checked with Daddy to see if he needed anything before going out to the porch. It was a blustery, cold morning, and the sun hid behind thick white clouds. A layer of frost covered the ground, caking the grass white.

I grabbed a woolen blanket and my comfiest cowboy boots before sitting out on a porch chair. I laid out my laptop and notepad, and took a sip of coffee. The smoky liquid warmed me up.

This was my happy place—sitting on our porch in the fall. I loved the cool mornings when the weather was changing, the bite of the coming winter in the air. There was nothing so cozy.

George curled up in the chair next to me and I patted her head.

"Alright, Georgie," I murmured as I opened my laptop and pulled up a search page. "What's your mama going to do?"

I started by searching for jobs in Aston Falls, lazily scrolling through the postings, but I had no clue where to start. Now that Ted and I were broken up, I no longer had a set plan for my life. For so long I followed the steps, checked the boxes I needed to check. I put on the nice clothes and smiled pretty at the country club, and I was what he wanted me to be.

Now, it felt like I was floating around, aimless.

I shuddered as I thought about when he dropped by Sweets n' Sundaes a few days ago. It was unexpected, to say the least. We hadn't seen each other at all since the breakup, but apparently, he wanted to return my box of things and thought dropping by unannounced was the way to do that.

Our conversation was stilted and awkward and, by the time he left, I exhaled a relieved sigh. It was always uncomfortable to speak with your exes, or so I'd heard. He seemed to be doing well, much better than I felt like I was doing…

I shoved the thought away, focused on my computer screen. It had been a long time since I'd done something for me. But where should I work? What should I do? Should I go to school, or work my way up in a company?

As I skimmed through the pages, not registering anything, I debated throwing in the towel and asking my friends for a job. Maybe Bowie had something at Bozeman Vibes. I could be a DJ.

Finally, after what felt like hours of fruitless, overwhelming searching, I sat back and took a big gulp of coffee. Ugh, it was cold.

My gaze wandered over the lawn before landing on the Barn.

I knew I should look away, mind my own business. Instead, I squinted. Was Christian creeping around in there? He hadn't been around to bother me lately. I'd barely seen him, and when I did, he just gave me a curt nod.

It was... unusual behavior, to say the least.

I finally spotted him walking around, moving from the kitchen to the living room. He was pacing, head bent. Finally, he threw up his hands and moved towards the stairs.

I could see him clearly now. See him reach for the bottom of his shirt. See him start to pull it up—

I looked away, cheeks flaming. I definitely shouldn't be looking.

And yet...

I leaned forward slightly. Enough to see a shirtless Christian grab something from the couch. As he moved around, I couldn't help but notice his golden skin, the taut, defined muscles of his shoulders and arms.

Christian West was *ripped*. More than I would've expected.

Not that I expected anything.

Or ever thought about Christian without a shirt on.

"Morning, sweetie."

I let out a squeal and practically leapt out my chair.

George reacted instantly and began to bark. My heart banged against my ribcage and my face was blistering hot as I looked at Ma.

Her eyebrows were raised in amusement. "Did I scare you?"

"Not at all," I stuttered, shifting my laptop to make it look like I'd been staring at it, and not the Barn.

Ma was silent for a beat and I avoided her eyes. My cheeks burned and I pulled up the hood of my hoodie. She sat in the chair next to mine. "What are you working on?"

"Just doing some research," I said, forcing my voice to be normal. Calm. Casual.

"Are you now?"

There was a note of suspicion in Ma's voice and I couldn't help but look at her. Notice her staring at the Barn. Thankfully, shirtless Christian had disappeared from view.

"Of course." I forced a laugh. "What else would I be doing?"

"I don't know, sweetie." Ma took a long sip of coffee and I averted my eyes again. Just as the front door of the Barn squeaked open.

"Hey Mrs. S. Jessica Jade."

I'd thanked my lucky stars too soon.

"Starboy." I nodded before turning back to my computer screen.

"Good morning, Christian!" Ma gushed. "It's lovely to see you. How are you doing?"

"Wonderful, thanks."

Ugh, I could hear the stupid, charming lopsided smile in his voice.

"I was actually wondering if I could grab some milk," he said. "I ran out yesterday and I'd love some for my coffee."

"Sorry, we're out," I said, raising my eyes to meet his in a glare. He was wearing dark jeans and a black long sleeve that was just a touch too tight. I refused to think about the muscles beneath the shirt. "No milk here."

"JJ," Ma admonished me. "We're a *dairy* farm. We have more fresh milk than we know what to do with."

I shrugged innocently. "Oops."

Ma smiled at Christian. "There are bottles of milk in the fridge, so help yourself. You can even take some back to the Barn with you, if you'd like."

"Thanks, Mrs. S." Christian shot Ma a heart-stopping smile before stepping towards the house. I kept my eyes firmly riveted on my laptop while he walked. I wouldn't give him even a second of my time if I didn't have to.

"Actually, I have an idea." Ma's voice was chirpy and bright. "Why doesn't JJ show you how we get the milk?"

My head snapped up. "Me? Oh no, I couldn't. Way too busy, you know…"

"Nonsense. That laptop has been on sleep mode the entire time we've been out here."

I checked the screen. She was right, a green and blue northern-lights-style screensaver was twirling and swirling around. Oblivious to the problem it had just caused me.

"Come on, sweetie." Ma smiled at me and very obviously nodded towards Christian. "Be a good hostess and give the boy a taste of real farm life, hm?"

I opened my mouth to utter another, very definitive "no."

But Ma was a step ahead of me. She opened her eyes wide, mouth puckering. "You could feed the cows while you're at it, too. Save me a chore given how busy things are these days…"

Dang it. She knew just which string to pull.

I couldn't say no when she asked for help.

I pressed my lips together. "Fine. Okay." I turned to Christian, squinting against the lone sunbeam shining behind his head. Like he was an angel or something. "Get your coffee, change into something less... fancy, and meet me here in fifteen."

12

CHRISTIAN

When I woke up this fine fall Thursday, I had a whole list of things I expected to get done. Feeding cows with JJ Sutton was *not* on that list.

But, here we were, at the urging of her mom, walking towards the cowshed in a slightly uncomfortable silence.

Okay, *really* uncomfortable silence. On my part, anyway.

I'd followed through with my resolution to stay out of JJ's way. When she wasn't working at Sweets n' Sundaes, I either kept to the Barn or went into town, and I stayed away from the main house as much as possible. I saw her from a distance a few times, wandering through the house, out on the porch, or working around the farm.

I had a feeling that these tactics wouldn't last long though. Mrs. Applebaum and Ms. Rodriguez had been checking in about our Christmas Carol performance—did this mean we were doing it? Together? And if so, what was the plan?

In any case, I didn't want to push JJ. Which was why this little expedition felt so awkward. I didn't know what to say, didn't really want to poke fun and tease her like I normally would. Not after what Austin told me about the breakup.

JJ seemed preoccupied anyway. Lost in thought. She stared at the ground as we walked, brow furrowed. I couldn't help but wonder what she was thinking about so intently.

The silence draped over us like a heavy blanket until we were standing outside the cowshed.

"You can go," JJ said. "Despite my mom's... uh, enthusiasm, you really don't have to do this."

"That's okay." A slightly stilted chuckle escaped my lips. "Besides, I put on my best cowboy getup for this."

JJ's gaze dropped down my body. "Aren't those designer jeans?"

"Used to be."

"What does that mean?"

I smiled, ran my fingers over my silver chain absentmindedly. "They're so faded and full of holes, they might as well not be. My mom bought these for me from a thrift shop when I landed my first gig. She and I used to play together when I was growing up."

JJ's eyebrows popped up in surprise and I pressed my lips together.

Way to overshare.

"Your mom sounds lovely," she said, hesitant.

"Just like yours."

"Hopefully a little less nosy?"

"Oh, she definitely had her moments."

JJ's face twitched as she registered my words. The past tense.

In the years since Mom died, it never got easier to tell people about my family. I kept it hidden, going out of my way to divert the tabloid spotlight from digging too deep. It just wasn't anyone else's business.

So what urged me to share this little bit of my past with JJ? I couldn't tell you. Maybe to even the playing field. I knew something personal about her, it was only fair that she knew something about me.

JJ's mouth twitched in sympathy as she shook her head. "I'm sorry. But really, you don't have to help, I'm used to doing this alone."

"I want to. Your mom asked us to, and I always keep my word."

A flash of something crossed JJ's face, but she didn't argue. Instead, she slid the heavy door open and we walked into the huge, ventilated cowshed. The smell hit me first, followed by the sight of a crowd of cattle, all staring at us. JJ went over to a couple of them and murmured kind words as she pet them.

"Watch your step," she said before heading towards the back of the shed.

I followed suit, silent and completely out of my element as I kept an eye on the straw-covered ground. I wondered why the cows weren't outside—probably something to do with the falling temperatures. The cowshed was warm and toasty.

JJ walked out the back door and gestured towards a set of controls, each with a green and red button.

"Hay silo." She pressed the green button on one control and moved down the line. "High moisture grain. Corn silage. Conveyor. And," she pressed the last green button, "belt feeder."

I raised my eyebrows, waiting for her to go on. When she didn't, I asked, "that's it?"

"Sure is. Unless you were thinking we feed them by hand?"

Yes. "No."

JJ laughed, rolling her eyes. "Alright, Starboy. Want to try it your way?"

Not really.

But, JJ was on a mission, so I followed her back inside. She moved around the cows, petting them, speaking to them softly. JJ was right about one thing—I was a city boy through and through. I'd never seen a cow up close before. They were actually pretty cute.

JJ grabbed a handful of feed from one of the troughs and gestured for me to follow her to a cow standing on the edge of the group. JJ murmured as she approached her, then turned to me. "You've fed horses before?"

I narrowed my eyes. Shook my head.

"Dogs?"

Another shake.

JJ's eyebrows raised. "Cats?"

A final shake.

"You've never had pets?"

"Never had time for them." I shrugged. "I always wanted a dog, though."

JJ looked at me like I'd spontaneously grown another head. Then, she gestured to the cow. "This is Missy. Now, you don't normally feed cows like you do other animals, but because you seemed so curious, Starboy... Why don't we try it."

I frowned. "We really don't have to."

"Sure we do."

She carefully balled her hand into a fist with some of the feed sticking out. "The most important thing to remember is to never lay your hand out flat or she'll try to eat it. Got it?"

"I guess?"

"Great." She smiled, sweet as pie. "Your turn."

My eyes went wide as she held out some of the feed.

"Come on, Starboy." She blinked innocently. "Missy won't bite. Or maybe she will."

"You're *really* enjoying this, aren't you?"

"So much."

I rolled my eyes, but I wasn't about to back down. I took the feed from JJ and approached Missy hesitantly, patting her awkwardly on the head. JJ snorted and I shot her a look.

Then, I copied her movements.

"Good girl," I murmured to Missy as I held out my hand...

And immediately dropped the feed when the cow's eager, surprisingly rough and slimy tongue slipped over my skin. "Yuck!"

Missy gave me a very clear, very annoyed stink eye while JJ burst into laughter. "You're a natural." She hiccuped between breaths.

I rolled my eyes and wiped my hands on my jeans. "You did that on purpose."

"Maybe. Just a bit."

I couldn't help but chuckle at her satisfied expression.

While the cows ate, JJ showed me the holding area where they milked them and told me a little about the herd. All dairy cows, all extremely well taken care of. Earl Sutton apparently inherited this place from his parents and had a real soft spot for all farm animals. Their herd was spoiled.

Right before we left the cowshed, JJ smiled at me. "Feel like trying something?"

I smirked back, kinda happy to see her so in her element. "The cow tongue thing wasn't enough?"

JJ made a face and then went over to a small paddock where a couple of adorable baby calves were laying around. When they saw her, they came close, and she scratched their chins and ears. Then, she turned to me. "Hold out your fingers."

"What?"

"Your fingers."

"Is this another trick to get them to slobber all over me?"

"You won't regret it." Her eyes sparkled. "I promise."

I had absolutely no reason to trust her, no reason to do what she said. And yet, I held out my fingers anyway. She told me to step closer to one of the calves and put my hand near her face. All of a sudden, a big pink tongue latched around my thumb and my hand was suctioned towards the calf's mouth.

"Woah!" I said as the calf's little mouth clamped down. She made cute sucking sounds and I blinked in surprise.

"What do you think?" JJ giggled, watching my face.

"Weird... But I don't hate it."

After a few minutes, I eased my hand away from the calf's mouth, and JJ and I returned to the cowshed to turn off the feed controls.

JJ seemed happy enough so it seemed as good a time as any to bring up the Christmas Carol. "So. Should we talk about this whole singing thing?"

At once, JJ sighed. "Guess so. We're both doing it then?"

"I'd like to. It's been a long time since I properly celebrated Christmas, and putting on a show for Aston Falls seems like fun."

JJ shook her head and a smile tugged at her lips. "You're in for a ride. Aston Falls goes all out for Christmas. Think a Holiday Parade and a Hot Chocolate Festival, and lights decorating the street, and a huge tree, and baked goods everywhere."

I smiled. "Sounds like a movie."

"It kind of is. Aston Falls is the place to be at Christmas."

"This should be... fun, then."

JJ set her jaw. "Fun might be stretching it. But I can't drop out now, I can't exactly let 'the entire town' down."

"You don't *really* think that would be the case, do you?"

"Maybe." She shrugged. "I know that Mrs. A and Ms. Rodriguez are counting on me."

I frowned. "You shouldn't feel like you have to do something you don't want to though. You do have a voice in this."

JJ's brow darkened for a moment, and I found myself wanting to know what was happening behind those golden eyes of hers. Then, she shook her head. "It doesn't matter. So how should we do this? It's going to be a little hard to avoid each other if we're both living here *and* doing this caroling thing together. I think we need to lay down some ground rules." She noted my blank expression and rolled her eyes. "You know, a game plan, boundaries, a list of what's allowed and—"

"I know what rules are."

She shot me a look. "I'm thinking that the only times we see each other are for this Christmas thing. How about if we meet quickly tomorrow morning before my shift to get a playlist sorted out and schedule a meeting with Mrs. A. If we have a couple details hammered down, she might finally stop pestering me about it."

"Then what?"

"Then, we'll only have to see each other for rehearsals closer to Christmas." JJ nodded once. "And otherwise, we'll divide up the farm—you stay on your side, I'll stay on mine."

"My side being...?"

"You can have the Barn and the front yard section. I'll get the upstairs and everything out back where the cows and horses are." She bit her lip. "I think that's a fair split. You'll have paths to walk around and do whatever it is you rich folk do, and I'll have the stable and cowshed."

"I think that makes sense."

"It's a deal, then."

JJ extended her hand and I assessed it for a moment. I never expected to agree on anything with Princess JJ, but here we were.

"Deal," I responded as I took her hand in mine.

Immediately, a spark lit up my fingers. An electric shock.

I started, surprised, but JJ didn't seem to notice. It was probably just static or something.

I pumped her hand up and down, surprised at just how small her hand was. Mine literally dwarfed hers. Her skin was cool and soft, except for the inside of her palm, which was slightly callused. It occurred to me that we'd never touched for this long before.

Finally, she dropped my hand and nodded at me before marching towards the house. I watched her go, hands in my pockets, weird electricity still radiating through me.

13

CHRISTIAN

Where I Belong.

That was the name I'd given the song. I had a feeling in my gut that this was *it*. This was the single I'd release to set myself apart, redefine who I was in the country charts. But even so, I couldn't shake the feeling that something was missing. It didn't feel right—the bones of the song were there, but it wasn't complete.

It wasn't a chart topper yet and I couldn't figure out why.

I frowned at my guitar, thinking.

With a sigh, I walked into the kitchen and took out a can of iced tea, downed the whole thing. It was 8am—JJ should be dropping by soon for our little Christmas Carol meeting. I had to admit that a small part of me was excited to see what she could do. The girl was an enigma—full of surprises at every turn.

As I stood there, I realized how quiet the Barn was. How empty it was.

This wasn't normally something I'd notice or pay any attention to. I was used to being alone—going from one generic hotel room to another on my tours, spending time on my own at my condo in LA. Most of the time, I savored the quiet. It was the reason I came to the Suttons' farm in the first place.

But I kind of missed noise. Not the noise of the city, but the sound of feet in the house, laughter and giggles, even friendly bickering. I hadn't had much of that since Mom died.

It was kind of nice being so close to the main house. So close to a family that I knew loved each other. Even though it was technically off limits per the "ground rules" JJ and I had agreed on—I wouldn't break a promise.

The silence seemed awfully loud all of a sudden. I needed a walk. Just a quick one, before JJ arrived.

I went upstairs and layered up. Light flecks of snow were falling outside and I couldn't be happier about it. Winter was coming, and I actually found myself looking forward to all those funny little events that JJ had described yesterday. A parade? Festival? Baked goods? It really did sound like a Christmas movie, and I'd be lying if I said I wasn't curious to see what the fuss was about.

After throwing on a thick cream wool sweater, my leather jacket, my beanie and boots, I ventured outside.

The sky was gray and clouded over, and the snow was falling quickly, layering the ground in white. I shoved my hands deep in my pockets as I started my walk towards the grove of trees in front of the house.

I wasn't used to the cold, but I kinda liked it. Liked the winter breeze brushing against my cheeks, the way the air sparkled and shone, the cold in my lungs waking me up.

"You're out early."

The deep, rough voice startled me and I turned to see Earl Sutton striding towards me, massive bundle of firewood stacked under his arm.

He came to a stop in front of me, barely panting despite the obviously heavy load he was carrying. The man was just an inch or two shorter than me, but that had more to do with his age than anything else.

"Cold morning for a walk," he said gruffly.

"Yessir."

"Have to respect a man who gets outside first thing in the morning, no matter the weather."

I shifted from foot to foot, oddly touched by his praise. "Ah, it's a nice day anyway."

"Sure is." He nodded once, then tilted his chin up slightly. "I've noticed you going for walks lately, even when the wind's strong. Not what I would've expected for a city boy. I admit I may have misjudged you." He cleared his throat. "Good on you for doing that."

I bowed my head. Getting a compliment like this from Earl meant the world to me for some reason. "Thanks, Mr. S. Need a hand carrying that?"

At this, Earl's stern exterior cracked and he emitted a short but warm laugh. "Don't be silly. I've been doing this for forty years. I'm sure a couple more won't hurt me."

He smacked my arm good-naturedly, turned on his heel, and off he went towards the house again, whistling. The ton of wood under his arm didn't seem to phase him one bit.

I continued my walk, going over Earl's kind words. He was tough on the outside, but I bet he made a wonderful father to JJ.

I never knew my own. He skipped out before I was born, leaving Mom to raise me alone. It was part of the reason we'd been so close. She worked full-time as a nurse when I was growing up, but she did her best to manage her shifts so we could have dinner together every night. We didn't have much, but we had music. Sometimes, all we had was music.

I lost track of that in high school when I fell in with a bad crowd, but Mom brought me back. We'd sing together and play on the ancient guitar she'd never given up. She had an amazing voice, and I had no doubt that she could have had a career in music.

I always wished she had. Especially after she died.

I did a quick loop by the fields, then walked back to the house. I liked to think that I skated near JJ's boundary line a couple times, just to bug her. I had a feeling that she'd find me if she sensed me crossing to "her side."

By the time I got back to the Barn, I saw that I was right.

JJ was standing outside waiting for me. She was wearing a huge black puffer jacket and a bright pink beanie, and there was a large scarf wrapped around her neck, almost covering her face.

She looked kind of adorable.

"Don't think I didn't see that." She placed her hands on her hips and puffed out her chest. But how could I tell her that she looked as scary as the Pillsbury Doughboy?

"See what?" I asked innocently.

"You crossing to my side."

I bit back a smile. "Were you watching me or something? Because that's kind of a stalker move."

"You would know."

I chuckled. "You're early."

JJ tucked her chin into her scarf and stared me down, defensive all of a sudden. "Is that a problem?"

"Not at all. I like being early too. Makes me feel like I'm on top of things."

"Exactly." I could've sworn I saw a flash of a smile, but it was hard to tell behind her scarf barrier.

"So, you ready?" I asked as I approached her. Close up, she was somehow even cuter. Her eyes were like melted honey mixed with amber, and snowflakes dotted her eyelashes. Light freckles dotted her nose and cheeks like stars illuminating the skies. She had a freckle just above her full upper lip that I suddenly wished I could touch.

JJ rolled her eyes, breaking me from my reverie. "Lead the way, oh famous one."

14

JJ

*I*f someone had told me a few weeks ago that my sworn nemesis would be living in my beloved Barn—and that I'd be sitting in there with him, like I actually approved of this situation—I would've thought I'd walked into a nightmare. But here I was, perched on the edge of the Barn's denim-blue couch, with Christian West on the other end.

I scooted further away.

See, something had clearly gone wrong when we went to the cowshed together yesterday—my brain had fallen out of my body or something. Because even though we'd agreed to stay in our own lanes, it was like I'd become tuned in to his presence. I looked for him as I went outside to help my parents with the horses, wondered if he might be in the house when I got back.

I ended up going to Sweets n' Sundaes in the evening just to get my mind off him.

I had to admit that it was pretty entertaining to see Christian so out of place when we were feeding the cows.

How could a man who sang country songs not know *anything* about cowboy culture?

Though to be fair, it wasn't like he ever sang about farms or small towns. Just about heartbreak and the quest for true love. I did wonder whether the guy had ever been in love himself. Whether he was in love with someone right now.

Not that it mattered. All I cared about when it came to Christian was that he stuck on "his side" and I stuck on mine.

And yes, I knew that our rule system was kind of petty and arbitrary, and it had no set boundaries. But it was the principle of the thing.

He'd come very, very close to crossing the boundary line this morning. I was enjoying a cup of coffee and helping Daddy light a fire when I saw him walking around outside. As he got closer to "my side", I threw on my winter clothing and ran out the door to give him a piece of my mind. Start another little bicker war.

It occurred to me briefly that maybe a part of me actually *liked* arguing with Christian West.

I banished the thought.

Now, I wrinkled my nose as I cast a glance around the Barn. "I love what you've done with the place."

At some point in the last few days, Christian had received a shipment. A huge one. Boxes littered the living room and kitchen—some were big, some were small, most were weirdly shaped. What on earth did he get? A massive lego set?

I was also surprised that I'd missed the delivery. I might've liked to see him bringing these huge, heavy things inside, the muscles of his arms and shoulders working...

Nope. No need to hop abroad that particular train of thought.

"Thanks, my interior designer is pretty great," he deadpanned, his full lips twisted up in that lopsided smirk of his. Couple that with his intent, smoldering gaze and my heart slammed. The man had no right to look so attractive in a fluffy white sweater.

Instead of offering any explanation as to what the boxes contained or why they were scattered around, he stood and walked to the kitchen counter. Picked up a stack of papers.

"So, what's the plan?" I asked, also rising to a stand. Staying seated while he was standing automatically tipped the power scales in his direction.

"For the Christmas thing?" He shrugged. "How about we choose a few songs, maybe sing one together now to see how we sound."

I took off my scarf and jacket, then stood strategically on the other side of the counter, hands clasped behind my back like I had all the confidence in the world. "Hmm, yes. I'm definitely thinking that we want to do *Have Yourself a Merry Little Christmas*, and maybe *O Holy Night*..."

Over the next few minutes, Christian and I managed to get down a short list of Christmas songs for the Carol. We'd run them past Mrs. Applebaum next Tuesday evening—the day we'd picked for our meeting.

Christian checked the time. "That didn't take long at all. Do we have time to get a song in before your shift?"

I grimaced. Right, now we actually had to *sing* together...

I walked past him and into the kitchen, grabbed a glass of water. Stalling.

Christian's dark eyes scanned me. "JJ, honestly, if you're not comfortable doing this performance, you don't have to. I can do this alone. I'm used to it."

His use of my preferred name threw me off for a

moment, but I recovered fast. "Bah!" I exclaimed. "You'd like that, wouldn't you?"

He took a small step towards me and I realized just how tiny the kitchen was. We were very, very close to each other, and he towered over me, all tall and broad-shouldered. There was something about him that felt magnetic, and I wondered whether he somehow had his own gravity field.

And did it just get extra hot in here? Apparently so, because the next instant, he took off his sweater. A corner of his light gray henley pulled up at the bottom, revealing a slice of tanned skin. A tattoo on the inside of his right bicep. I gulped and looked away.

"I just want to make sure you feel comfortable." Christian said this so sincerely, so seriously, apparently unaware of the effect he was currently having on me. He even raised a hand, looking like he might place it on my shoulder in reassurance, but then dropped it.

Immediately, I was reminded of the warmth that traveled the length of my arm when we shook hands the other day. His hand was so big wrapped around mine.

Was he actually being... nice right now?

No, no way.

"I'm comfortable," I croaked. "I'm very comfortable. Don't you worry."

"If you're sure." Christian's eyes were intent on mine. They were the exact color of dark chocolate, with just a fleck or two of gray. "We might as well get started."

His deep, hypnotic voice washed over me, and shivers rose on my skin. "What?"

"Let's play a song together." Christian's eyes grew concerned at my silence. "You okay, JJ?"

That was the second time he'd called me "JJ" in the last few minutes.

I blinked furiously, dropped my gaze. Took a big step back, away from whatever bizarre hold he had on me. "Of course I'm okay. Let's get this over with."

He shot me a slightly concerned look, and gestured towards the couch before picking up his guitar. "Is there any song in particular you want to sing?"

"Hang on, we're singing right *now*? Not even doing like... vocal exercises or something?"

"We can if you'd like. But this is just a test run." He smiled. "So what song?"

I pursed my lips as I wracked my brain. It was like when someone asked your favorite show or movie. I always went blank, like I had no idea what those things even were in the first place. Only one song came to mind—it had been in my head all morning. I blurted it out before I could think. "*I'll Be Waiting For You.*"

Christian's eyebrows popped up. "Really? One of my songs? I thought you were the President of my Haters Club."

Drat! Of all the songs I could've blurted, why, oh why, did my stupid brain go there?!

If his head wasn't already inflated to the size of a small country, this would do it.

"I was kidding, ha ha!" I burst out manically. "Obviously, I wasn't serious. That was a joke."

Christian nodded once, a smile playing on his lips. "Just checking. How about we do something Christmassy. *Silent Night*?"

"Great." I sat tall in an attempt to retain some sense of dignity. "I'll take the high harmony."

As Christian strummed the first note on the guitar, the gravity of the situation hit me square in the face.

Oh, no. This whole thing had gotten away from me. I didn't *actually* want to *sing* in front of Christian West!

In recent years, there weren't many people who had heard me sing—only my closest friends and family, the occasional Sweets n' Sundaes customer. I never imagined that I'd be singing in front of a talented musician. Because yes, as much as I hated the guy, he was very clearly talented.

Rude and arrogant Christian West, I was comfortable with. But singer-songwriter Christian West? That was a different story.

What if I messed up and sounded awful? What if I gave him more ammunition in our little war?

I looked at him, more uncertain than ever. But when I met his sure and confident gaze, my fears were soothed a little. He was looking at me encouragingly. Like he believed in me, for whatever reason.

But who cared what Christian West thought?

This was a challenge, and I wouldn't be the first one to give.

I opened my mouth, and started to sing.

15

CHRISTIAN

I almost dropped my guitar.

Seriously.

JJ's voice was like sweet velvet as she sang the opening verse to *Silent Night*. Rich and silken in places, but with playful high notes in between. I could hardly believe it. And when it came time for me to sing with her, I almost forgot to.

I was locked in, completely taken by her voice. It hit every note, fluttered over the words like waves crashing onshore. This was JJ—the same girl who used this same voice to argue with me and call me out.

Her eyes were closed and she swayed softly with the song, her hands clasped tight in her lap. I found myself leaning in towards her, captivated. Her shoulders were back, her posture straight, like she was shining in her element. Her face showed every expression, her brow creasing and releasing with the words. Her full lips marked every lyric with sweetness and in her voice, I heard something that sent shivers across my skin.

Every breath was laden with emotion, passion and love.

Even though this was a Christmas song, she was putting her all into it.

All at once, something lit in my chest—a small flame waving and blowing in the breeze.

Almost like my heart was defrosting, beating along with the song.

Her passionate singing, her dedication inspired me. Took my breath away.

By the time I played the final note, I was craving more. More of her singing. More of this.

"Wow," I whispered. "That was…"

JJ tucked a strand of hair behind her ear. "Pitchy, right? I probably didn't need to lean into it so hard."

"No, absolutely not," I said quickly. Why on earth would she think that? "That was perfect, JJ."

Her cheeks were tinted pink and she bit her lip. That weird flame in my chest burned all the brighter. Then, she jumped to a stand. "Anyway, I should probably get going, or I'll be late."

I stood with her. I couldn't take my eyes off her for some reason. "Can't have that."

"Right." She grabbed her things and shuffled towards the door. I went with her. "I'll let Mrs. A know that we've got a playlist, and we're set to rehearse on Tuesday."

I opened the door for her. "Absolutely."

"Great." She pressed her lips together and her eyes met mine. That electric current hit me again, striking down to my toes and back up again. It made me a little breathless. Then, JJ looked away. "See you Tuesday."

"See you then and not a minute sooner." I winked. "You know, with your-side, my-side."

"Exactly." JJ shifted from side to side. "Well, bye."

She took off towards her pickup, scrambling into her

coat and scarf. I stood in the door and watched her go. It felt like something big had just happened... but I wasn't yet sure what it meant.

After JJ got in her truck and drove off, hair blowing in the breeze of the open window, I went back inside, my mind racing.

16

JJ

The following Tuesday, there was a snowstorm.

Nothing major, nothing like the big blizzard that was due any day now. But the snow was coming hard and fast, thrashing down from the sky and coating the peaks and fields in a thick layer of white.

When Christian and I agreed to have our meeting with Mrs. Applebaum this evening, I did not consider the fact that I had the day off from Sweets n' Sundaes. Which meant that we would both be driving out from the farm at around the same time.

I didn't realize the repercussions of this until Christian and I nearly ran into each other outside of the farmhouse.

"Hey," he said. Even such a simple word sounded annoyingly gorgeous in that gravel voice.

I pressed my lips together. "Hi."

I felt awkward, I couldn't help it. We hadn't seen each other since singing together in the Barn the other day—which, I had to admit, had been a terrifying experience but also kind of great. It'd been so long since I'd put my all into singing, and I sang at the top of my lungs. I used to do that when I was alone at the apartment, but I hadn't since I'd moved back home. I missed it, I really did.

That it all happened in front of Christian West was pretty weird and surreal. It was a vulnerable place to be, singing with a stranger. Especially a stranger you hated.

And unfortunately, that experience only seemed to heighten the problem I'd been having before. Over the past few days, I found myself thinking about Christian a lot. Like, a lot a lot. Mostly negatives of course. But I didn't particularly enjoy his intrusion in my thoughts.

But, he'd apparently kept his word after all, and was sticking to his side of the farm. Though, in all honesty, it seemed like he'd barely left the Barn at all except to go for walks or runs. What was he working on so hard? And what on earth was in those boxes?

"Excited for this?" he asked now, sticking his hands in his pockets. His scruff traced the angles of his jawline and cheekbones. I'd never dated anyone with a beard before—Ted always said it wasn't for him. But I had to admit, there was something about his scruff that seemed rugged, masculine. Maybe even attractive.

"So much." I twirled my finger sarcastically, then grabbed my car keys. "See you there, I guess."

"Well, do you..." Christian trailed off, turned away, then looked at me again. "Should we drive together? We're going to the same place."

I narrowed my eyes. "Why would we do that?"

He chuckled. "I don't know. For the environment maybe?"

Ugh, he made a good point. I couldn't exactly say no now.

Besides, my driver's side window was still broken, and as much as I didn't want to be driving around town with Christian West, I also didn't love the idea of having snow fall directly into my lap.

"It's a pretty spacious car," Christian said now, eyes dancing. "I promise we won't have to touch elbows. Won't even have to speak or look at each other, if you don't want to."

I pretended to think hard for a moment, then I threw up my hands. "Fine. Twist my arm. Just as long as you stay far away from me."

I meant it—I didn't want to be distracted by his weird gravity.

We got into his fancy SUV which was, of course, already warm thanks to his remote starter. I sneakily pushed my seat heater on max as we took off towards Sweets n' Sundaes.

Surprisingly, we ended up talking and joking most of the way. Mostly just taking jabs at each other. Christian was kind of funny, whether he meant to be or not. And he seemed... normal at times, nice even. Which was weird.

We made it to Sweets n' Sundaes in record time—in fact, we were early. I couldn't help but smile as I looked around Center Street—the Christmas lights had gone up today, along with the huge Christmas tree at the end of the road. I could almost taste the peppermint hot chocolate.

Christian turned off the SUV, but didn't get out of the car. Instead, his brow furrowed as he stared at the dash. "JJ, can I ask you something?"

Uh oh. What was this about? I pursed my lips, suspicious. "Maybe."

"I'm wondering if you can help me with something."

"What kind of something?"

"Well, the other day when we were singing, I had an idea. But I would need your help."

I blinked in surprise, taken aback by his show of vulnerability. Christian and I didn't engage on this level. Ever. I decided to lighten the mood a bit, take another light jab at him. "Wait. So the great Christian West is asking for *my* help? I didn't realize the prince would stoop so low."

Christian glanced up, eyes playful. "So, you finally admit that I'm a prince?"

"Sure. Just stay far away from my kingdom."

He laughed.

"Why should I help you?" I asked.

"To be a good person? To help out an eternally-grateful person?"

I raised an eyebrow, skeptical, and Christian chuckled. He ran his fingers through his hair, then reflexively touched the silver chain that always dangled around his neck.

"If you help me, I can finish what I'm doing and get back to LA. Which means that your barn will be free sooner rather than later."

Those were the magic words. I gave him my brightest smile. "Why didn't you say so?"

Christian chuckled, then reached directly in front of me and opened the glove box. I could feel the heat of his body, so close to mine. His spicy cologne, warm and masculine, made my head spin.

He grabbed a set of papers and then sat back in his seat. I could swear I saw a shift in his expression, a shadow, but a second later, it was gone. He held out the papers. "Read this."

I narrowed my eyes again, then took them. Turned on the light above the seat and leafed through the pages slowly.

I noted the scribbles, crossed-out words, and highlighted sentences. Above every line was a series of musical notes.

"What is this?" I asked.

"Exactly what it looks like."

I glanced at him. "A new song. But what does this have to do with me?"

"I want to try harmonizing with you. If you'd be up for it."

My jaw hit the floor and I almost dropped the pages. "You what?"

"I want to sing it with you."

I had no idea how to take this. Suspicion and skepticism seemed like a safe route. I wrinkled my nose. "Why?"

"I think we'd sound good."

I looked at the paper again. Was this for real?

"Listen." Christian turned to face me and in the glow of the Christmas lights outside, I saw how serious he was. "If you don't want to, I get it, but I think it's worth a try. You have a beautiful voice, JJ, and I think this could be amazing." His tone then took on a familiar teasing, challenging lilt, which I felt much more comfortable with. "The sooner I have a demo to pitch, the sooner I can leave. And I have a good feeling about this."

My breath caught in my chest. I looked around awkwardly. "But there's no music. You can't play guitar in here, it's too cramped."

He smiled at me then. The kind of smile that could melt even the coldest of hearts. "We don't need music. Just you and me."

Those four words hit me funny, sent my heart lurching through my chest and my stomach into freefall. Oof, might need to ask Austin about that. My cheeks were also suddenly warm and I hoped Christian couldn't see my face.

I gazed intently at the pages and I was grateful he knew the words by heart so he couldn't see just my hands shaking.

I was nervous. Just nervous.

Christian began to hum softly, and the melody filled the car. It hit me, hard, and all of my anxieties seemed to melt away.

He began to sing, and I found myself singing with him.

Our voices intertwined and played off one another, the gravel in his voice mingling with the smoother notes of mine. It was incredible. I sang the words like I didn't need the lyrics, like I'd memorized them already.

And as we sang, the strangest thing happened. My body felt light, weightless, like gravity had forgotten all about me.

The words were stunning, beautiful. Poetry. I lost myself in it, threw myself into the song so completely so that, by the end of it, it was like I could barely breathe.

Woah.

I looked at Christian and he looked at me, and some unbelievable force seemed to lie between us. Like we shared a secret only the two of us could know.

The intensity was too much and I had to look away. I tucked a strand of hair behind my ear, my heart racing and blood soaring through my veins. It felt like I'd woken from a dream—an amazing dream.

"That was..." I started. "That was fine."

Christian chuckled once. "Fine, huh?"

"Yeah. Alright."

"It was alright with me, too."

I shot him a smile, suddenly shy, and his smile back made my heart beat even harder.

I cleared my throat and looked outside. "Uh, we should go. Can't leave Mrs. A waiting."

"Absolutely not," Christian agreed, his eyes sparkling.

He got out of the car, but I stayed in for a moment, waiting for the shivers and the numbness in my limbs to subside.

What just happened? Singing that song together, without even a guitar to keep us on track, had to be one of the most powerful, emotive things I'd ever done. I had to do it again, I was hooked. And I had Christian West to blame.

17

CHRISTIAN

"So, how long did it take for you to unpack those crazy boxes?" Austin asked as we walked into Aston Falls' brand new Bell-King stadium.

It was a cool, windy day, but the sun was out and the stands were already filling with crowds of people. The energy was high, and the loud rumble of conversation and laughter surrounded us. The intermingling smells of popcorn, hot dogs and french fries made my stomach growl.

"Too long," I said, then smiled ruefully. "But honestly, the worst part was getting everything set up. That took me the better part of a night."

"I'm sorry, man. I would've stayed longer but Ella and the girls were waiting for me. We always make dinner together on Wednesday nights."

"Don't worry about it. I'm just glad you and Nicholas helped bring the boxes over from the station."

"Happy to. Plus, the promise of pizza and beer afterwards didn't hurt."

I laughed as Austin and I settled into the chairs Nicholas

had saved for us at the front edge of the field. If we were at an NFL game, this would've been the VIP section, and while I'd been seated in that section a few times since hitting the big-time, something about this game felt more exciting. More meaningful.

Maybe because it was my first King's Kids Championship game.

I watched the kids group around Nicholas as he gave them what seemed to be a very spirited pep talk. They were a mixed team of ten to twelve year olds, and they looked up to their ex-NFL-quarterback coach—the great Nicholas King himself—with wide, eager eyes.

I smiled to myself. I didn't have what you'd call a "normal" childhood, what with Mom working all the time and my dad being out of the picture. My friends used to talk about the football or soccer or basketball they played after school, and I was jealous. I always thought that, if I ever had a kid, they could do whatever activity they wanted—rugby, synchronized swimming, circus clowning.

I'd never really thought about having kids though. I was always too busy, and I'd never dated anyone who felt that serious. But as I watched Nicholas and his team, it occurred to me that maybe I did want kids someday. I wanted the chance to be the dad I always wished my dad had been.

"Hey, guys," Nicholas called as he jogged over after the pep talk. "Glad you could make it!"

"Thanks for the invite." Austin bit into a fry then jerked a thumb my way. "We were just talking about Christian's little barn makeover."

"Hey now, it's not a makeover. Imagine how JJ would feel about that. I like having all my limbs attached to my body, thanks."

"You think you'll be able to work there?" Nicholas asked.

"Definitely." I grinned as I thought about the Barn's living room. Or what used to be a living room, and now served as my very own private, mini recording studio.

When I found out last week that the closest recording studio was in Bozeman, I went ahead and bought some top-of-the-line equipment online. Antonia had it delivered to Aston Falls, and the random assortment of boxes had cluttered the Barn for the past week. Thankfully, the Barn's living room ended up being the perfect size for a mini studio. The acoustics in there weren't half bad either.

I'd have a demo prepared in no time. No less because I finally found the secret ingredient I'd been searching for.

"Are you, Christian?" Nicholas's voice broke through my thoughts.

"What was that?"

"I was asking if you're still coming to Thanksgiving dinner at our place on Thursday." A whisper of a smile crossed Nicholas's lips. "Gracie's excited to try some new Morning Bell cake recipes on you."

"Oh, right." I nodded. "Absolutely. I'll be there."

"What were you thinking about, bro?" Austin asked. "Your face went all serious and... are your cheeks red?"

I slapped my palms to my face and my cheeks were actually a little warm. Probably just the sun. Or the cold wind.

Before I could say anything, Nicholas smirked. "Maybe it's not so much a 'what' as it is a 'who.'"

Now, an unmistakable wave of heat rose up my neck. What was going on with me? "You don't know what you're talking about."

"Maybe not," Nicholas said, though his expression indicated the opposite.

I rolled my eyes. The guys had been bothering me about my love life lately. A lot. The evening we were moving the boxes into the Barn, I practically went hoarse insisting that I hadn't dated anyone in over a year. That I hadn't wanted to.

"Come on." Austin wiggled his eyebrows, rehashing the argument. I shifted in my seat, getting comfortable. If history was any indication, we'd be here for a while. "I remember how things were in LA—it was like date after date for you. You can't honestly tell me that no one's after you."

"I didn't say that."

Sure, I did alright, back in the days when I was dating. Mostly fellow artists and other celebrity types. Though my fan base consisted mainly of women, one rule I had was that I would never date fans. I figured there would be an automatic power imbalance—like she might not feel comfortable being honest and vulnerable with me because of who she thought I was.

Not to mention the minefield of issues around wondering if she actually liked me for *me*.

"No one has piqued your interest?" Nicholas asked. "Not even a little?"

One person comes to mind, a little voice whispered. I hushed it immediately and pressed my lips together. "Nope."

"That's a real shame," Austin went on. "I always thought that you and a certain fiery, strawberry-blond ice cream server would make a pretty sweet couple."

"JJ?" I forced a chuckle even as my heart slammed. I rearranged my expression to appear cool and confident. "You're nuts. The girl hates me and has been plotting my demise ever since we met. The fact that someone so shouty has the voice of a literal angel was a complete surprise to me."

"What did I tell you?" Austin said smugly as he bit into another fry.

Nicholas raised an eyebrow. "Wait. So you and JJ sang together? That's pretty huge."

"Well the thing is, we actually sound good together. Like, really good. Now that the recording studio is set up, I'm thinking of asking her to record with me."

Austin paused mid-bite. "Really."

"I thought you always 'worked alone.'" Nicholas put this last part in quotes.

"I always have, in the past. But I have a good feeling about this."

Nicholas crossed his arms, bit his nail to hide a smile.

Austin, meanwhile, didn't even attempt to mask his glee. "Of course, you two are teaming up! The girl and the guy *always* team up." Me and Nicholas stared at him with matching perplexed expressions. "What? That's what happens in those chick flicks Els watches."

I snorted. "This is as far from a chick flick as can be. Besides, let's not get ahead of ourselves—JJ's probably going to say no. As a general rule, she wants nothing to do with me. I doubt she's going to want to spend *more* time with me on top of the caroling stuff."

I picked at my fingernail. Though I believed my words, I also hoped they weren't true.

The memory of singing with JJ in the car before our meeting at Sweets n' Sundaes a couple days ago still burned bright in my mind. I was nervous to show her my lyrics— though I'd struggled with writing the song, it still felt intensely personal. Showing them to the girl who hated me felt about as risky as walking a tightrope over a pit of angry tigers.

But in the end, I was so unbelievably glad I did. JJ didn't laugh or poke fun at my words, she actually sang them. Did them justice. She could've used the opportunity to give me a hard time, and instead, she harmonized with me like she already knew the song by heart. It felt like I was seeing another side of my nemesis.

I'd never sang with someone before—not like that. But singing with JJ felt weirdly right.

While we sang, I couldn't help but follow her movements. I was locked into her, mesmerized. She was exquisite. Her expressions changed with the song, and I heard the love, the sincerity in her voice. It was like I was seeing another part of her soul, another part of who she was.

And despite what I'd said to the guys, I definitely didn't hate it. Not at all.

The craziest thing was that her vulnerability, her passion for the music, lit something within me. Suddenly, it was like I was coming back to my roots, and slowly, something I'd lost long ago came to me—the part of myself that I'd hidden and buried over the years. The part of myself that I'd had trouble tapping into.

By the end of the song, there was no doubt in my mind.

The song needed her. Jessica Jade and her incredible, sweet-and-silken voice.

Now, I had to hope that she might want to record the song together. See if we sounded as good when we were taped, and had instruments behind our voices.

God had to be laughing. What a crazy twist of fate that the person who hated me most on this planet was the one person I was relying on? The one person I couldn't get out of my head?

"So you haven't asked her about this recording thing yet," Austin said.

"Not yet, but now that everything's set up in the Barn, I'll try to ask her after her shift at Sweets n' Sundaes tomorrow. Praying on my lucky stars she'll say yes."

18

JJ

"JJ, dear. Your shift ended a half hour ago, you should get home," Mrs. A said as she spun around the counter with an armful of packaged gumdrops and gingerbread sticks—the first of our Christmas toppings. It was just after 5pm, and while Mr. and Mrs. A usually covered the evening shift on Fridays, I felt bad leaving when customers were in the shop. Even if there were only two.

I filled a napkin holder. "I don't mind, Mrs. A."

"What would we do without you?" She placed a warm hand on mine, then seamlessly took over the task. "But Gerald and I can take it from here. Besides, don't you have a certain celebrity heartthrob to get home to?"

My face heated and I made sure to keep my gaze averted. "I don't know about 'heartthrob.'"

"Oh, my girl, you'd have to be blind not to see it. Those brooding, mysterious eyes, that little smirk..." She sighed. Literally sighed. "I can't tell you how excited I am for our caroling rehearsals. That should give Christian an excuse to come here more often—I noticed he hasn't been by as much as he was on his last trip to Aston Falls. He used to come in here every single day."

"Probably easier for him to bug me at the farm now," I said under my breath, but a small smile played at my lips.

"What was that?"

"Oh, nothing."

Mrs. A gave me another squeeze, then patted my back. "Now, off you go. I need you rested and ready for the Carol. Tuesday's meeting went so, so well, and I think once we settle on the first song to open the performance, we'll be set."

"Right. So we'll meet again in a couple weeks from now?"

"Excellent. And if you see Christian, do let him know. Now go on! I'm sure you have much better things to do than to hang out here with Mr. A and I."

I smiled though it didn't reach my eyes. There was one thing I *should* do but had been avoiding for days.

This Christmas Carol thing actually served as a perfect distraction from my "job search." Which had effectively stalled. I couldn't help but feel overwhelmed whenever I tried to look for a new career. I teeter-tottered between feeling like I had too many options while also not having enough.

I'd considered working in retail, opening my own design firm, being a plumber, going back to school... I'd thought about managing our farm, but Ma and Daddy loved the farm, and they were still young. If I ever did take over the farm, it would probably be years from now.

And then, there was singing.

A warm, bright, traitorous glow filled my heart as I thought about singing with Christian in the car.

There was no explanation for what had come over me. I

had to be catching a cold or something, because that bizarre, weightless feeling—as wonderful as it was—had to be an indication of something being terribly wrong.

I'd never felt that way in my entire life. Not even when Ted finally proposed on our eleventh anniversary.

Okay, so it happened at the country club in front of his parents and their friends—the stuffy McPhersons. The photos looked great, but the uncomfortable heels and itchy tights I was wearing would be forever burned in my memory. Even still, *that* was meant to be the best day of my life.

The fact that I'd felt so happy, and in the presence of Christian, of all people, just served to further twist my brain. It all felt surreal—some hazy, wonderful dream, but a dream nonetheless. The only hint that any of it had been grounded in reality was the fact that I truly didn't think my imagination could come up with anything remotely close to that.

The worst thing about all of this, though, was that I really was hooked. I was addicted, and all I'd been able to think about was singing with him again.

In some wildly illogical way, nothing had ever felt so right.

I had to bottle that up, though. Shut those thoughts away. I couldn't get my hopes up, couldn't begin to dream of something that was completely out of reach. I had to find something else to pursue. Even if that thing didn't make me feel half as excited as singing did.

After changing into my blue sweater dress, I went back to the front of the shop. I picked at the tag on the back of it —Ted had encouraged me to get this dress awhile ago, specifically for cool winter days around town. He always preferred me in dresses to jeans and slouchy sweaters.

"You sure you don't want me to stick around?" I asked Mrs. A.

"We've got this, dear. Now, go!" She practically swatted at me, so I laughed and made for the door. "Oh, and JJ, would you ask your mother to call me? She's in charge of decorations for the Christmas Carol, and I've had the most wonderful idea involving fake snow and tinsel. The Aston Glow will be completely transformed!"

I gave her a small salute as I pushed open the door. "Will do, Mrs. A."

Christmas Eve was fast approaching now, and our performance was just one tiny part of the massive organization that went into planning the Christmas Carol and party. The planning committee this year consisted of my mother and Mayor Davis, and was spearheaded by Mrs. A and Ms. Rodriguez. They all took their jobs extremely seriously.

I drove home in silence, forcing myself not to think of Christian. Or singing. Instead, I focused on George and what we might do this afternoon. George loved being on the farm, having all that space to run around. A layer of snow was building on the fields and George loved to bound through it for hours. We hadn't had our first blizzard yet, but I could feel it coming.

Back when I lived at the apartment, I always felt bad leaving her alone during my shifts. Dogs like George deserved a big backyard... Though this particular opinion always led to an argument with Ted.

As much as I loved our apartment, I always imagined I'd settle in a nice two-storey house, maybe a log house like my parents'. Something with high ceilings, huge windows, a red roof, and a big porch overlooking an even bigger backyard. Ted wasn't sold on the idea—he wanted something ritzy and modern, an apartment full of chrome and glass.

My teeth clattered loudly and I bundled myself further into my scarf and jacket. Darned window, I had to get it fixed and fast. The mechanic was insanely busy these days and said it could be a couple more weeks.

I was driving up the road to the farm when I saw a lone figure rounding the corner of the house. They wore black running tights under black shorts, a light gray sweatshirt, and a black beanie.

Christian.

He hadn't seen me yet, and I took a moment to look at him. The muscles in his legs worked as he ran, and puffs of white exhalation floated in front of his face.

As I watched, he hit a patch of ice and slid. But before he could fall butt-first into the mud—which would've made me cackle—he caught himself and continued on. Graceful as ever.

"Nice save!" I called out.

Christian startled, almost slipped again, then removed his earbuds. He spotted me and smiled his lopsided grin. "Nice of you to notice."

I smirked back at him, then continued up the driveway.

But Christian seemed to have taken my comment as an invitation. He started to jog my way. "How was your shift?"

I stopped the car and he came to my window. Dang it, if he didn't look gorgeous even after exercising. His dark hair escaped his beanie in whisps and his eyes glowed. His scruff was perfectly trimmed and I suddenly had the almost insatiable urge to reach up and run my fingers over it.

I kept my hands firmly on the wheel. Tilted my head. "What's it to you?"

"Can't a guy ask a girl about her day?"

"Not when the guy has a secret hidden agenda."

Christian laughed. "How could you tell?"

"Your eyebrow always gets all poppy when you want something."

His smile widened and heat rose up my neck. Uh oh, why did I say that? It probably sounded like I spent tons of time watching him or something. Which I hadn't.

But he didn't elaborate and a loaded silence sat between us. His gaze was firmly planted on mine and I looked away, feeling warm. "I'd better go. You know, better things to do."

"You always drive with your window down?" he asked suddenly.

"What?"

"You've always got the window down. No matter how cold or windy or snowy it is."

I shrugged a shoulder, feigning nonchalance, though I was really just snuggling further into my scarf. "It's broken. I'm waiting to get it fixed."

Christian's eyebrows popped up. "I can take a look."

At this, I fully snorted. "Yeah, right. You're a celebrity, not a mechanic. You probably have a team of the world's best NASCAR mechanics on speed-dial or something."

"Well." Christian winked. "I'm no NASCAR mechanic, but I do okay."

"Whatever you say, Starboy."

Christian stepped back, took a quick look over my truck. Then, he clapped his hands. "Meet me in the garage in fifteen minutes. Bring a toolbox."

Ten minutes and twenty seconds later, I was standing outside of our garage, toolkit in hand.

I bit the inside of my cheek. What was I doing? Why was I trusting Christian with this? The guy had a silver spoon in his mouth, there was no way he could fix my broken car window. Maybe I just wanted to see him fail and poke fun at him, I reasoned to myself.

Besides, I was mildly curious to know what he wanted from me—not that I would *do* whatever this thing was. But I couldn't help but wonder what was happening in that mind of his. The guy seemed to be full of surprises.

I placed the heavy toolbox on the ground with a *clank*, then grabbed the doorknob. Paused.

Back when we were together, Ted was always late. Always. If we were going to one of his ritzy events, he dressed it up by saying we were "fashionably late" or "making an appearance." It drove me mad because I liked being early. Liked having plenty of time to get ready so I didn't show up frazzled and flustered.

As Christian said the other day, being early made me feel like I was on top of things.

Ted used to say that this was one of my most annoying qualities.

I paused for a moment, unsure if I should go inside or not.

Then, the doorknob turned for me and the door swung open. I jumped back. "Ack!"

"Hi." Christian blinked. "Perfect timing."

He picked up the toolkit like it weighed nothing, and then gestured for me to follow him inside the garage. His hair was damp from the shower and he'd changed into dark jeans and a well-worn black shirt that was half a size too small. He must've bulked up since the last time he'd worn it. Unfortunately—or maybe, fortunately—the shirt seemed to emphasize every muscle of his torso.

Christian had pulled my truck inside—surprising given

that it was manual transmission and I would've assumed he drove automatic. Or had a driver.

Without a word, he opened the toolkit and took out a variety of drills and screwdrivers. Within minutes, he'd removed the driver's side door panel, exposing the inner workings of the car window. He didn't say much as he poked around.

Finally, he stood, wiping his hands on a towel. "The gears are crusty." He gestured to a stool he'd pulled up next to the truck. "Take a seat."

I frowned. "Why?"

A whisper of a smile crossed his face. "So you can see that I'm not sabotaging your car."

I sat on the stool. Close enough to feel the heat coming off him, the faintest smell of his spicy cologne after his shower. Why was that making me lightheaded? And what was it about hot guys fixing cars that was probably the most attractive thing ever?

"First off, I'm going to put the window crank back on," he explained. "Just like this."

Over the next half hour, Christian walked me through fixing my car window, step by step. It was actually kind of fascinating to see how the window worked, and I found myself leaning in, asking questions. To my biggest surprise, Christian answered almost every one. If I didn't know better, I'd say that he really did have training as a mechanic.

After adding oil to the gears and testing the window a few times, Christian painstakingly put the car door back together. Then, he tapped it twice, satisfied. "Good as new. Want to try?"

"Sure." I hopped up from my stool and joined him by the door, rolling the window up and down with ease. "Wow! That's much better."

Christian's smile widened. "Glad to hear it."

I matched his smile, forgetting for a moment that I was supposed to hate him. The guy *did* just save me from becoming hypothermic on my drive home one of these days.

"Thanks," I said, and I meant it.

His chocolate gaze melted into mine and my heart skipped. For a moment, the world disappeared and it was just me and Christian. His presence took over my senses, and all I was aware of were his eyes, his smile, his masculine scent, the heat of his body. We were standing just inside the door of my truck, our bodies almost pressed together.

For some reason, I had the urge to wrap my arms around him, close the gap.

And call me crazy, but as his eyes scanned my face, I had the sense that he wanted to do the same. Like he was also feeling the force pulling us together.

I blinked. Looked away. Took a step back.

"What do I owe you?" I asked, my voice cracking slightly.

"Oh, uh... Nothing. Nothing at all."

"No, really."

"Yeah, really." He shrugged. "I'm happy I could help you."

I gestured towards my truck, refusing to meet his eyes. "How'd you know how to do this? Youtube?"

Christian chuckled. "I used to do a ton of random jobs around LA. Landscaping, construction, pouring cement." He nodded at my truck. "Fixing windows."

My eyebrows shot up. Was he serious?

I had Christian pegged as the guy who didn't know what it meant to work hard. Especially not physical work. I always assumed that he'd been born rich and didn't know anything different.

I would still believe it had he not just fixed my car right in front of me.

"I had no idea," I stuttered lamely. "So, you really *did* fix the coffee machine the other day."

"And the shower. Didn't the bursts of cold water ever bug you?"

Yes! But, I wasn't about to tell him that. Ted wasn't particularly handy, no matter how much he promised to help. And I always meant to ask Daddy, but I didn't want to pile more onto him when he was so busy.

Was Christian—the devil's spawn—really going around fixing things without being asked?

"I should pay you, it's only fair," I insisted.

Christian waved a hand. "It's my pleasure, Jessica Jade. It's been awhile since I did this—it feels good to get back to my roots."

For the first time, I ignored his infuriating use of my full name. There was something hidden in his words that made me want to know more. What did he mean by that? I held back from asking, rolled my eyes. "Well, I'm glad I could help you too."

I lifted my hand in a bit of an awkward wave and turned to leave.

"You know, if you wanted to help more, you could sing with me again."

I froze mid-step. Turned slowly. "Ah. There it is."

Christian shook his head. "Let's get it straight, you don't owe me anything. I was just thinking that you might've had as good a time as I did the other day, and maybe you wanted to sing together again."

My mouth went dry as Christian dangled the poisoned apple in front of me. Of course I wanted to sing again. But was it smart to go down this road when it could only lead to a dead end? It wasn't like I was about to launch into a music career at this point in my life. I was really only giving myself false hope.

And yet...

Christian's eyes met mine and I felt myself falter, my resolve breaking into pieces. For so long, I held back, sacrificed my happiness for the sake of "our future."

Well, there was no "us" anymore and I was on my own. Did I owe it to myself to go down this road, at least a little bit?

"Okay," I whispered.

Christian raised a hand to his ear. "What was that?"

"Okay!" I giggled. "I'll sing with you."

"Good." His eyes sparkled. "I think you'll *really* love what I did to the Barn."

19

CHRISTIAN

Nerves jumbled in my stomach as I walked with JJ from the garage to the Barn. I hadn't felt this sort of anticipation in a long time. There was nothing I loved more than working on a passion project. And, after singing with JJ, I couldn't wait to get started.

As we walked, JJ and I teased each other, poked fun at each other, but things were different now. Lighter. I could almost believe that we were having a good time. She had a nice smile, a tinkling, sweet laugh, and between her bouts of glaring and sarcastic comments, it was kind of fun to have her smile directed at me.

I hoped she wouldn't run away screaming when she saw what I'd done to her barn.

Fixing the window of her truck had been a breeze—the town mechanic must've been wildly busy not to have time for such a simple fix. I truly didn't expect anything from JJ when I offered to help—I had some experience working on cars, and it didn't seem right that she should drive around with her window open given how cold it was. Maybe that big blizzard Mrs. S warned about was on its way.

I'd planned on asking JJ if she wanted to record "Where I Belong" later—maybe when she was changed out of that dress with the tag that she kept picking at—but as she turned to leave, I blurted it out. Couldn't help myself.

And as soon as I did, I saw the look in her eyes. The same spark that I recognized in myself—passion, excitement. She enjoyed singing with me just as much as I had, and I knew I had her.

"Here we are," I announced grandly as I opened the door to the Barn, stomach twisting. How angry would she be with me?

Her jaw immediately hit the floor. "What the...?"

I saw the living room through her eyes—the blue couch and coffee table pushed to the side, the rugs rolled up and propped by the window, the lamps and plants lining the far wall. And, in the midst of everything, a huge black desk with a state-of-the-art laptop for mixing, the audio interface, the studio monitors and speakers, the keyboard, the mics.

And, of course, cables. Everywhere.

In truth, I could see why JJ loved the Barn so much, why she insisted on calling it "home." With its wood beams and big windows and rich dark wood walls, it was a cozy spot. Exactly the sort of place I might've imagined for my family home, complete with a big backyard, of course.

I scanned her face. For the first time—maybe because we were actually getting along for a minute—it deeply mattered to me if JJ was upset. "Well, what do you think?"

Her mouth was still hanging open. She looked cute, all stunned and perplexed. Finally, she cleared her throat. "I just..."

I held my breath, waiting for her to tell me off.

Instead, she exhaled loudly. "I've never seen a recording studio before."

My chest deflated and I smiled. Gestured into the room. "Here we are."

"But how?"

"I had it all shipped here."

"The boxes..." she murmured. "*This* was packed inside all those boxes?"

I nodded. But JJ didn't say anything else and my smile faded. I was usually pretty good at reading people, but I was lost when it came to her. Finally, I had to ask. "What are you thinking?"

Her brow darkened. "I guess I'm confused."

"About what?"

"About why I'm here."

"Because I want to record a song with you."

This time, JJ looked at me straight on, her eyes wider than ever. "With me?"

I shrugged. "If you're interested."

"Of course I'm interested," JJ said in a rush, the words tumbling out. Then, she shrugged, tucked a strand of hair behind her hear. "It just... seems too good to be true."

Her words, the crack in her voice, bothered me for some reason. The girl was an incredible singer, and she clearly had a lot of passion for it. Something told me there was more to her words than she was letting on.

"It might seem like it's too good to be true," I said slowly. "But your voice deserves to be heard."

She looked at me then, and something dark crossed her face. A sadness, a hint of pain. But it passed quickly and she smiled. "Twist my arm."

She bounded over to the equipment and ran her fingers over the keyboard, the speakers, the mics. Almost like her touch confirmed that all these things were real. I watched her, watched joy and curiosity cross her face. She looked like a kid in a candy shop and I kind of loved it.

Finally, she placed her hands on her hips, all business. "Where do we start?"

I pulled up a kitchen stool, then grabbed a set of headphones. She sat and I knelt down so we were eye-level, her honey gaze sparkling gold in this light.

"Hold still," I said as I placed the headphones gently on her head. Though JJ didn't seem like the type to worry about it, I didn't want to mess up her hair. Or have the headphones pull or anything. My fingers grazed her cheek, right by those adorable freckles, and her breath caught. Electricity shot through my body.

We were close, literally face to face. I felt her eyes travel over my features and I wondered what she was thinking. She smelled like an intoxicating mix of strawberries and vanilla. She didn't have any makeup on, but she was absolutely stunning, just as she was.

As soon as the headphones were securely on her head, I pulled back with an ounce of reluctance. JJ had this pull on me, this way of drawing me in. A part of me wanted nothing more than to be close to her, though I knew this was insane.

I handed her the lyrics, picked up my guitar, and started up the rest of the equipment. I'd usually do a run-through of the track before recording, but I figured we could wing it.

I sat on the stool next to JJ's, my guitar propped on my lap. She was silent, watching me. It was unusual for her to be so quiet, and it made the moment feel all the more significant.

"Ready?" I asked her.

A smile crossed her full, pink lips as I strummed the first note.

And, once again, I was blown away. JJ and I fell into the

song together, like diving off a cliff and into clear blue water. Our voices rose and fell, skipped and floated over the words. Seamless.

My blood raced with how incredible this felt, how *right* this was. As JJ threw herself into the music, I knew she felt the same. She even went off-page a few times, tried something different, and I loved it.

Whenever she glanced at me, shy or embarrassed, I nodded at her, urged her to do what felt right to her. That was the beauty of making music—you just followed your heart.

It was one of the things I used to love. Still loved.

We neared the end of the song too early, and I took a breath. Heat and adrenaline pulsed through me. JJ looked at me, smiled, and my heart thudded. Hard.

We were exactly where we were meant to be. I could only wonder if she felt it too.

20

JJ

I snuck down the stairs, dancing around each and every noisy step, then stuck my head around the corner into the hallway.

Coast was clear.

I tiptoed across the hall and laid my back flat against the wall. Took a breath, squeezed my eyes shut, then peeked into the kitchen.

Empty.

Phew.

I relaxed and padded into the kitchen. I didn't turn on the radio and I moved about quietly, listening for the telltale creak of the front porch step. There was only the light tap-tap-tap of George's nails on the hardwood as she came to greet me.

"Morning, Georgie." I scratched the sweet spot behind her ear. Her fur was damp and cool—she must have just come inside.

She followed me around the kitchen as I took out a mug and started the coffee machine. I sat on the floor and took advantage of the dog cuddles while the coffee dripped into the pot. But my gaze was on the hallway and I stayed alert.

I was, once again, avoiding Christian West. This time, for very, very different reasons.

A wash of shivers raced across my skin at the memory of *that* afternoon, and my hand paused in George's fur.

A week ago, Christian and I recorded a song. We actually worked together to create something that felt... beautiful. I should never have said yes in the first place, should never have agreed to record "Where I Belong," because I hadn't been able to get it out of my head. Not even for a minute.

I lost myself in the song, was swept away again. With the guitar playing and the two of us harmonizing, my walls broke down. I threw all of the pain and frustration and disappointment that had been building for months—if not years—into the lyrics. I'd even improvised a little, hit different notes than he'd written, tweaked his lyrics.

I assumed he hated me changing what he'd created, but every time I went off track, he'd just smile that heart-stopping grin of his. Like he trusted me, believed in me.

For the first time in a long while, I felt free. Like I was safe—encouraged, even—to do what felt right. To be myself.

How was it possible that the person I hated most was the very same person who, for a shadow of a moment, made me feel so... me?

The experience was exhilarating, terrifying, incredible. I was completely vulnerable, exposed in a way that I'd never been before. Like I was standing on a precipice in nothing but my bathing suit, ready to jump.

And it all happened with Christian West.

Talk about embarrassing.

I didn't stay to listen to the song once we'd stopped

recording, couldn't bear to see his face or hear his words if he didn't like it. If *I* didn't like it.

I ran out of the Barn and hadn't seen Christian since. He'd probably listened to our song by now, and I wasn't ready to face him, hear his thoughts. I knew I wouldn't be able to help myself from asking.

So here I was, sneaking around my house like I was an intruder. Tiptoeing through our halls and peeking around doorways to make sure there weren't any Christian-West-surprises waiting for me. I had no idea what I'd do when we had our first rehearsal for the Carol this upcoming week, but that was a bridge I'd have to cross whenever I came to it.

"We need to stay away from Christian, don't we, Georgie?" I cooed as I scratched under her chin.

She just smiled wide and panted, shiny pink tongue sticking out.

Ah, George couldn't lie. I'd seen her trot over to Christian's door when he left the Barn, spread out in front of him for belly rubs. She was obsessed with him. Little traitor.

At that moment, the front porch step squeaked.

I froze, blood pounding in my ears, then scrambled to a stand. George, meanwhile, ran to the front door, barking her head off. Was it Christian?

I grabbed my mug of coffee and hurried towards the stairs. But unfortunately, the mug was filled to the brim and a gush of hot coffee splattered onto the floor.

Drat.

The slam of the front door echoed through the house.

Double drat.

Heart racing, I placed my mug on the counter, dashed across the kitchen, grabbed a towel and mopped up some of the mess. I'd have to clean the rest later.

There was no time to run upstairs, which meant my only option was the living room.

The footsteps down the hall were getting closer, so I bolted around the corner.

"Georgie, Georgie, you were outside just a few minutes ago," an unmistakably light voice was murmuring. Then, "Oh, my. What happened here?"

I exhaled a sigh of relief and walked into the kitchen. "Morning, Ma."

"Eek!" she screeched, almost dropping a stack of papers she was holding right onto George.

"Sorry, didn't mean to scare you." I helped her place the papers onto the counter—mock-ups for the Christmas Carol invitations.

"What were you doing, hiding around the corner like that?!"

"Long story." I shook my head and grabbed a cloth to finish cleaning the mess on the floor. Time for a subject change before she could dig any further. "Any good contenders for the Christmas Carol invites?"

Ma rubbed her hands together. "Well, I think we have some very strong options. Now that I'm doing decorations *and* invitations for the Christmas Carol, I really wanted to step up my game. So I had a couple mock-ups made of the original designs, along with something a little different."

She held up one of the invitation mock-ups. It looked exactly the same as the original ones, as far as I could tell, complete with an adorable snowman surrounded by sparkling gifts and big snowflakes. "What's different?"

Ma frowned. "Look at the snowman!"

I leaned in closer, squinted at the snowman. Then, I saw it—he was wearing a plaid scarf instead of his usual tartan. I shot Ma a thumbs up. "Looks good!"

"I think so." Ma smiled. "Alicia and Sue seemed excited for the change as well."

Together, we unloaded the groceries she'd picked up in town, including a bunch of red and green-colored sprinkles and cute cookie cutters. The first week of December, after we'd finished the last of our Thanksgiving leftovers, we started our Christmas baking. Ma and I would take over the kitchen, turn on the radio, and soon enough, the house would smell like cloves, ginger and cinnamon. There was nothing like it.

"So, JJ," Ma said as we sat at the kitchen table with our cups of coffee. I felt better being here with Ma—even if Christian *did* walk in, he wouldn't dare bring up the recording. "I've been meaning to ask you a question."

"What's that?"

"Well." Ma shifted in her seat. "You and Christian seem to be spending time together lately. How're things going with you two? Are you...?"

"Are we...?"

"Ah, what is the term you kids use these days." Ma tutted, then her eyes lit up. "Doing the Netflix and Chill?"

I almost spilled my coffee. "What?! No! Ma, do you even know what that means?"

She frowned. "Dating, right?"

I sighed. Shook my head. "Not quite. Just... don't use that term. Ever."

"Alright, alright. Well, I saw you coming out of the Barn with him last week."

"I was helping him with something. For the Carol."

Ma smiled this serene smile. Like she knew something I couldn't possibly know. "That's awfully nice of you."

"I can be nice. Sometimes."

"And he's nice too, isn't he?"

"Sure." I shrugged. Then, I muttered, "for being the devil."

But, the words didn't have the usual punch and venom to them. A lot of my insults were becoming more muted recently. I even found myself smiling when I thought about him fixing my car window—it was kind of him.

Hanging out with him last week was... pleasant. He was funny enough, and our banter was nothing if not entertaining. I couldn't say that I'd ever met anyone who could spar with me quite like Christian could. He matched me perfectly—word for word, shot for shot, insult for insult.

And yes, I admit that I may have misjudged him when I assumed that he'd never had to work hard. Clearly, the guy had a knack for fixing things, and I respected the fact that he came from more humble beginnings.

But that didn't mean I liked him. That didn't mean we were friends. It just meant that, while he was still a loathsome creature, he wasn't *as* loathsome.

Especially when taking into account the very confusing and unsettling feeling that he knew something about me no one else did—he'd seen me sing my heart out in a supremely vulnerable way.

There was one thing I would say, though. I still wasn't sure who I was or who I was supposed to be, but I could always count on Christian—whatever he stood for, I was on the polar opposite end of the issue. Easy.

I smirked to myself as I finished the rest of my coffee.

"What can I do today, Ma? My shift at Sweets n' Sundaes doesn't start until later."

Ma tapped her nails on her mug, frowning. "I've been meaning to check on the horses. We're running real low on grain, but another shipment should be coming in today from Bozeman."

"Got it." I smiled, then put my mug in the sink and made for the stairs.

"Oh, and JJ? Wear layers. It's getting cold out there, I think some weather's coming in."

"Will do."

21

CHRISTIAN

The track faded out and I pressed "Play". Again.

I closed my eyes as the strums of the guitar filled my ears. Then, JJ's sweet, melodic voice.

I'd been listening to our recording of "Where I Belong" all morning. I couldn't stop. Just as my gut instinct had predicted, the song was perfect. And not because I'd written or composed it, but because of what JJ brought to the music.

This morning was the first time I'd listened to it. After recording, JJ made a hasty excuse and practically ran out of the Barn..I wanted to follow her, insist that we listen to the track together, but she was long gone by the time I made it out the door.

A week had passed now without a sign of her and I couldn't wait a minute longer. Now that I'd heard it, I wanted nothing more than to show it to her. Show her what we—what she—had done. She had so much to be proud of.

My chest inflated with excitement as I rifled through a stack of papers on the desk. Pages filled with scribbled notes. More lyrics. More songs. More music.

I'd more or less been holed up in the Barn, writing.

Words and melodies came to me, flowed onto the pages. All of a sudden, I was able to access that well of emotions I'd locked up for so long. I was able to feel things I thought I'd buried forever. Nothing had ever felt so good.

Now, I had about 3 or 4 songs. And I wanted to sing them with her, if she wanted to.

Some of these songs were just... made for her.

I pressed "Pause" and stood from the table. It wasn't right for me to be doing this—I had to find her, bring her here to listen too.

I threw on my jacket and beanie and stepped outside. George appeared from nowhere and lay at my feet.

"Hey, girl," I said, scratching her side. George was one of the sweetest pups I'd ever met. She always came to greet me when I left the Barn, and she'd even joined me on a couple of runs.

After petting her for a few minutes, I walked towards the farmhouse. I crossed JJ's invisible "boundary line" and wondered if that might somehow summon her.

No dice.

I knocked on the front door, but there was no answer. Then, I noticed that the door to the stable was open. Was JJ in there?

I jogged over and popped my head in. "JJ?"

I saw her right away, standing at one of the horse stalls. Her hair was pulled up into a high ponytail and she had a huge blue scarf wound around her neck. She wore cowboy boots, a black puffer jacket, and worn-in jeans that hugged her gorgeous curves.

She looked cozy and warm. Adorable.

I watched her grab an empty bowl from the horse's stall and walk to the bag of grain in the center of the room. She filled the bowl, then put it back in the stall, speaking sweetly to the horse. The black beast whinnied happily as it dove into its food, and JJ giggled before going to the next stall.

She hadn't seen me so without a word, I copied her movements. Walked into the stable and grabbed a bowl from the horse stall across the way. I was heading to the grain bag when JJ finally looked up.

"You!" she shrieked, dropping the empty bowl.

I chuckled. "Good morning to you too, Jessica."

I was rewarded with a smirk. "Good til you came along, Starboy."

"Ooh, you got me." I clutched at my chest.

"Can you blame me? I wasn't exactly expecting to see you this morning. Especially not here. I thought you'd gotten over your stalking ways, but we may have a relapse on our hands."

I laughed. JJ used to give me a hard time for visiting Sweets n' Sundaes on my past visits to Aston Falls. I hadn't been on this trip except for the one meeting we'd had for the Carol. I never thought about going, not when I could talk to JJ here.

Did that make me sound like a stalker? Hope not. I'd always enjoyed talking to JJ, even before this whole... singing thing. I liked that she challenged me, put me in my place.

"At the risk of confirming your accusations, it's been awhile since I saw you," I said carefully. I wasn't sure how she'd take this particular subject change. I had a feeling JJ scared easy when it came to more personal topics.

"So you *have* been keeping tabs on me." JJ smirked. She grabbed an empty bowl from another stall and I did the same.

"Well." I took a deep breath. "I listened to the track this morning."

JJ froze, the bowl of grain poised in her hand. "Did you?"

"It's good. Really, really good."

JJ's cheeks were turning a sweet pink color. She turned away. "You don't mean that."

"I absolutely do. It's amazing, JJ. You should listen to it."

"I—I don't think I can."

"What are you talking about?" I frowned. What could possibly be making her so hesitant? "I think you'll be really impressed. I would actually... well, I would love it if we could record a few more songs together."

She whirled around to face me. "*More* songs?"

"I've got three written so far."

"And you want to sing them... with me?" JJ's voice was almost a whisper, her eyes wide as saucers. The flecks of amber in her irises shone brighter than ever, and her skin practically glowed despite the fluorescent lights. I was once again struck by how beautiful she was.

"I do." I nodded definitively. Then, I dropped to my knee, hoping to lighten the mood. "JJ Sutton, would you do me the honor of collaborating on an album with me? We can even do a Christmas album, if you'd prefer."

I couldn't tell you exactly what I expected to happen. Maybe for JJ to be surprised, excited, happy. For that gorgeous smile of hers to light up her face. At the very least, I expected an acknowledgement of what I'd said.

Instead, JJ turned away like I hadn't said a word.

"JJ?" My voice seemed to echo despite the crunching from the stalls. "Did you hear me?"

She stayed silent, crossed her arms. Her body was straight as a board as she faced away from me.

I suddenly wondered if I'd said something wrong, if I'd offended her in some way. The thought bothered me and I approached her slowly. "It's okay if you don't want to. You shouldn't feel pressured or anything."

I placed a hand on her shoulder and gently turned her around in time to see a tear streak down her cheek. I reacted without thought, stood directly in front of her as though to shield her from whatever thing had hurt her.

"Are you okay?" I asked urgently, scanning her face. Her eyes were closed, light eyelashes brushing her cheeks. "What's wrong? Did something happen?"

JJ opened her eyes. Her gaze met mine and a jolt of surprise shot through me. In her eyes, I saw something I'd never seen before—especially not in JJ Sutton.

She seemed... afraid.

What happened next was purely instinctual.

I took another step forward and pulled her towards me. Wrapped my arms around her and held her body against mine. She resisted for a moment, pressing her fists against my chest. But then, she gave in. Her body sagged and she leaned into me. Her hands twisted onto my jacket, holding on, and she buried her face in my chest. Her shoulders shook, and I stood firm, supporting her.

It wasn't quite a hug, but it also wasn't nothing. I tried not to notice how her body folded so perfectly into mine, how I could rest my chin on the top of her head, how her fruity shampoo made my head spin.

I wasn't sure how long we stood there, holding each other. But, as JJ leaned into me, I realized I was also leaning into her. As if a part of me needed this as much as she did. It occurred to me that it had been a long, long time since I'd held someone like this.

Finally, she pulled back and I let her go. She sniffed and I noticed how tired, how wary she looked. It broke my heart.

I raised a hand to her face, cupped her cheek. Our eyes

met and I used my thumb to lightly wipe the tear that remained.

JJ's eyes searched mine and her lips parted. My gaze fell to those full lips of hers and an incredible wave of heat rushed through my body. I was hit by the almost untameable urge to pull her against me again. Press my lips to hers.

Just one kiss—

"JJ, you there?"

The voice was like a bolt of lightning and JJ and I sprang apart.

I knocked into the bag of grain and it toppled to the ground, spilling horse feed all over the floor. JJ made to rush forward, sweep it up, but I gestured towards the door, where Mrs. S would appear at any minute.

"I got this," I murmured even as my heart was racing.

She blinked once, then shot me a small, tentative smile of gratitude. It was easily one of the most beautiful things I'd ever seen. Because there was JJ—the real, no-walls-up JJ.

"Sweetie?" Mrs. S called again and JJ ran towards the door.

"Yes, Ma, I'm here."

"Good. I need your help." Mrs. S appeared at the door, slightly out of breath. Her face twisted in bewilderment when she saw me, but she shook her head like she didn't have time to ask what I was doing kneeling on the floor, sweeping grain into a bag. "We have a BIG problem."

22

JJ

"What's going on?" I asked, trying and failing to focus on Ma. Though we were several feet away from him, all of my attention was on Christian. My mouth was dry as the desert and my skin tingled and sparked.

It was a miracle I heard Ma's response over the frantic beating of my heart.

"The blizzard's here," she said, wringing her hands.

That got my attention. I frowned as I peeked over her shoulder—the sky was overcast, but it wasn't snowing. "Now?"

"Well, it's not here yet," she said impatiently. "But it's coming. From Bozeman. Which means..."

The blood drained from my face. "Oh no."

"Which means what?" Christian asked and I reflexively glanced towards him. His handsome face was twisted in confusion as he came to stand next to me. Shivers ran the length of my limbs and the side of my body closest to him—mere inches away—lit up with his proximity.

I kept my face neutral, staring at Ma. "We're on the last bag of horse grain. We'll run out by the end of the day, and if this blizzard is a big one, it could be awhile before we get more."

I felt Christian's frown more than I could see it. Ugh, how was I so tuned into him?

"Do you have any neighbors who might have extra grain?" he asked. "And, horses eat apples and carrots, don't they? Can they have that for a few days?"

Ma took this question. "We adopted our horses from shelters and sanctuaries. Most of them are getting old and we buy a special grain to keep them healthy and strong. Yes, they can eat regular grain for a couple days, but if this blizzard takes out the Express for longer than that, I'm afraid our babies won't be in good shape."

Ma crossed her arms over her body, mouth pinched. My insides squeezed with dread as I went over to my horse, Starlight, and pet her nuzzle affectionately. "We won't let that happen to you, girl."

Daddy appeared behind Ma, placing his hands on her shoulders. "It'll be alright, Mary. These blizzards usually pass quickly, and there's no way to know if the Express will break down in the first place. If it does, the crew are prepared for it. There's no need to worry."

Ma tapped her foot impatiently. "If only Mayor Davis could get that darned roadway put in."

"He's making progress."

"Well, if wishes were horses..." she trailed off. Then, she stood straight and a determined look crossed her face. "There's only one thing we can do—hop on the train right now and get the grain ourselves. We've got to beat the blizzard!"

She pumped her fist in the air. Like she had any chance at competing against an extreme weather event.

Daddy squeezed her shoulders gently. "You know it's not a good time for you to leave the farm, dear."

Ma deflated. "I know. There's a whole list of chores to get done before the blizzard hits."

"Maybe I can go," he said. "I'll help bat down the hatches here, and then hopefully, I can catch the second last train. Make it back in time..." He trailed off as he and Ma looked at each other with matching, resigned expressions.

"I'll go." My voice seemed blaringly loud as I stepped forward.

Ma and Daddy looked at me like they'd forgotten I was here.

"That's very kind of you to offer, sweetie," Ma said. "But, I'm afraid it isn't a one-person job anyway. If it was a question of just a bag or two of grain, it would be fine, but we've ordered enough to get us through the next few months of winter. You can't do this alone."

"I'll go with her."

That familiar sweet gravel voice shook me to my core, and it took everything I had not to stare at the man next to me. From now on, I decided, I would treat Christian like I did the sun—never look at him directly.

"We can't ask you to do that, son," Daddy said, shaking his head.

Son? Since when were Daddy and Christian on such good terms? Daddy always called Ted by his first name, and almost reluctantly at that. Apparently, Christian was now the golden child.

"Why not?" Christian asked. "I'm not doing anything else today, and I'm happy to lend a hand. Besides..." In the corner of my eye, I saw him shoot me a glance. I kept my gaze on my parents and far away from those melted chocolate whirlpools just waiting to drag me under. "I've been meaning to get a workout in. Those bags of grain are no joke."

Ma and Daddy laughed. Real, belly laughs. Of course Christian had charmed the absolute pants off of them.

"Well, only if you're sure…" Ma said hesitantly. "I don't want to put you out, by any means. You're our guest after all."

"It's no trouble."

I stood still as a statue, unable to move, unable to say anything. I had hoped that going on this trip alone—being away from the farm for a few hours—might give me space and time to clear my head. To clear my body of what had almost happened between Christian and I.

Because, for a heady, unbelievable moment, it seemed like Christian might kiss me.

And for that same heady moment, I almost wanted him to.

Christian freaking West.

Now, he was basically inviting himself to join me on this lengthy, tedious chore. It was kind of him to offer—and to help my parents and our beloved horses—but it also created a huge problem for me.

Because neither my body nor my brain were in order when I was around Christian. And there was a chance that being trapped with him for half a day would seriously mess with me. Who knows if I could ever come back from that?

But the decision had been made. The train had left the station, so to speak.

"You'd best hurry," Ma said now, grabbing my arm and shooing me out the door. "Those clouds are coming quick and we don't have much time."

Christian was right behind me. "We'll take my car?"

I nodded once. "Fine."

And that was how I ended up on an hours-long trip to Bozeman with Christian West, head spinning, heart racing, and lips tingling with the memory of his face so close to mine.

23

JJ

"Scoot over?"

I looked up in surprise. "Excuse me?"

Christian raised his eyebrows, his dark eyes giving nothing away. He nodded at the space on the bench seat next to me. "Mind if I sit?"

I looked around the empty train car and wrapped my jacket tight around me in an effort to ward off the cool air. The Express was deserted—Christian and I were the only passengers on this journey back to Aston Falls from Bozeman. "There are a ton of seats open for you and your fancy jeans."

He smirked, eyes twinkling. "Maybe these fancy jeans want to sit next to you."

I blinked, taken aback by his flirty response. But I moved over, made space for him.

His warm, firm side pressed against mine as he sat. His masculine smell of cedar and spice threatened to unleash the gang of butterflies that were perched in my stomach.

Why were they there anyway? Probably just some lingering side effect from what happened in the stable.

It *had* been months since I'd been kissed.

Not that I wanted Christian to change that.

I'd spent the entire train ride to Bozeman pretending I was asleep. I didn't want to face him, to talk about *that* moment. And it seemed like Christian was the type to want to talk about it. I thought most men weren't good at communication? Christian was showing himself to be the opposite.

By the time we arrived in Bozeman, I'd come to one conclusion—I didn't *actually* want to kiss Christian West. The moment when I almost leaned in? It was all rooted in my missing Ted and grieving the end of my engagement. It was the only explanation because there was no way I'd ever feel Christian's lips on mine.

The guy was still the enemy. Sure, he wasn't exactly who I assumed he was, but that didn't mean he was a good man. He'd literally made his career on breakup songs. There was no way that mine was joining his list. Especially seeing as my split from Ted was so, so fresh.

I shifted slightly, trying to move away from him and his bizarre gravitational pull. But it was a small seat, barely big enough for the two of us.

For the millionth time in my life, I cursed my curves. If only I was slight and willowy, like Grace, or petite, like Ella. I'd never felt completely comfortable with my body, no matter how confident I tried to act.

"Tight fit." Christian chuckled.

"Hence why I told you to sit somewhere else."

"Hence? You're starting to sound like Ella."

I put on a thick accent. "Just because I grew up on a farm doesn't mean I don't know nothing about proper English."

Christian suddenly went serious, eyes locked on mine. "I didn't mean it like that. You're very well-spoken, JJ."

His compliment took me off guard and I crossed my

arms. I felt off-kilter, like Christian was beckoning me to meet him in the no man's land between our battle zones and I had no idea whether I should put down my weapons or look out for traps.

"Anyway," Christian continued with a smile, oblivious to the confusion he'd triggered within me. "I find trains a little drafty, don't you? I figured I'd sit close, we could share body heat."

His words lit a flame in my stomach that skyrocketed to my face.

His expression changed as his words registered. "That came out funny. It's just that trains can be chilly, and I noticed you shivering in your sleep on the way to Bozeman. I just wanted to say that—"

I snorted, letting him off the hook. "It's okay, Christian. I got it." I snuck a glance at him. "And thanks."

He smiled that lopsided grin of his and the butterflies I'd been trying so hard to hold back burst free. My stomach flipped in a warm topsy-turvy kind of way, while the butterflies continued down my extremities, gathered by my toes.

Keep it together, JJ.

"It's pretty impressive that we made the last train." I shifted awkwardly.

"Amazing what a bit of stress and high pressure can do."

I rolled my eyes, then thought back to seeing Christian load the bags of grain from the feed store to the cab, and then from the cab to the train. I couldn't say I hated watching his muscles strain and work to move the heavy bags.

No wonder his biceps and shoulders were so sculpted—the guy was strong. Very strong.

By the time the train set off for Aston Falls, the blizzard

was upon us, and Christian and I were apparently the only ones idiotic enough to risk riding the train.

At that moment, a gust of wind slammed into the side of the train car.

I squeezed my eyes shut and clenched my hands together. I couldn't fake sleep on this journey, not when a storm was raging. Which meant that Christian and I would be trapped together, awake and aware, for the next three hours and twelve minutes.

Fantastic.

"Nuts?" Christian asked, holding out a bag of trail mix.

I frowned. "Where'd you get those?"

"I stopped at the vending machine before we boarded the train. Picked up a few things." He reached into the pocket of his leather jacket, pulled out chocolate peanut butter cups, cheesy crackers and salt n' vinegar chips. "Boy scout motto says to always come prepared."

Salt n' vinegar chips were my kryptonite. But the train shook again and my appetite went out the window with the force of the wind. "I'm good."

"Suit yourself."

Christian continued to munch through his trail mix. Normally, the sound would annoy me, set me off. But oddly, I found it comforting. I was glad that I wasn't alone on this terrifying train ride, and a part of me was relieved that Christian was here. I had a feeling he'd be good in a crisis.

Plus, I could use his body as a human shield if something bad were to happen.

Another gust of wind blew, hitting the train car so hard it almost came off the tracks. My heart jumped to my throat and I squeaked, closing my eyes tight.

"I hate storms," I muttered.

Christian stopped his crunching. "We don't get snowstorms in LA."

"There's a lot of things you don't get in LA."

Christian smirked, then popped another nut in his mouth. He leaned forward to stick the empty package into his pocket and, as he moved away from me, cold air hit the side of my body. I let out an involuntary shiver.

Okay, he was right—if he hadn't been sitting next to me, I'd probably be curled into a ball to conserve heat.

"If you hate storms," he said, "why don't we talk? Distract ourselves?"

Red alert! Red alert! Get out of there!

Panic set off through my body and I stiffened. Talk about *what* exactly? The weird hug he gave me in the stable? Why I was crying, and why he then wiped a tear from my cheek so tenderly? The moment when I thought he might bend down and kiss me?

"So now that we're alone, what do you *really* think about my scruff?"

I blinked. Exhaled in one fell swoop. "What?"

"Well, I figured if we die tonight, we might as well take the opportunity to be honest. So scruff is a yay or nay?"

I couldn't help but snort, fully distracted. "Nay."

Then, as though God knew that I was lying, the train lurched violently and my stomach rose up to my throat. I squealed, clenched my eyes shut. "Okay, okay! It's a yay."

Christian chuckled. "What an enthusiastic answer. Guess I'll keep it then."

I shot him a glare.

"Alright, another distraction... How long have you been singing for?"

"Excuse me?"

"Your voice and breathwork are amazing. You've clearly been singing for a long time."

The wind pummeled the side of the train and I held my breath. My mind was quickly approaching a dangerous spiral involving train crashes, yetis, and being buried alive in a snowbank. Anything had to be better than going down that particular path of anxiety…

Even having an actual, no-jabs conversation with Christian West.

"Since I could talk," I said through clenched teeth.

"And you never considered pursuing it?"

"Never had the opportunity."

"I don't believe that."

I bit my lip and looked out the window. The world was pitch black with nightfall; it was probably for the best that I couldn't see anything. I started picking at my nails. "I might've had a chance, once upon a time," I said, then quickly added, "but it's not worth talking about."

Christian faced me, but stayed close so I could continue stealing his heat. "Why not?"

I exhaled a laugh, but it came out choked. I'd only ever told one person about what had happened that day, and my story had received a pretty negative reaction. There was no reason for me to tell Christian West. Not really.

But he looked at me patiently, not pushing or expecting anything, and it occurred to me that maybe I wanted to tell him. No less because, if I died tonight in some freak blizzard-train-yeti incident, I'd regret never telling anyone else about this.

I took a deep breath, my eyes cast downwards. "It was after I graduated high school. I got the job at Sweets n' Sundaes, but in the evenings, I used to do open mic nights, small performances for birthdays and celebrations, stuff like that."

I took another breath. Focused on the exhale. Christian didn't move.

"I was singing in a mall in Helena around the holidays. It was your typical Christmas gig—I was wearing an elf costume, singing next to Santa. After finishing my set, a man approached me. He said he was a talent agent from New York, in town visiting his mom for a few days. He offered to sign me on the spot. Assuming I was ready to pick up and move to New York by the end of the week."

I smiled sadly, remembering how excited, ecstatic, I felt. It was a dream come true, a fairy tale come to life. And the first person I wanted to tell was Ted.

When I got home that night and told him about the offer though, his expression had turned sour. He insisted that I couldn't move to New York, *we* couldn't move to New York. We had a long conversation about why we both needed to stay in Aston Falls. For our own good. For the good of our future family.

"Long story short, I didn't end up going," I said to Christian, still staring at my hands. The sharp pain of regret and sadness took my breath away. It had never abated, not in all the years since. "Ted didn't think it was right for me to go, and I agreed with him. I stopped singing after that—it was easier to stop believing in my dream than fight for something impossible."

I didn't dare look at Christian's face. I couldn't imagine what he'd say. Would he make fun of me for thinking I actually had a shot? Would he say that I was stupid to believe, for a second, that I could do it?

Finally, he took a deep breath. "I admire you."

I had to look at him then. "Are you joking?"

"Not at all. You gave up a lot for love. That must've been an almost impossible sacrifice."

I was embarrassed to feel tears prick at my eyes. He was right. It was almost impossible.

"Fat load of good it did me," I whispered.

Christian was silent for a long moment. He shifted and I thought he might put an arm around me. A part of me actually wished he did. "At least you tried, JJ. At least you loved."

I blinked back my tears, but it was too late. It felt like my chest was caving in. Because the truth was that love wasn't even on my radar when I turned down the offer to move to New York. It simply felt like what I was supposed to do—settle down, buy a house, get married.

"Did I?" I whispered.

"What do you mean?"

I squeezed my eyes shut again, hardly believing what I was about to say. Maybe it was the hunger, or the head-spinning moment in the stable, or the fact that the train might topple off the tracks at any moment, but a part of me wanted to be honest. To stop hiding. To stop fighting.

"I've been engaged. But I don't think I've been in love."

24

CHRISTIAN

JJ's words bounced around inside my head. I couldn't understand what she said, I must've misheard. Over the years, JJ had gone out of her way so many times to show me just how perfect her relationship was with Ted.

"I didn't get that," I said, almost cracking up at my ridiculous misunderstanding.

JJ, however, wasn't laughing. The words tumbled from her mouth. "I don't know if I've been in love."

Any urge to laugh disappeared.

I frowned, eyes traveling over her face. Her fingers were clasped in her lap so tight that her knuckles were white. Part of me wanted to reach out, grab her hand, release her grip, maybe take some of her pain as my own.

"What about Ted?" I murmured. For some reason, my heart was slamming against my ribcage.

"I... I don't know," she started. Then, she exhaled a shaky breath. "Can I tell you something?"

I tilted my head. This was new territory for us—JJ and I usually had an ocean of snappy remarks and comebacks separating us. But I realized that I wanted this. I wanted to know her, know more about her. "Of course."

"You remember that time we met? In the Aston Falls river?"

Like I could forget. "Yeah."

"I didn't lose my engagement ring while walking George," she whispered. "I threw it."

I startled. Looked at her blankly. "You...?"

"Threw it. I threw my engagement ring in the river."

JJ shifted in her seat, her face unnaturally pale. I didn't want to press her, didn't want her to feel any sort of discomfort. I just wanted to be here with her. So I was silent, giving her the space and time she needed.

"It wasn't like Ted and I had a fight or anything. It was actually one of our good days." She shook her head. "As soon as the ring splashed into the water, I came to my senses. I was shocked at what I'd done, and unbelievably angry with myself. The last thing I needed at that moment was to be 'saved' by some devastatingly gorgeous stranger who, I found out later, happened to be one of my favorite artists."

My eyebrows shot up and I couldn't help but smile. "Devastatingly gorgeous, you say?"

JJ rolled her eyes. "Don't flatter yourself. You were gorgeous until the moment you opened your mouth and told me that I was too young to get married."

"I didn't say that."

"Sure you did."

I frowned, genuinely confused. "Whatever I said, I didn't mean it that way."

"What did you mean, then?"

"Honestly? I was thinking about how lucky you were." I ran my fingers through my hair. "You were so young, but you'd already found your place, found where you belonged. I haven't felt anything like that since my mom died."

I caught myself, surprised that I was telling JJ any of this. But I wanted to tell her, it felt right that we should talk like this. For as long as I'd known her, JJ had challenged me, been my eternal rival. I'd always counted on our verbal sparring.

But now? I couldn't stop thinking about how much I wanted to kiss her.

I took a breath. "I do want to thank you, JJ."

"Thank me for what?"

"For years, I've been feeling like a spectator in my own life. Like I've been sleeping and I can't wake up. And because of that, I've been lying."

"Lying to who?"

"Everyone." I shook my head. "My friends, my manager, and worst of all, my fans. They expect truth and honesty in my songs, and I used to be able to deliver that. But I haven't been able to for months. Until you came along."

JJ sat back... as far back as she could on our impressively small bench seat. "Me?"

I nodded. "When I met you, I felt something. And every time I came to Aston Falls and spoke to you, I felt something. Even if it was just annoyance and irritation."

I winked and, to my intense joy, she rolled her eyes.

"It was like talking to you was medicine, the thing I needed every few months just to keep going. I relied on that, relied on coming back to Aston Falls and seeing you. Remember when I filmed that music video?"

"How could I forget." JJ laughed ruefully. "You came by Sweets n' Sundaes every single day."

"I wanted to see you." I smiled, fingering the silver chain around my neck. "Things were moving quickly in my life, so quickly I barely had time to think. Or write. Barely had time to miss my mom. That was the lowest point for me."

I trailed off, shame biting at my insides. But JJ didn't interrupt. Didn't berate me or give me a hard time.

"When we sang together the other day... Well, that was the kicker. Because of you, I felt excited and passionate about music again. You were the one who brought me back, and I can't thank you enough for that."

I closed my eyes. My stomach was twisted into a knot and beads of apprehension gathered on my skin. I felt like I'd just divulged all of my secrets to the enemy, but it strangely didn't feel bad at all. I was exposed and armorless.

At that moment, a small, warm palm pressed against my hand. Lightly, gently. Just to show that she was here.

Without a thought, I intertwined my fingers with hers, like it was the most natural thing in the world.

"Can you feel this?" she murmured.

I looked into her eyes, her gorgeous golden eyes. I let myself fall into them, fall into her sweet and open expression, the relief of touching her. A smile crossed her lips, and my heart slammed.

Then, the train ground to a halt and the lights went out.

25

JJ

Growing up, I'd heard many things about what it meant to be in love.

There was the prince rescuing the princess from the tower, the two kids who find love despite the blood feud between their families, the girl standing in front of a boy asking him to love her.

As I got older, I wondered to what extent love was glamorized, made to look a certain way. Because what I felt for Ted never came close to what I expected. Don't get me wrong, I loved Ted—loved him for being stable and steady, loved him for loving me, loved him out of habit. But, I'd often questioned whether I was *in* love with him.

Maybe that was why I'd broken off our engagement.

These were the thoughts flying through my head when the lights of the train went out.

As I shrieked in fear, it occurred to me that my last thought couldn't possibly be about some dragon holding a princess hostage.

"JJ! JJ, you're fine!"

A pair of big, warm hands clasped my wrists and I jolted in surprise. Stopped screaming. Opened my eyes.

"Can you see me?" Christian's voice was right in front of me. My eyes adjusted to the darkness and I saw the faint outline of his body.

"N-Not really," I stuttered, either from cold or from fear. "You're a blob."

Christian snorted. "Gee, thanks. I think I liked 'devastatingly gorgeous' better."

I narrowed my eyes, but fear released its grip on my throat. "You would."

He chuckled again and my shoulders relaxed a touch. As long as I kept my eyes on the blob that was Christian, I was okay. I was safe.

"What happened?" I asked.

Christian shifted, but didn't move his hands. They were wrapped around my forearms gently, calming me. I could feel the light, rhythmic tap-tap of his heartbeat through the skin on his wrist. I stayed focused on that, let my breathing sync with his.

"I'm not sure," he said. "The conductor should—"

"Good evening, passengers of the Aston Falls Express." The speaker crackled. "I'm afraid we've encountered a problem. Due to the blizzard, the train is stuck and we won't be able to continue to Aston Falls until conditions improve. We realize this is terribly inconvenient, and we'd ask for your patience. The dining car is open and there are blankets available for your use at the front of every car. Please make yourselves comfortable... It could be awhile."

I squeaked and sat back just as the lights came back on. Christian was kneeling in front of me, his body almost covering mine. Weirdly, he was smiling his lopsided smirk, eyes dancing.

"Think this is funny, do you?" I asked.

Christian took this opportunity to stand, unfortunately severing the connection between his hands and my forearms. "Not so much funny as it is an adventure."

"Do you always put such a positive spin on things?"

"Only when a situation seems particularly bad." He walked towards the front of the train car, opened a cupboard, and took out a pile of wool blankets. "Might as well do what the conductor says and make ourselves comfortable. I've never slept in a stalled train before."

Christian placed a blanket next to me, then began to lay out a blanket on the floor in the aisle.

"How can you possibly be so casual at a time like this? We could die here."

"We won't die. We might just... freeze a little." Christian smirked.

I fixed him with a glare. "I don't think this is funny, Christian. I have a family to get home to, horses to feed, a job I need to work tomorrow morning."

"Bully for you."

At this stage, my panic and fear were compounding my anger. I stood from the bench seat. "Look. You might be incapable of taking anything seriously, but this isn't a joke to me."

As soon as the words were out of my mouth, I regretted them. Before the train had stalled, Christian was telling me something so personal, so private—so *serious*—and here I was throwing it back in his face.

"Oh man, I'm sorry," I stuttered, shaking my head. "I didn't mean that."

But it was too late. Christian faced me, any trace of humor gone from his expression. "No, go on. Tell me what you really think. You're going to do it anyway, aren't you?"

"What's that supposed to mean?"

"I think you know, Jessica."

"Don't call me that. You shouldn't have come with me today."

"I would never have forgiven myself if you went through this alone."

Any anger I felt evaporated instantly. I blinked, lost for words.

He was standing so close we were almost pressed together in the aisle. That same tension I felt between us in the stable began to crackle and pop. A hot ball of emotion sat at the base of my throat.

But as I stared at him, stared into those lovely brown eyes, all rationality and thought went out the window. My mind went quiet—wonderfully, blissfully quiet.

Without permission, my eyes dropped to his lips. And when I looked up again, his gaze was slowly traveling over my face, like he was memorizing my features.

My heart lurched and the butterflies came back in full force. This time, there was no doubt about it—I *definitely* wanted to kiss Christian. Right here, right now. In a broken down train car.

I wanted nothing more than for him to bend, for me to rise on my toes, to wrap my arms around him. I wanted him to pull me close, sweep me off my feet...

Just when I thought I might die if he didn't, he stepped away.

Looked down. Dropped another blanket on the floor.

"You take the bench seat, I'll take the aisle," he said gruffly, avoiding my eyes. "If we stay close, we'll stay warm."

I exhaled a breath I didn't realize I was holding. My face was red-hot and I felt lightheaded. I fell back onto the bench seat without a word. Laid down, turned away, closed my eyes. But I was all too aware of Christian—the soft sound of his jacket as he took it off, his movements as he laid down in the aisle.

My heart continued racing and I squeezed my eyes shut. Shivers erupted over my body, though I couldn't say if it was due to the cold or the intensity of that moment.

I barely noticed when he tucked a blanket around me before I fell into a fitful sleep.

26

CHRISTIAN

The first thing I noticed was the smell of strawberries and vanilla.

The scent was everywhere, permeating my senses, infiltrating my dreams and making them sweet.

I blinked my eyes open and was nearly blinded by a bright, yellow beam of light shooting through the window. I shut my eyes again and shifted slightly, causing the left side of my body to explode in painful pins and needles.

Then, I felt a small, warm presence pressed along my body. Curled around in front of me.

What the...?

My eyes shot open again—wide awake this time—and I saw the mess of strawberry blonde hair falling across my outstretched arm. The familiar bright pink beanie and black puffer jacket. A small hand grasping my forearm.

JJ.

Sometime in the night, she must've gotten cold and joined me in the aisle of the train. My body was wrapped around hers, and we were pressed against each other in the small space. She was facing away from me, her head resting on my bicep. Which explained why I couldn't feel my arm.

Uncomfortable tingles shot down to my fingers, but I didn't want to move. Didn't want to disturb her. I watched her for a moment, registered the easy rise and fall of her side, her rosy right cheek and slightly parted lips. Even in sleep, she was beautiful.

The smell of her hair made my head spin, and I couldn't help but smile. I felt her light heartbeat through the layers separating us, and I thought back to last night. When we were arguing one moment, and the next, I almost kissed her.

I still wasn't sure why I didn't do it. Pull her close, hold her, trace my fingers across her freckles.

Maybe because, in the heat of that intensely-charged moment, it occurred to me that it might not be enough. It *wouldn't* be enough. A few stolen moments every couple of months, the occasional conversation. Just one kiss...

Maybe I wanted something more than that with JJ.

She snuffled—the cutest noise—and rolled onto her back. Her side was pressed into my front, but her face stayed away from me. My eyes traveled the lines of her profile, her straight nose and her light-colored eyelashes fanning across her cheek.

Part of me wanted her to wake up so I could see those gorgeous golden eyes again, and part of me wanted to let her sleep, let her dream.

Maybe I did like JJ. Liked her *a lot*.

But the moment she woke up, would she hate me all over again? Was I supposed to hate her too? I wasn't sure, but for better or for worse, my heart was racing and I couldn't tear my eyes away from her.

At that moment, JJ's eyes popped open. Before I could

lay my head down—pretend I was asleep, *something*—she turned to me. Raised an eyebrow. "Morning, stalker."

I snorted. "Morning to you. Someone get a little cold last night?"

"No," she said quickly. Then, registering our bodies pressed together, she smiled sheepishly. "Okay, maybe yes."

I took in her glowing skin, her messy hair, and—finally—her eyes. Red lines criss-crossed her cheek from where her face had been pressed against my sleeve, and I wanted to trace each and every one.

A loaded silence settled between us as JJ noticed me staring at her. She smiled a small, shy smile, and looked away. But that smile drove me wild, and I knew that I wanted to ask her out. Not only that, I wanted to make her feel special—JJ deserved better than a rushed kiss in a stalled train.

"What?" She tilted her head.

"You look so pretty right now," I murmured without thinking.

JJ's eyes widened and pink rushed to her cheeks. Then, she lifted her head, covered her eyes against the beam of sunlight. "Looks like the storm's passed."

I took the change of topic in stride. "Guess so." I got to my feet. Cracked my back. Held out a hand for her. She assessed me for a moment, like I might whip my hand away as soon as she reached for it. "Don't worry, I'm not going to drop you. You can trust me."

JJ smiled ruefully, then hesitantly placed her hand in mine. I held tight and helped her up, watched her as she brushed off the front of her jeans.

"There's not a lot of people who keep their word these days," she said quietly, almost like she didn't intend for me to hear. Then she glanced at me. "Thanks."

I wondered what she meant by that—maybe something having to do with Ted? But the confidence she'd shared with me last night felt sacred and I didn't want to push it. "Anytime."

Screeeeeee!

The train grunted and squeaked. Jerked forward.

JJ grasped onto the wall as the train began to move.

"Ladies and gentlemen, good morning." A voice spoke over the speakers. "Good news—due to the hard work of our dedicated crew, the tracks to Aston Falls are now clear and we are ready to proceed. Please take your seats for the remainder of the journey."

JJ squealed and collapsed into the seat close to the window. Her face lit up as she watched the landscape pass us by—slowly at first, then more quickly. "Finally," she breathed. "We're going home!"

I smiled as I took a seat across from her, enjoying the glee and excitement in her voice. The storm had left a sparkling white blanket on the foothills and mountains surrounding Aston Falls, and the sun was shining bright. But despite how beautiful it was outside, nothing could compare to the glow in her eyes. After last night, it felt like I was seeing everything in a brand new light.

"We are," I said quietly.

27

JJ

Christian West thinks I'm pretty. In the morning. With sleep lines on my face.

His words—said in that rich timbre—ran through my mind on repeat for the rest of the day. I was thinking about them as Christian and I got off the train in Aston Falls and loaded the bags of horse feed into his SUV. I was thinking about them when we drove home in a comfortable silence, our forearms resting tantalizingly close on the center console. And I was thinking about them when he touched my hand before I got out of the car, asked me to meet him at 6pm in the Barn.

"Wear something that makes you feel most like yourself," he'd said with his heart-stopping grin.

Cryptic as could be.

Now, it was 5:32 and I'd just finished blow-drying my hair. I was wrapped in a towel dress, no makeup on, and staring at the clothes I'd laid out on my princess bed. My stomach was in a knot and I couldn't stop fidgeting.

Because Christian asked me to the Barn and I had no idea why. But I *did* know that he thought I was pretty.

I bit my lip, my body warming as I thought back to this morning. Waking up next to Christian in the train was surreal. Despite the woolen blanket draped over my body last night, I woke up in the early hours, freezing cold. I couldn't stop shivering long enough to get back to sleep. My only option was to get on the floor, lay next to him.

Lucky for me, the man was a furnace. Being close to him heated me right up.

Unlucky for me, sleeping-JJ apparently couldn't get enough of the heat, seeing as we woke up practically spooning.

I couldn't speak for Christian, but I hadn't slept next to many people in my life—only my best girlfriends when we had sleepovers in the Barn. Ted and I had never fallen asleep together... unless you counted dozing off to a movie on either end of the couch.

And yet, there I was, basically cuddling with Christian West of all people—the man who was supposed to be my greatest nemesis.

Logically, rationally, I realized that he'd probably only asked me to the Barn to go over something before our Christmas Carol rehearsal. Or to record more music. Nothing special. But I couldn't get over the mess of nerves and butterflies in my stomach at the thought of seeing him again.

I checked the clock next to my bed and bit my pinky fingernail. I had 35 minutes to go, and no idea what I should wear.

What did "wear something that makes me feel like myself" even mean?! Christian might as well have sent me a riddle through a crossword puzzle.

I could wear a dress, like I always did when I went out with Ted. To be fair, he always dressed nicely himself. Neat, combed-over hair, sweater tied loosely tied over his shoulders, khaki pants. I called it his "golfing at the country club" outfit, and he expected me to join in like I was his country club wife.

In reality, I felt more like the country wife. Complete with cowboy hat and dusty flannel shirt.

As much as I loved some of my dresses—particularly the fun, light, summery ones—none of them seemed well-suited to this situation. Which left...

"Jeans." I sorted through the pile of pants I'd stacked on top of my pillow. For some reason, I wanted to look good tonight, so I picked out a pair of black ones that fit like a glove. And by that, I meant that they were so tight, it was hard to sit down.

I started to wiggle myself into them, then thought back over Christian's words—did these make me feel like myself?

If I was being honest, *no*.

I settled on my favorite pair of worn-in, faded blue jeans with a hole in the knee. High-waisted and with white embroidered flowers on the back pockets. I threw on a simple white t-shirt and a black cardigan. I ditched the fully-made-up look and went for a simple foundation, mascara and lipgloss combination.

I walked to the mirror, checked the final product.

"Looking good," I said to my reflection, shooting finger guns like I was a dude in a Western movie.

And I did look okay. Casual, laidback. I was far from glamorous or sexy, but I did feel like me. This was what I would wear if I was sticking around the house, or seeing Ella and Grace.

I checked the clock.

5:50. It was still early.

But, Christian wanted me to be myself... and JJ Sutton was always early.

"Ready or not," I said, checked my reflection again, and went downstairs.

※

The air was cool and crisp as I shut the front door behind me. Small, sweet snowflakes fell from the sky and landed on my eyelashes. The soft crunch of snow under my feet was wonderfully familiar as I crossed the few yards from the main farmhouse to the Barn.

The blizzard had hit Aston Falls last night as well, covering the ground with a solid foot of snow. When I spoke to my parents earlier today, they said the storm wasn't nearly as bad here. The snow fell hard but gradually through the night with relatively no wind. Or shaky train cars.

Lucky them.

They were in town for the evening, at a planning committee meeting for the Christmas Carol. Which left me and Christian alone on the farm.

I reached the Barn and knocked on the door three times. Even though this was, technically, my space growing up, something felt different now and I couldn't explain how or why.

Within seconds, the door swung open.

Christian was standing just inside. He'd ditched his usual jeans and leather jacket for casual black slacks and a gray pull-over. His hair was tousled and his silver chain was on full display, dangling around his neck. When he saw me, his face lit up and, suddenly, all of my anxieties surrounding my appearance disappeared.

"You're here," he said, his gravel voice making my insides turn to mush.

"Am I too early?" My voice was a croak.

"Never." He gestured through to the Barn. "Come in."

I stepped inside and my jaw dropped.

Once again, the inside of the Barn was completely transformed. Fairy lights were strung around the living room and up the stairs. Scented candles burned on the tables. Some of the recording equipment had been pushed aside so that the couch and coffee table were back where they belonged. A fire was roaring in the small wood stove that I'd long ago written off as being non-functional.

On the dining table, there were takeout boxes from Morning Bell cafe.

It was a fairyland. A cozy little cocoon, protected from the cold.

"What is this?" I asked, my stomach jumping into my throat. I had a feeling I knew exactly what this was, but I didn't want to jump to conclusions.

"Whatever you want it to be." Christian was suddenly standing right next to me. "A truce, an agreement of friendship. Or... a date."

My head snapped up as I looked at him in surprise. He was smiling at me shyly, his eyes lowered. He seemed young, at that moment. Vulnerable. Nervous.

Like he was worried about what I might say.

I was taken aback. I almost wanted to laugh at whatever crazy twist of fate had brought me here, to this moment. Not only was Christian West—my nemesis, the most talented musician I could ever dream of meeting—asking me on a date. But he was nervous about it, waiting to see what my reaction would be.

"What do you want it to be?" I breathed.

Christian shook his head once. "I think it's clear what I want. But whatever you want to call it, you should know that I... care about you, Jessica Jade Sutton."

Christian used my full name, but I didn't hate it. In fact, I kind of loved it. Because behind his words, I heard the emotion, the care. I heard something that made me almost want to cry.

A strange feeling began to bubble up inside me, some strong emotion rising to the surface. My breath came in short, light gasps and I squeezed my eyes shut.

When I opened my eyes again, I knew the answer as sure as I knew my own name. I faced Christian and smiled shyly. "A date. A date works for me."

Christian's face lit up and he took me in his arms, swung me around. I held on tight, enjoying being so close to him. I giggled as he put me back on the ground. Helped me out of my jacket.

"You look beautiful," he said as he took in my outfit.

I clasped my hands behind my back, shrugged. "This feels most me."

"It's perfect."

I bit my lip. "You look..." My words faded out. He looked amazing, as per usual. But something was different tonight. He was different.

Christian chuckled, gestured down at himself. And at once, I realized what it was—he seemed vulnerable again. He wasn't used to this either. "Tonight, you're seeing the real Christian West."

His sweet tone made my heart race. "I like it."

He matched my smile. There was something so vulnerable in this moment, it almost made me break out in a full-body blush. Here we were, two people who were so used to acting, dressing, behaving a certain way for others. It was comforting to know that, with each other, we could just be ourselves.

I met his gaze and, for the first time ever, I didn't run from those chocolate whirlpools. I dove in, headfirst and willing. And it occurred to me that fairytales undersold how amazing it is to look into the eyes of someone who really sees you, understands you.

Because looking into Christian's eyes? There were no words to describe it.

28

CHRISTIAN

"Shall we?" I gestured towards the dining table because if I stared at JJ for a second longer, there was a very real chance that I wouldn't be able to hold back from kissing her.

She tucked her hair behind her ear and bit her lip. Which made the whole holding-back thing all the harder. "Absolutely."

JJ led the way to the dining table, where I'd laid out takeout boxes from Morning Bell. My stomach was jumping with anticipation. I'd been nervous when putting together this "hopeful-date". I wanted everything to be perfect, wanted to do something that felt quintessentially JJ, as I thought I knew her.

Fairy lights, candles, her favorite food. And, the Barn.

Once everything was set up though, I started second guessing myself. What if I had it all wrong? By the time I opened the door for her, I was seriously considering whisking her off to one of the two fine dining restaurants in Aston Falls before she could see what I'd done to the place.

But the minute she saw the Barn and her mouth dropped open, I knew I'd done the right thing.

Now, as we sat down to enjoy the food—all of JJ's favorites, according to Grace and Ella—I couldn't be happier. I'd told JJ to come as she felt most comfortable. She looked amazing.

While we ate, we laughed, teased, joked, and talked. And despite it all happening in what was essentially a renovated barn in middle-of-nowhere Montana, it was hands-down the best date I'd ever been on. I didn't have to be "Christian West, the music star" around her, I could be myself. In the most ironic twist of all time, I was able to let my guard down —be vulnerable—with the one person who hated me most.

JJ had a way about her—something that made you want to seize every moment, live life as an adventure, instead of letting things pass by. I couldn't get enough of the way she talked, the sound of her laugh.

"Mayor Davis came into Sweets n' Sundaes today," JJ was saying while we did the dishes—I washed, she dried.

"What was it this time?" I didn't know much about Mayor Davis, but I *did* know that he always had an agenda.

"He wanted to interview me about being stuck on the train. Thinks it'll help get the roadway project approved."

"He's like a dog with a bone."

"You have no idea."

JJ put the last dish away and I took her hands. She made a face and started swinging our arms back and forth, like we were kids on the playground. I swung our arms higher, high enough to twirl her. Dip her. Twirl her again. We both laughed.

"What do you want to do now?" I asked.

JJ's brow furrowed for a moment, then she nodded towards the living room. "Do you have your guitar?"

"Want to play something?"

"There's a song I'd like to try with you."

I raised an eyebrow, joking. "Another Christmas jingle?"

"Not quite." JJ's face went serious all of a sudden and she looked away. "It's... something I wrote."

I gently tilted her chin so her eyes would meet mine again. "I'd love to hear it."

I grabbed my guitar and we sat on the couch. She took one of the pillows and placed it on her lap, like she was stealthily trying to hide behind it.

"I wrote it in school," she said quietly, avoiding my eyes. "It's probably garbage."

"I doubt that," I said sincerely.

But she still seemed unsure, biting her pinky nail.

I took her hand and met her eyes. "It's just you and me, J. I'm right here with you."

She dropped her hand, her eyes swirling oceans of emotion. "Promise?"

"Promise."

She smiled a small smile and the crease in her eyebrow disappeared. I propped the guitar on my knee, ready when she was.

She closed her eyes, took a deep breath, cleared her throat. Then, she started singing.

Her voice rang out through the Barn, bouncing off the walls and filling the space. Once again, I was blown away by the passion in her voice, the way she threw herself into her words.

The song was a love song as well, but it questioned whether soul mates were real. It shook me to my core. As the words and melody tumbled from her mouth, I caught on. Began to play.

I harmonized with JJ, letting the strums of the guitar rise

and fall with her. I sang softly behind her, my voice only meant to enhance hers.

I was completely tuned into her with every fiber of my being. The melody filled the room, our voices complementing each other perfectly.

By the end of the song, I'd closed my eyes too. When I opened them, all I could see was JJ. See her blush, the rise and fall of her chest, the emotion still carved in the furrow of her brow.

I couldn't tell you exactly what happened next. If JJ or I made the first move.

All I know is that, suddenly, we were moving towards each other.

Our bodies crashed together and my lips met hers feverishly, hungrily. Those same sparks erupted through my body, like we were two stars that had collided. My arms locked around her body, drawing her closer as she tangled her fingers into my hair. She even tasted like strawberries.

I was aware of her—only her—as we fell deeper into the kiss. All thoughts went out the window as her lips moved against mine. There was something so perfect in this, something I could only describe as divine. Because in a weird way, it felt like we were supposed to end up here. Like all of those months of bickering and arguing and fighting were leading up to this moment.

For the first time, I considered that maybe all those croony love songs were right.

Because this felt as close to heaven as I'd ever been.

29

JJ

Nothing could've rivaled my first kiss with Christian West.

Except maybe the second. Or the third. Or every kiss thereafter.

Over the past two weeks, every time he took me in his arms, held me close to his body, pressed his lips to mine, I saw stars. Fireworks. All the things that princesses in fairy-tales talk about. Things that I'd never felt before, or even thought were truly possible. But after two weeks of those amazing kisses, I got it now. A hundred times over.

Following our date in the Barn, Christian and I were inseparable. We went for walks together on snowy mornings, mugs of hot cocoa or coffee warming our hands. When I was working at Sweets n' Sundaes, we'd drive into town together, and he'd sometimes stay and entertain me during a lull (to the delight of Mrs. Applebaum and her "social media marketing").

We worked around the farm and I showed him how to care for the cows and horses. Christian West was becoming a pretty convincing cowboy, it turned out. He and George were best friends and she followed him around obsessively. Which I had to say, I couldn't blame her for.

In the evenings when we were free, we had dinners in town—my favorite being the night Christian booked out Morning Bell so we could have a candlelit dinner, just the two of us. We went on a horse-drawn carriage ride by the river, and ice skated at the town rink surrounded by fairy lights. We had games nights and watched Christmas movies together, then talked until I had to creep back into the farmhouse in the early hours of the morning like I was in high school or something. And in between all of that, we wrote songs together, sang together, rehearsed for the Carol together.

In short, my life had become a beautiful montage of music, romance and toe-curling kisses. And it was all thanks to Christian West.

Tonight was another rehearsal night. We were getting closer to the performance and we'd bumped up our rehearsals to twice a week. Which was why we were at Sweets n' Sundaes after closing, performing to an intimate audience of three people.

As I finished the last verse of the last song on our playlist —*O Holy Night*—my voice rang out across the parlor. Our audience burst into applause.

"Brava. Phenomenal. Truly excellent," Mrs. Applebaum gushed.

"You two sounded spectacular!" Ms. Rodriguez joined in.

"Now," Mrs. Applebaum said soberly, her brow creased. "We need to hammer down that opening number for you two. I'm happy enough with *Silent Night*, but ideally we could find something even better."

"Oh, it's fine, Sue." Ms. Rodriguez tutted. "It'll do."

"I suppose you're right." She sighed dramatically. "The show must always go on."

Christian and I looked at each other and shared a secret smile—this had become Mrs. A's motto.

Meanwhile, Ma stood from her stool and came over to me. She gave me a hug, squeezing me tight. When she spoke, her voice cracked. "My girl, you are amazing. I am so, so happy that you're singing again."

"Thanks, Ma." I looked up at Christian, who took my hand. "I guess I was just waiting for the right person to sing with."

Ma threw her arms around me again, then extended one hand to grab Christian by the lapel of his shirt and drag him into the hug.

Finally, she released us and returned to Mrs. Applebaum and Ms. Rodriguez, who had moved onto arguing about the color of the garlands they'd hung up at the Aston Glow Inn in preparation for the Christman Carol. The three of them disappeared down the hall towards the office.

Christian turned to me and took both my hands in his. Sparks immediately ran the lengths of my arms. We'd spent literally every free moment together over the last few days, but I still couldn't believe the magnetic connection between us.

"I have a surprise for you," he said quietly.

"What kind of surprise?"

"The good kind." He smiled that lopsided grin of his that liquified my insides like hot caramel.

"When it comes to you, there's only the good kind." I stood on my tip-toes and kissed him, running my fingers against his scruff.

Christian disappeared to the back of Sweets n' Sundaes and I briefly wondered if he was joining the older ladies in their conversation. Then, I heard a crackle over the speakers —speakers that I'd believed, until this second, had been purely decorative.

I probably shouldn't have been surprised that Christian had somehow made them functional again. The guy had a knack for fixing things that were broken.

The crackle was replaced by the familiar strum of a guitar.

A melody I recognized instantly.

Christian stepped back into the room. His eyes were locked on me, like the entire world had disappeared around us.

"What..." I trailed off as one of my craziest, most outlandish childhood dreams came true.

The song I'd written in high school was playing through the speakers. Christian and I had perfected it and recorded it earlier this week. Tears pricked my eyes as my voice echoed around the room, complemented by his gentle guitar, Christian's deeper tones. He'd edited the track slightly, added some percussion and a stronger bass. But our voices were untouched, natural.

"We sound... good," I whispered, choked.

Christian smiled as he came to stand in front of me, his eyes keeping me hostage in the best way possible. "We really do."

"I had no idea."

Christian nodded and, in his eyes, I saw the complete and utter faith he had in me. "I did." He took my hand, squeezed it gently. "If you want, I'd love to show this to my record label. I think they'd love it. But only if you want."

My eyes widened, and I felt the response I would've usually given bubble up in my throat—that he should do whatever *he* wanted. I held back. Christian was the one person I'd always been able to be honest with. The one person to whom I could say what I wanted, when I wanted.

In the past, those had been primarily fighting words, now we'd entered new territory together, but I appreciated that one aspect of who we used to be. With him, I didn't have to act or be a certain way. With him, I could be myself. He *wanted* me to be myself, for better and for worse.

"I don't know what to say." My voice was breathy and uneven. "I mean, I'd love that. Being considered by a record label would just be... wow."

As soon as I said the words though, a pit of nerves soured my stomach.

Christian picked up on my expression. "What's wrong?"

I bit my lip. "What if they don't like it? What if they think I sound awful?"

He chuckled. "They'd have to be tone deaf to think that. But even if they did, it wouldn't matter. You're incredible JJ, and a wonderful singer."

Christian's words, the pure, aching sincerity behind them, washed over me like warm ocean water. And for the first time, I let myself bathe in it. Let myself believe for a second that he was right. That I could do this. Really do this.

That, maybe, my dreams could come true.

"I couldn't help but overhear..."

Chrisian and I startled apart.

Mrs. Applebaum was peeking at us from the doorway. She was quickly joined by the heads of Ms. Rodriguez and my mother.

"Did you say that you want to take this song to your record label?" Mrs. Applebaum asked, her eyes glowing as she looked between Christian and I. "Does this mean we might have *two* music stars in our midst?"

"Let's not get ahead of ourselves, Mrs. A."

"Could you imagine! Our little Aston Falls Christmas Carol would be the first live performance featuring Christian West and JJ Sutton." She gasped. "Oh my stars, that's it. The opening number!"

I frowned. "What about it?"

"It should be one of your new singles!"

Christian looked at me. "This one would actually be perfect, J."

I bit my lip, overcome with emotion. Was this actually happening right now? Christian and I might get to perform one of our songs live? "I love this idea, but we should do "Where I Belong." It's a little more upbeat and romantic."

Christian was gazing at me so sweetly, so lovingly, I almost forgot where we were. "Deal."

"Wonderful!" Mrs. Applebaum exclaimed. "Any chance we might be hearing this song on the radio before Christmas? What a way to amp everyone up."

Christian put his arm around me. "Afraid not, Mrs. A. With the rehearsals and the performance, I won't be able to get back to LA and give them the demo until after Christmas."

"Ah yes," Ma piped in. "When you go back to LA. Does this mean JJ will be going with you?"

And with those words, time stopped. My body stiffened and Christian froze for a moment, his arm locked around my waist. We hadn't talked about this particular issue... what would happen between us after Christmas. Everything had been going so well, I was happy living in my little fairytale bubble with my prince. Who was not a toad after all.

But this was the glaring question, one that I'd been trying *very* hard not to face.

Now that it was presented to me, I had no idea what to say.

Luckily, Christian didn't seem to have the same problem. He looked down at me with a tender smile that sent my stomach into freefall.

"We'll figure it out," he said in that gorgeous gravel voice. His tone was so firm, so sure—like any other answer was completely ridiculous.

At that moment, I decided to believe him.

We could make this work, couldn't we? No matter what happened, me and Christian could weather the storm. If I'd learned anything from our relationship—which had its fair share of bumps and bruises—it was that he would always surprise me. In the best way possible.

Christian West always kept his word. It was one of the things I loved most about him.

30

CHRISTIAN

*T*he day after the rehearsal at Sweets n' Sundaes, I woke up at dawn.

Thwack! Thwack!

Mr. S was chopping wood again.

Through the skylight above the bed, I saw the slightest tinge of gray. Clouds. It was going to be another cold, blustery day, which meant that Mr. S would be chopping wood for the fireplace in the main house for awhile.

A smile crossed my lips as I considered the comforting, smoky smell, the crackle and glow of the embers. I didn't mind the occasional gray days in Aston Falls, not when it meant setting a roaring fire. I'd turned on electric fireplace in my penthouse in LA on multiple occasions. But even with its "state-of-the-art" label, I could fully verify that it was not the same as having a wood-burning fire.

Cleaning out the wood stove and getting it functioning again was one of the best fixes I'd made in the Barn.

With that tempting thought, I got out of bed. Threw on a few layers and stepped outside to join Mr. S.

I followed the sharp crack of wood around the back of

the Barn and into the small thicket of trees. As expected, it was cold and I stuck my hands deep into the pockets of my jacket. Snow had fallen through the night and piled up against the walls of the Barn. My exhales were white floating clouds and my inhales stung.

"Morning!" I waved to Mr. S as I approached.

"Hey there, son." Mr. S shot me a smile, then blew air into his gloved hands. He placed the axe on the chopping block, stretched his back. "Hope I didn't wake you."

"I was up anyway."

It was only a half-lie; I hadn't slept well.

Over the past two weeks, things between me and JJ had been out of this world. Surreal. The stuff you only heard about in love songs.

It was like every song I'd ever written about relationships—every belief I'd had—was blown out of the water. When it came to JJ, I would've done anything to make her smile. Bantering with her, talking to her, kissing her. I couldn't get enough.

I wasn't sure what she'd think about the demo I put together with her song. Would she hate it? Think it was too much? She'd mentioned in passing at one point that she wanted to hear herself sing on the radio someday. Playing our song for her in Sweets n' Sundaes wasn't quite at radio level, but I hoped she enjoyed it anyway. And if she truly wanted our song on the radio, I would find a way to make it happen. I'd do anything for JJ.

When her mom brought up LA, she went stiff. No, we hadn't talked about our future yet, but I wanted to make things work with her. Assuming that was what she wanted too.

After that awkward moment, the rest of the evening was normal enough. JJ and I packed up at Sweets n' Sundaes and drove home together. We sat on the couch in the Barn and watched *The Grinch*, her legs tangled around mine.

It wasn't until the end of the evening that I noticed how distracted she was. Her eyes kept glazing over during the movie, like she was lost in thought. When she went back to the farmhouse, she didn't meet my eyes, just kissed me on the cheek before darting off.

I couldn't help but wonder if her distraction had something to do with the whole LA question. If it was bothering her, I wanted to talk about it. Which I was ready to do as soon as she was awake.

"Ever chopped wood before?" Mr. S asked now.

"Does fixing broken cabinets count?"

Mr. S chuckled gruffly. "Give it a go."

He handed me the axe and stepped back. I fixed a piece of wood onto the chopping block, then positioned myself in front of it. Just like I'd seen on Youtube. It was the kind of thing most men learned from their dads, but I'd have to make do with what I remembered from video tutorials.

I lifted the axe. Slung it right into the piece of wood.

Sliced the wood clean in half.

"Nicely done." Mr. S nodded. "Next time, make sure your legs are shoulder-width apart. It'll save your back."

"Will do," I said, grateful for his advice. I ran my fingers through my hair. "Do you happen to know if JJ's up yet?"

"She is, though she already left for Sweets n' Sundaes. Right before you came outside, actually. Said Sue—Mrs. A—called her in early this morning. Holiday Parade and all that."

I raised my eyebrows. I usually drove into town with JJ, kissed her goodbye. But I'd heard a lot about the Aston Falls Holiday Parade—it was one of the town's biggest events of the year, alongside the Christmas Carol and the RiverSpring

Carnival—so it made sense that JJ and the Applebaums had to do extra prep before opening the ice cream parlor for the day. "Right. I guess I'll meet her there later."

"You and JJ going to the parade together?"

"We're meeting Nicholas, Grace, Ella and Austin. Should be fun. JJ's been talking about the parade all week."

Mr. S shot me a small, rare smile. "You care about Jessica, don't you?"

"I care about her a lot, sir."

"I can see that." He slapped my shoulder. "Well, I'm glad for you both. She seems happy when she's with you. More... herself. Just make sure you don't hurt my baby girl, hm?"

I may have had a couple of inches on Mr. S, but his words—the serious glint in his eye—communicated the warning pretty effectively. And he wasn't even holding the axe.

"I have no intention of doing so," I said sincerely. "I'm planning on sticking around as long as she'll have me."

"Good." Mr. S nodded once. Then, he winked, stepped back and grabbed the axe.

After helping Mr. S bring a couple of loads of wood to the farmhouse, I returned to the Barn, lost in thought. Our conversation rolled through my head.

I meant what I'd said to him, every word of it.

Though I don't think I understood at the time just how literally I meant it.

Because I had every intention of sticking around. For the first time, my career wasn't my biggest goal, my sole focus. JJ meant more to me, she was my priority now. When I told her I wanted to bring the demo to my record label, I wasn't thinking about whether this would re-establish my name in the industry. I was thinking about her—I wanted to help her advance her career and her dreams.

It was time I told her that. If she wanted me to stay after Christmas, I would. It was time we got it all out in the open.

I threw open the door to the Barn and went upstairs to get ready. I'd meet her at Sweets n' Sundaes after her shift, maybe ask her to walk by the river where we met before we went to the parade.

I wasn't about to let JJ go. Not when I'd just found her.

31

JJ

I was wiping down the last table when Mrs. A spun into the room, bags of sundae toppings tucked under each arm. "JJ dear, that table is beyond spotless. Go get changed and clock out, you've done more than your share today."

I forced a bright smile. "But it's parade day, Mrs. A."

"Oh, psh. You know that on parade days, we're only open in the morning. I appreciate that you started early today, but it's all the more reason for you to head out now. Mr. A and I have this under control. Besides, I don't want you overworking yourself—we need you to be in tip top shape for the Carol next week. Understand?"

"Absolutely." I nodded, trying to match Mrs. A's grave tone.

"Good." She waved a hand like I was a pesky fly. "Now, away with you!"

I held back a chuckle before I grabbed my stuff from behind the counter.

I'd managed to avoid seeing Christian this morning, left

the farm earlier than usual. It wasn't that I wanted to avoid him but—as much as I wished it wasn't the case—I couldn't stop thinking about LA. Now that Ma had asked the question, I couldn't escape it. What *would* happen after Christmas, which was now just over a week away? Were my days with Christian numbered? Would he want to break up?

The thought was like a knife to the stomach. A twist.

I'd been with Christian for far less time than I'd been with Ted, and yet, I had no idea what I would do if we broke up. I couldn't imagine not seeing him every day, not talking to him. But it wasn't like I'd ever ask him to stay. I was asked to give up my dreams once, I couldn't do that to him.

I had to talk to Christian about what was bothering me. Tell him how I'd been feeling since the rehearsal yesterday. It was a risk to have this conversation, a risk that might lead to heartbreak. But if it meant a chance at happily-ever-after with him, it was a risk I was willing to take.

Christian knew what time I finished work, and we were meant to meet with our friends for the parade. Maybe we could talk before we met up with them.

With a determined sigh, I checked my reflection in the mirror, puffed out my lower lip to blow the hair out of my eyes. Minimal makeup. Cozy black leggings. The gray pullover Christian had been wearing the night of our first date —it still smelled like him. And reindeer antlers.

By the time I returned to the front of the shop to say my goodbyes, Mrs. A had put the "Closed" sign on the door. The parlor was empty—Christian was running late. Unsurprising given how busy Center Street usually was on parade days. I probably should've warned him.

I was grabbing the rest of my things when the front door opened.

He's here. Heart in my throat, I pasted a smile on my face and looked up.

Immediately, my body stiffened.

"Ted?"

"Hey, JJ," Ted drawled as he came up to the counter. His brown hair was cut short and neat, and he was wearing dark dress pants and a prim blue blazer. It looked like he might've been trying to grow a beard as well, which was unlike him. I would know, given that we were together for sixteen years.

And yet, as I stared at the man, he suddenly seemed like a stranger.

Ted leaned his elbows on the counter and his brown eyes—light brown, nothing like Christian's dark chocolate ones—moved slowly down my body and back up again. I idly wondered if he'd say something about my slouchy sweater and leggings. Or maybe it was the antlers.

"You look... good," he said.

"Thanks." I smiled wide, like I hadn't noticed his hesitation. "Can I help you with something?"

"Maybe." He matched my smile. Stood straight. "I thought I'd drop by, see how you're doing."

He half-turned to look at the keychains next to the cash register and the light caught something plastic on his waist. Was that an ID card?

"I'm doing well, thanks. You?" I asked mildly, hoping that he would get on with what he wanted so this conversation would end soon. Ted and I had only seen each other once since the breakup and that conversation wasn't exactly fun.

Ted didn't say anything, just shifted slightly to check out more keychains. As he did so, the light caught the plastic on his waist again, so I pointed at it. "What's that for?"

"This?" he asked, fingering the card. "It's from R&R. You know, Russell & Randall. The big accounting firm." He met my eyes, smiled. "Got a job there. A CPA job."

My eyebrows shot up. "Wow, Ted. That's wonderful! I'm so happy for you." I meant every word—I knew how much Ted wanted to work in accounting and I was genuinely happy to see him succeeding. "You were looking for a good job for so long."

"Thank you, JJ. Yes, it was a long time coming." He chuckled, ran his fingers over his patchy scruff. Then, he leaned in. "What about you? You doing okay? I heard through the grapevine that you've been singing."

I pressed my lips together. Nodded once. I knew how Ted felt about my singing. "Yes I have. It's been a pretty... intense experience."

"I bet. Well, I'm happy for you. It's good that you're trying out the whole singing thing."

My mouth twisted at his half-hearted words. "Thanks. So, is that it?"

I stepped towards the door in an effort to end the conversation, but unfortunately, Ted was faster. He cornered me by the end of the counter, his overpowering cologne an unpleasant reminder of our past. Where was Christian? Or Mrs. Applebaum and her (normally) inconvenient interruptions?

"Listen, I've been doing a lot of thinking," Ted started. Took a breath. "I think it's time we reconsidered our breakup."

"Reconsidered it how?"

"Like, we should get back together."

My stomach clenched up tight and I stepped away, putting more distance between us. "I'm sorry, Ted, I just don't think that's a good idea."

"Why not?" His voice was almost a whine. "You and I are made for each other, we were together, like, forever. I can give you everything you could ever want and need. Now that I have a job, I'll move out of my parents' place. We'll find another apartment. We can do this, we can have a good life together."

They were words I'd heard before, words I'd hung my future on. Words that, ultimately, came to nothing. I shook my head again, more adamantly this time. "I'm sorry."

Ted's smile turned into a grimace. "Is this about that Christian character? I thought I heard that the two of you were dating but I didn't think it could be true."

I bit my lip. "This isn't about Christian. But yes, we are dating."

His jaw dropped, but he recovered quickly. Smiled. Adjusted his hair. "I see. Well, I want you to know that I'll wait for you, JJ. Whenever things don't work out and you decide you're ready to settle down with someone who's actually serious about you, I'll be here."

With that, he turned on his heel and left Sweets n' Sundaes. I wasn't sad to see him go.

"I'll wait for you, I'll be here."

Those were words that the prince in a fairytale might've said, or the hero in a romantic movie or book. Coming from Ted's mouth, the words felt... false. Disingenuous.

All the same, my legs were numb and I leaned back against the counter. Though it was hard to believe anything Ted said, I couldn't stop my doubts and anxieties from rising to the surface like a tidal wave. Begging to be seen and acknowledged.

Was I delusional? I was a girl from a tiny town in Montana, did I really think I could make it as a singer? Not to mention carry on a relationship with a country star from LA?

It sounded like a fairytale. Wonderful, heart-warming... and completely unrealistic.

32

CHRISTIAN

I heard the buzz and hum of the crowd gathered on Center Street before I even reached town.

I should've expected that driving through Aston Falls during the parade would be a chaotic mess. Rivers of people flooded the streets, putting any sort of traffic to an automatic standstill. In the end, I gave up on driving and parked my SUV streets away from Sweets n' Sundaes. It would be faster to walk.

I took out my phone and shot JJ a text to say that I was a few minutes away. I hoped she wouldn't mind, I knew how much she appreciated being early.

As soon as I stepped out of the car, I could almost physically feel the Christmas spirit wrapping around me like a warm, cinnamon-scented blanket. I jangled my keys as I walked towards Sweets n' Sundaes.

Center Street was an absolute hive of activity. Booths were set up along the road, selling hot cocoa, gingerbread houses, deep-fried pastries and other festive treats. Groups of people milled about, scoping out potential home-made Christmas gifts, while children bobbed and weaved around them, their giggles filling the air. The rumble of happy conversations was almost deafening here. The parade was scheduled to start soon, and floats were already beginning to line up at the far end of the road.

It took me awhile to get through the crowd—I was stopped a few times by people I knew looking to catch up, or by visitors wanting photos. As predicted, the sky was gray and moody, but the hordes of bright lights along Center Street did more than enough to compensate for the dreary weather.

As I drank in the festive spirit—and the genuine kindness and love across Aston Falls—a funny thought occurred to me. Though I'd never lived in a small town, I felt weirdly completely at home here. A certain person made me feel at home here.

Though, in all honesty, the thought of living in Aston Falls did make me feel pretty "merry". Or maybe that was just Christmas getting to me.

By the time I made it to the other end of Center Street, I was officially late. I cursed under my breath as I checked the time before picking up my pace. I was jogging around the corner when I ran into someone.

"Sorry, man." I held out a hand to steady the person I'd run into, but when I saw who it was, I dropped my arm.

"Ah, it's you," Ted Bigby muttered, tilting his chin up. The guy was about my height so all this did was give me a pretty unwelcome view up his nostrils.

"Hey, Ted." I nodded once. Formally. "How you doing, man?"

Ted ignored the question. Glanced towards the ice cream parlor. "Going to see JJ?"

"I am."

"Good, good." Ted suddenly smiled, but it didn't reach

his eyes. "I heard the two of you are dating now. Congrats. I hope you're happy."

His words were kind, but there was an edge to them I didn't like. "We are, thanks."

"She was always a firecracker, that one." He barked out a laugh. "I loved that about her, but she was also really hard to take sometimes. Hope you're not having the same issue."

Was Ted trying to... bond with me? Over JJ? Like we were friends with a common interest? My jaw clenched, but I kept my voice level. "Not at all. JJ's wonderful."

"Oh, sure she is. Absolutely. I just mean that she's a little all over the place. Doesn't quite know what she wants."

"I think she knows better than either of us could ever give her credit for."

He snorted. "What makes you think that?"

"Listening." I shrugged. "Talking to her."

"Come on, bro." Ted's use of the word "bro" was so unnatural, it was almost laughable. "That's all nice and sweet. But nothing compares to sixteen years' worth of experience."

"It's amazing what you can learn about someone in a few months if you're paying attention."

Ted's lips pinched slightly, then he leaned in. "Listen, I'm going to tell you this for your own good. I actually *know* what will make JJ happy in the long run. Sure, she might enjoy dating you now, and she might like this whole singing thing. But it's not what she needs. She needs stability, someone to give her direction and guidance. Face it, man. I've known JJ since we were kids. When you leave her, where do you think she'll be then? She'll come right back to the person who knows her best."

Ted jerked his thumbs out towards himself.

Meanwhile, I had to restrain myself from going back to

Center Street, buying a large pie layered with whipped cream, and lobbing it at him.

"Guess we'll see, won't we?" I said instead, my voice so cold, it was practically Antarctic. "It's JJ's choice, and I'll respect whatever she wants."

"Well," Ted said. "I think we both know what she'll choose."

With that, he brushed past me, knocking into me with the clear intention of pushing me into the wall. Unfortunately for him, the guy was slighter than me, and his push ended up ricocheting him into the street instead. He disappeared into the crowd on Center Street without looking back.

I officially had a bad taste in my mouth. Ted was about as interesting as a beige towel on a good day, but clearly, he had a bite in him that I would've been happier knowing nothing about.

Where had he come from in such a rush anyway? There were only a few other shops on this street—did he come from Sweets n' Sundaes?

Did he go to see JJ?

A sudden, strong protective instinct surged through me and I ran the rest of the way to the ice cream shop. JJ could take care of herself, I knew that. But Ted was clearly still a tender subject—he better not have upset her.

When I walked through the door, JJ was leaning against the counter, chewing her lower lip. She looked adorable as ever in her leggings, reindeer antlers, and the gray sweater I'd let her steal from me—it looked better on her anyway.

When she saw me, she smiled and, as usual, that gorgeous smile lit a fire in my chest.

"Sorry I'm late, J. Center Street is insane right now."

"I figured. You ready to go?" she asked.

"Absolutely." I studied her features but her face gave nothing away. I decided to be direct. "Was Ted in here a minute ago?"

I saw the small stiffening in her posture. Then, she shrugged. "Yeah, he dropped by."

"You okay?"

"Absolutely." She smiled wider, then rolled her eyes. "Just seeing an ex, you know. Never fun."

"Guess not."

I scanned her face, trying to see if she really was okay, but she dropped her gaze. Gestured towards the door. "We better head out. Gracie and Els are probably waiting for us."

At once, I remembered what I wanted to talk to her about before my unpleasant conversation with Ted. Maybe a walk would be good anyway, give her time to talk if he'd said something to bother her. "How would you feel about going to the river first? I want to talk to you about something. About LA and—"

"Is this about the demo?" JJ cut me off, waving a hand. "I was going to say—do what you want with it. It's yours after all, and I know how important your next single is to your career. So if you want to give it to Crown House, go for it. I don't care either way."

I blinked, taken aback. "What?"

"Give it to them, don't give it to them… It doesn't matter. Do whatever's best for you and your music, Christian."

Her voice was calm. Too calm. Where was this coming from?

I stepped forward, heat rising through my chest. "Did Ted say something to you?"

"No, no. Nothing like that." She stepped forward and placed a hand on my cheek, running her fingers along the stubble tenderly. "I just think that you need to do what's best for you."

I frowned, my eyes searching hers. But where her golden eyes were normally sparkling and light, it was as though they'd gone flat. I pressed my hand to hers on my cheek. "J, you're what's best for me."

An unreadable expression crossed her face before she stepped away, just slightly. "Ah... well maybe I'm better off scooping ice cream."

"You don't actually believe that."

"How do you know?" She shrugged. "It's not like we've known each other very long."

She said this in such a casual, indifferent way that my stomach immediately curdled. "Of course I know you... And you know me."

She chuckled humorlessly. "Christian, we were sworn enemies up until a couple weeks ago."

My brow darkened. It was like I was watching her build her walls back up in real time, bit by bit. "Yeah, we were enemies then, but these have been the best weeks of my life, J. You mean so much to me."

Her eyes finally met mine and a small smile crossed her lips. "The feeling's mutual," she said, her voice barely above a whisper. Then, she dropped her gaze to put on her jacket. "So shall we go? The parade's starting soon."

We might've been standing a few feet from each other, but it felt like a chasm had opened up in the middle of Sweets n' Sundaes. "JJ, talk to me. What did Ted say?"

No answer. She fiddled with the zipper of her puffer jacket.

"Look, if this is about LA, I need you to know that I'm crazy about you. If it wasn't obvious over these past couple weeks, I want to be with you. Whether we do this crazy demo thing or not, I just want you."

At this, JJ looked at me squarely, but her expression was blank. Like I was speaking a language she didn't understand. Her expression softened and she opened her mouth, then apparently thought better of it and shut it again. She turned away to grab the rest of her things.

What was happening? Couldn't she hear me? My eyes searched for hers, but she was avoiding my gaze. A part of me wanted to take her hands, shake her, something. But she seemed far, far away.

That scared me almost more than anything. I would rather JJ hate me with a fiery passion than for her to be indifferent.

All of a sudden, she took a deep breath and made for the door. "You know what? I'm not feeling well, I think I'm going to go home. Can you tell Ella and Grace and everyone that I'll see them another time?"

With barely a glance in my direction, she left Sweets n' Sundaes. The door slammed behind her, and only the faintest smell of strawberries and vanilla remained.

33

CHRISTIAN

I stared at the closed door of Sweets n' Sundaes, bewildered. What on earth just happened? What would set JJ off like that? Send her spiraling back to not believing in herself?

Ted. The scumbag obviously said something to her.

I started to go after her when my phone vibrated. I reached into my pocket and checked the screen, hoping it was her.

Austin Bell.

Dang it, we were late meeting everyone for the parade.

I answered the call as I ran out of Sweets n' Sundaes. "Hey, man. I can't talk right now—"

"Hey!" Austin shouted, loud enough that I had to yank the phone away from my ear. In the background, I heard screeches, screaming and laughter. "Where are you? You and JJ on Center Street yet?"

"Not yet." I grit my teeth as I looked around, but JJ had disappeared. I jogged back towards the crowd, searched for her.

"What'd you say? Hang on." I heard Austin fumble with

the phone, and the noises in the background faded. Finally, he came back on. "Sorry, couldn't hear you. Too close to the bouncy castle. Where are you guys?"

I craned my neck, heart racing feverishly. Crowds of people swarmed around me, but I couldn't see JJ's pink beanie anywhere. Finally, I sighed. "JJ went home, she's not feeling well."

"Oh. Sorry to hear that." Austin paused for a moment. "You okay? You sound weird."

"Yeah, I..." I ran my fingers through my hair. "I don't know. JJ and I just had this really bizarre conversation."

Austin clicked his tongue. "Look, me and Nicholas are here with Els and Gracie. Come meet us and we can talk about it?"

I thought about his suggestion. I wanted to go after JJ more than anything, continue our conversation. But the more I thought about it, the more my gut said that something else was going on. Something bigger than just me and her. And I had the distinct feeling that, as much as I wanted to go after her and talk to her her, it wasn't necessarily what she needed right now...

"Okay, fine," I reluctantly agreed. "But I need a favor."

"What's that?"

"Tell you when I'm there."

Austin gave me directions on where to meet them, and ten minutes later, I was walking up to Aston River park. I stopped for a moment and watched my friends. Nicholas and Austin were standing in the playground looking at a group of ducks that were passing by. Austin had one of the twins tucked in his arms while Nicholas held a laughing Dallas. On a bench nearby, Ella and Grace were talking while Ella gently rocked the other twin.

Over the years, these people had become the closest

thing I had to a family. Though I'd started out being closest with Austin, Nicholas and I were good friends now, and I loved both Grace and Ella. None of them lived in LA, but they were the people I relied on and trusted almost more than anything.

At that moment, Austin turned around and spotted me. "Hey!"

"Hey guys!" I waved as I approached my friends. Austin was holding baby Kali and she smiled at me.

"Glad you could join us, dude," Nicholas said. "Happy parade day!"

"Happy parade day. Though I'm not sure I'll stay for it."

"What's going on? Something happened with JJ?"

Austin tenderly placed Kali into her stroller and tucked her in. She continued to stare at me and blow spit bubbles, and I tickled her little belly. She laughed—a high, tinkling, joyous laugh. Man, she was cute.

But my mind was locked on JJ. I stood straight and ran my fingers through my hair. "She's definitely upset about something."

"On top of being sick?" Nicholas asked.

"No... I don't know. But, about that favor—"

"Christian, what have you done with our best friend?" Grace suddenly appeared next to us. "We heard JJ's not well. Too much rehearsing for the Carol, perhaps?"

I turned to Grace, and Ella just behind her. "Well, that's where I'm hoping you guys can help. I think she needs her best friends right now." I shook my head. "When I went to meet her, I ran into Ted just outside of Sweets n' Sundaes."

"Hold up." Ella's eyes went wide and she stopped rocking Gia. "Ted went to see JJ?"

"Yeah, I think he said something to her. She basically ran out just now."

"That's not good. They've barely spoken since the breakup."

"For good reason." Grace nodded. "They had their share of issues. Remember prom? When Ted was late?"

The group all murmured and tutted. I raised an eyebrow. "What happened?"

"JJ was so upset," Grace said, holding her finger for Dallas to grab. "He promised her he'd be early but he turned up forty-five minutes late. He knew how much she wanted to walk into prom together and get their photo taken. In the end, they missed the photographer altogether. He barely even apologized."

Ella nodded as she tucked Gia into the stroller next to Kali. Their little eyes were drooping and sleepy—they'd both be out in seconds. "What did he say to her?"

"I'm not sure." I went over the conversation in my mind. "But whatever it was, she essentially insisted that she was better off scooping ice cream than singing."

At this, Grace and Ella shared a look and I could swear some sort of secret best-friend-voodoo thing passed between them.

Grace turned to me. "We'll go after her."

"Are you sure?" I frowned, still feeling conflicted myself. "I hate to pull you away from the parade..."

"No, you did the right thing. This is a job for her best friends." Ella offered me a small, comforting smile. Then, she placed a kiss on her daughters' heads and wrapped her arms around Austin. "Be back soon."

Meanwhile, Grace turned to Nicholas. "Dal's snacks and bottle are in the diaper bag. If he starts crying, he's probably—"

"Hungry. I know, Ace. I even threw in some of his

favorite mashed carrots as well," Nicholas said smoothly, giving his wife a kiss.

"You know what," I blurted, stepping forward. "Maybe I should come with you guys after all. JJ might need something, and I want to see her."

Grace shook her head. "Don't worry, Christian."

"Yeah," Ella agreed. "We got this."

I pressed my lips together, torn. Was I doing the right thing? Finally, I exhaled. "Just please let me know if she needs anything and I'll be there. I'm not kidding, I'll drop everything to be with her in a heartbeat."

"We know." Ella smiled a small smile and squeezed my arm. And with that, they were gone. I stared after them, still feeling conflicted and unsure.

"Don't worry, man," Austin said as he checked the stroller, where Kali and Gia were now sleeping peacefully. "Gracie and Els know what they're doing. They've known JJ for years."

"I hope so. I just don't know what happened. Everything was going so well until last night."

"What happened last night?" Nicholas asked, bouncing Dallas.

"It all started when her mom said something about me going back to LA and whether JJ would come with me. I think it bothered her, but she wouldn't talk to me about it."

"Well, what do you want to happen?" Austin asked.

"I want to be with her, no matter what that looks like." I ran my fingers through my hair. "After the whole Ted thing today, I tried to tell her that. I said that I wanted to make this work, but she had no reaction whatsoever. It was like she couldn't hear me. I'm starting to wonder if I've misread the whole situation."

"Doubt it. JJ's a tough nut to crack, but she knows a good

thing when she's got it. And you two? Definitely a good thing."

"You think?"

"Absolutely." Nicholas and Austin said this simultaneously, their voices confident.

But as much as I wanted to believe them, trust that things would be okay, I couldn't help but wonder. Something else was going on, something none of us knew. The last thing I wanted was to push JJ, but I was worried about her.

JJ had a history I didn't fully know or understand, but I would do everything I could to support her and be there for her. Even if it meant not knowing the full extent of what had happened between her and Ted. Even if it meant sending someone else to be with her when I really wanted to be there myself.

That's what you do for someone you love—you're there for them, no questions or judgment. For better and for worse, through thick and thin, sick and poor. All the things those wedding vows talked about that I never really understood, but maybe now, I was starting to.

And maybe, later today, she might be ready to talk. If not, that would be fine too. I'd sit in silence for months as long as she was the one I was sitting next to.

34

JJ

I parked my truck in front of the farmhouse and cut the engine, then sat for a few moments in silence, my eyes shut.

What had I done? I shouldn't have left Sweets n' Sundaes like that. I'd finally pepped myself up to talk to Christian, tell him how I'd been feeling. Ask him about LA and our future. But seeing Ted had thrown me for a loop. Thrown my intentions off-course. I still felt like I was in the midst of some uncomfortable, nauseating roller coaster freefall.

Eventually, I got out of the car and went into the farmhouse, where a very overeager George was waiting for me. She jumped on me, yapping and barking with excitement. I knelt to her level and she licked my face, making me laugh. No matter how miserable or scared I was, George always brought a smile to my face.

"Time for a walk, Georgie," I said as I opened the door.

We stepped outside and began to walk around the farm. Small white flakes were falling from the sky, slowly but surely adding another layer of snow. There was no wind today, so the world felt peaceful and quiet. I stuck my hands in my pockets, relishing the bite of cold on my face.

I walked towards the stable first to see Starlight. My parents were at the Aston Glow Inn this afternoon, helping Ms. Rodriguez prep for the Christmas Carol and party.

The Christmas Carol...

Last night's rehearsal felt like years ago. It was amazing how much could happen in 24 short hours.

The stable was warm and welcoming when I walked in, and George trotted in after me. I checked that the horses had all been fed, then went to Starlight. A pang hit me as I considered the times that Christian and I had been here together. The time we almost kissed...

What would I say to him when he got back to the farm? Where would I even start?

I continued my walk, visiting the cows before looping back towards the house. George followed close behind. At this point, the sun was setting, casting a gray light over the landscape and the mountain peaks in the distance. The snow was falling a little more readily now.

I was about to climb the steps to the front door when I noticed the car parked next to mine. It wasn't Christian's black SUV, but a small blue sedan. With two carseats in the back.

I opened the front door and heard soft murmurs in the kitchen.

When I turned the corner, Ella and Grace were sitting at the dining table, each holding a steaming mug.

"Break and enter much?" I joked.

"Hey, J." Ella gave me a hug. "We were wondering when you'd be back."

"I hope you don't mind, we made ourselves some hot cocoa." Grace smiled.

"You know you're welcome to help yourselves." I took a seat, and immediately, my heart filled with warmth for my best friends. It had been a long while since we'd all gathered in my kitchen like this. I hadn't realized how much I missed having them around. Then, my brow furrowed. "Wait. Why aren't you guys at the Holiday Parade?"

"The question is, why aren't *you* in bed?" Ella tutted. "Christian said you were sick."

Right. Sick.

I coughed, rubbed my belly. "Yeah. Must've eaten something bad." I added a couple more coughs for good measure.

Grace cocked an eyebrow. "Weird. Food poisoning doesn't usually make me cough."

I smiled sheepishly. "So you saw Christian?"

"We did," Ella said. "For the record, he didn't buy the sick thing either."

"Hey now, I make a very convincing sick person."

"Sure you do." Grace smiled innocently. "When you're *actually* sick. You may be a good singer, J, but your acting skills leave much to be desired."

"Besides, what kind of a sick person goes for hour-long leisurely walks in the cold?" Ella added.

"The kind of person who believes that fresh air is the best kind of medicine?"

Ella shook her head. "Come on, what's going on? Christian mentioned that Ted came by Sweets n' Sundaes today. Is that why you came home?"

I pressed my lips together. They couldn't possibly know the truth. I never wanted to talk about it.

"Look, hun," Grace's voice was calm and sweet. The perfect mothering voice. "You don't have to tell us. I know it was probably very hard when Ted broke up with you, but we love you."

"Ted didn't break up with me," I blurted.

Oh no. So much for the whole "never talking about it" thing.

Ella and Grace both went so quiet that I swear I heard the soft patter of falling snow on the roof.

"What?" Ella asked.

"I..." I took a deep breath. I was in for it now. "I broke up with him."

"You...?" Grace started. "I thought... Well, I just assumed—"

"Yeah, I guess it seemed that way." I fiddled with my fingers, then sighed, defeated. "In all honesty, he might as well have broken up with me."

Ella tilted her head. "Why do you say that?"

I felt the emotions bubbling up, the terrible memory of that day. Our last day together.

"It was awful." I continued staring at my hands, which began to blur as my eyes stung. "He just said it so offhand, like it was the most natural, normal thing in the world..."

"Said what?" Grace asked gently, placing her hand on mine.

I bit my lip, tried to regulate my breathing. "We were having dinner. I made mac and cheese with a side salad—his favorite. I brought up the wedding, thought it was time we set a date." My heart squeezed as I relived it. "He didn't seem to have an opinion, didn't seem to care. So I made a joke about him not having anything to put in his vows. And he laughed. Said he hadn't thought about it, probably wouldn't write them until the night before the wedding anyway."

I took a deep breath in. A deep breath out. Tried to ignore the nauseating roll of my stomach.

"I was hurt. Told him that I'd already written mine, and

he brushed it off." I squeezed my eyes shut. "Said that vows don't mean anything. They're just pretty words you say for other people. No one really believes that 'forever' stuff."

Grace squeaked. "Oh, JJ—"

"That's not all he said though." I cut her off. The words were coming fast, I couldn't stop them. "Obviously that bothered me for the rest of dinner, and while I was doing dishes, I brought it up again. Told him that vows mean something to me. Told him that I meant forever when I said forever. He just laughed again, said that people leave each other all the time, the divorce rates speak for themselves. That chances were I'd leave him one day. Or he'd leave me."

You could hear a pin drop in the kitchen. I gasped for breath.

"He said it so plainly, like he was talking about the weather. Said that we would get married and have a good life together, but that he could find somebody else if he had to. Like I was disposable. After sixteen years together, a five year engagement. He could take me or leave me."

My entire body was shaking and I didn't even realize that tears were streaming down my face until I felt them pooling by my hands. Within seconds, two pairs of arms wrapped around me.

"JJ..." Grace whispered, and the pain in her voice made my heart squeeze all over again.

"How dare he," Ella spat. "The gall. The audacity."

Ella went on like that for a few minutes and I let myself crumble in front of my best friends. And they held me, squeezing tight while I cried. I hadn't had a good cry about everything that had happened. Not like this.

I needed this. Needed my friends.

"That was the night I walked out," I muttered. "And

today, Ted had the nerve to come back to Sweets n' Sundaes. Tell me that he wanted us to be together again."

"What a tool," Grace said sharply. "An absolute tool. He heard you were happy and moving on with Christian, and he just had to stop it."

"But what if he's right?" I whispered. "What if I am someone who's easy to leave, and Christian's about to leave me too?"

"Sweetie. I've seen you and Christian together," Grace said seriously. "The way he looks at you... it's like watching him fall in love every time your eyes meet. The boy would have to be clinically insane to leave you."

Ella grabbed a tissue and dabbed at my tears. "You should've seen the worry in his eyes today when he asked me and Gracie to come after you instead of going himself."

I blinked, sniffled. "Christian asked you to come here?"

"Yeah. He said he had a feeling you needed us."

I swallowed thickly, my throat tight. I didn't know what to say. How on earth did Christian know how much I needed this time with my friends? The man understood me better than I ever could've expected.

"JJ, here's the bottom line," Ella said, clapping her hands. "You want to be with Christian, right? So talk to him. Tell him what you just told us. What do you have to lose?"

Everything I've ever dreamed of.

But I didn't say that. Because both of my friends got their happily-ever-afters, got everything they wanted, but that didn't mean I'd be so lucky. That was the problem with wanting things—there was an automatic, inescapable risk. Wanting put you in danger of loss and regret and grief. For so long, I'd been happy enough to shove away my desires, to defer to Ted instead of pursuing what felt right for me.

It was a much safer way to live. Much less terrifying. And nauseating.

On that night, when Ted told that he could leave me in a heartbeat, it was like a trigger had gone off in my mind. I realized how miserable I was, how much I'd given up and deprived myself of wanting for so long. All in an effort to be happy.

I realized that not wanting didn't necessarily bring happiness either.

So, when I felt a tiny, hopeful shred of my heart wanting my friends to be right, I listened. And it was that shred that pushed me to wait in the Barn until Christian got home.

35

CHRISTIAN

The Holiday Parade was an absolute hit. At least, it was with the babies.

Dallas laughed and giggled and cooed as the floats rode down Center Street. Gia ended up bursting into tears from the noise and activity so close to the parade route, leading Austin to carry her to a quieter spot. Meanwhile, I held Kali, who watched the procession with wide, unblinking eyes.

Each float was more outlandishly decorated than the last, boasting elves dancing in front of Christmas trees, extravagant ice castles, and an imitation North Pole that was actually pretty realistic, in my opinion. Mayor Davis floated by on an ice throne, and the Applebaums were on a float that looked like a melted sundae covered with gumdrops and candy canes.

Finally, the very last float appeared—a huge, colorful sleigh featuring a waving Santa Claus in front of a towering pile of gifts.

Seeing the excitement on Dallas and Kali's faces—not to mention the pure joy that seemed to radiate from the parade-goers—almost made me forget about what was happening with JJ.

Almost.

I tried to smile and laugh along with my friends and the kids, but my mind was stuck on her like superglue. I couldn't help but think of how she should be enjoying this too. As much as I liked being here with my friends, these things were more fun with her. Everything was more fun with her. JJ managed to take the world and paint it over with a bright, brilliant brush.

As soon as the parade came to an end, the crowd dispersed—either heading to the river, where there would be fireworks, or home to put the kids to bed. The sun had set, but night hadn't fallen in Aston Falls—the town had enough Christmas lights to make the entire county shine.

"I'd ask if you want to grab a beer, but I should get the twins home," Austin said as he tucked Gia into the stroller next to a now-sleeping Kali.

Nicholas nodded. "It's way past Dal's bedtime too."

As if on cue, Dallas yawned and closed his eyes.

"I want to get back to JJ anyway. You think Els and Grace have worked their magic yet?"

"They better have." Austin chuckled. "Ella's bedtime's coming up too. She's pulling some seriously weird hours with *The Weekly Best* so she can spend time with the twins when they wake up."

I said my goodbyes to Nicholas, Dallas, Austin and the twins, then walked back to the SUV. Well, jogged. As much as I'd wanted to go after JJ earlier, I was grateful I hadn't. I had a gut instinct that JJ needed her friends, and I hoped I was right. Now, I knew exactly what I wanted to tell her. I just had to hope that the conversation would go better, and that JJ would hear me out.

By the time I got back to the farm, the sky was dark. The snow was falling, and I smiled fleetingly, wondering if we were about to get another blizzard. The first one wasn't so bad—it was, after all, the reason JJ and I ended up cuddled together on the floor of the train.

As I drove up the driveway, I spotted JJ's pickup. I parked next to it, then went up the stairs to the farmhouse, avoiding the creaky porch step.

When I walked inside, the lights were out and the house was silent.

"JJ, you home?" I called.

All I heard in response was the soft pitter-patter of paws as George ran down the hall. She promptly splayed herself at my feet, belly up.

I knelt to give her a scratch. "Hey, Georgie. Any idea where your mom could be?"

George proceeded to bark and dart outside. I followed her, and that was when I saw the light on in the Barn. I swear, that dog understood English.

"Thanks, George." I ushered her back into the house and she went with some reluctance. Then, I went to the Barn, opened the door. "JJ?"

"I'm here."

She was sitting stiffly at one end of the couch, legs crossed. She was fiddling with her fingers, the index of her right hand tracing around the third finger of her left. Left-over nervous habit, I supposed.

I walked towards her, took her hands in mine. Her fingers were frozen. "I've been wanting to talk to you all day."

"I want to talk to you too." Her voice was practically a whisper. "You go first."

"Are you sure?" I asked. "How did things go with Ella and Grace?"

"Good." She smiled again. "I really needed them, so thank you for sending them. What did you want to say?"

I grinned, just happy to be near her, to see her smile. "I know that things have been weird with us today, but you have to know that I meant what I said earlier. I want to be with you, JJ. No matter what."

Her brow furrowed slightly. "What about LA? Your music career?"

"I don't care about LA. And I can make music anywhere." I took a breath, let it out. "Look, I've spent most of my life trying to find my place in the world, trying to find where I belong. When my mom died, I became even more ungrounded, which is why this silver chain means everything to me."

I released one of her hands to hold the chain around my neck. Then, in one swift motion, I took it off for the first time since I was a kid.

"I didn't think I'd ever find somewhere to call home. Until I met you." I placed the chain in her palm, closed it tight. "You're my home, JJ, and if I know anything, it's that I belong with you. The first time we met, the first time I ever laid eyes on you, I knew that my life would never be the same. And it hasn't been. For years, I felt lost and untethered, I wasn't myself, but you changed that. Since we've been together, I've been able to write and sing and actually *feel* again. And I feel so much for you, JJ. I care about you. I... love you."

I uttered the words I'd never said to anyone else, but there truly was no possible alternative. I loved JJ, loved her from the moment we met. Loved her through our fights and bickering, and loved her more with every day.

JJ gave me the gift of sight. She not only saw me for exactly who I was, understood me on every level, but she was the one who'd changed my perspective so completely. She helped me acknowledge the pain and sadness I'd experienced, but also the joy and pride and passion.

JJ's expression broke and she smiled a heartbreakingly sweet smile, pressed a hand to my cheek. Her eyes lingered on my face as though she was memorizing my features. "Christian, that means everything to me..."

She trailed off and a sour pit lodged itself into my stomach. I knew what would follow. "But?"

"But," her voice cracked. "How do you know that you won't change your mind?"

I searched her eyes, confused. "I couldn't change my mind, J. This is a matter of the heart. I can't just decide I don't love you anymore."

"No?" she whispered. "What if I can't make you happy? What if I let you down?"

I blinked. "You could never, ever do that. Don't you know that you already make me happier than I ever thought possible?"

She shook her head. And I realized that she still wasn't understanding me.

I took a different angle. "Okay, JJ. Answer me this. What do *you* want? Forget about me, forget about your friends or Ted or whoever else. What would make *you* happy?"

At this, JJ's eyes flashed. "It's not that simple."

"It doesn't matter if it's simple," I said, bewildered by this conversation. "JJ, the only way you can fight for what you want is if you *know* what you want. So, what do you want?"

"I want..." she trailed off, then hesitated. Frowned. "It doesn't matter what I want."

"How can you believe that's true?"

She set her jaw. "Experience."

"What experience? JJ, what are you talking about? Of course what you want matters."

"Really? What if you had to choose between me and your music?"

36

JJ

As soon as the words were out of my mouth, I regretted them.

I wished more than anything that I could inhale them back into my body, swallow them, banish them to the depths of the earth where they belonged. It was like my soul exited my body and watched from above, shouting at me like you would to someone in a horror movie opening the door to a serial killer.

Did I really just say that?

Gave him what sounded like an ultimatum?

Involving his music?!

Christian's face dropped, and the shock and pain in his eyes made my stomach jolt horribly. When I opened my mouth, I wasn't sure what would come out. "Ohmygoodness, I didn't mean that. Ignore me, Christian. I'm so sorry, that was—"

But he looked away, held up a hand to silence me. I shut my mouth. My stupid, ridiculous mouth where my foot had lodged itself once again.

Then, he turned on his heel and strode out of the Barn,

leaving me alone with my senseless words. I wanted to go after him, explain myself, but I was literally frozen. My legs were two blocks of cement, weighed down by my idiocy.

What had come over me?! It was like all of my fears and anxieties took over. And I'd gone and done the very thing that Ted did to me—what I'd said to Christian sounded like I was asking him to choose between me and his dreams.

I'd never do that, but some terrible, monstrous part of my past had risen to the surface.

Christian told me he loved me, told me he wanted to be with me, and instead of acknowledging his beautiful, sweet words, I blocked them out, refused to believe them, because I'd heard those words before. Heard those promises before.

Ted had told me so many times that he loved me. He'd told me every single day since we were kids.

And, in the end, it was all a lie. All of those sweet words meant nothing.

Christian wasn't Ted, and I knew that, but my stupid brain was living in fear. I'd given up so much for Ted, including who I was. I wore pretty clothes to dinners at the country club, bought an apartment when I craved a house, worked a job I wasn't passionate about to grow our "family's" savings.

I'd given up so much that, when we ended, I wasn't sure who I was. Or what I wanted. Or if what I wanted even mattered.

The only times I had an inkling of an idea was when I was with Christian. Whether we were bickering like enemies, singing together, or joking around, I always knew where I stood with him. I liked that I could be myself when I was with him. Christian pushed me, he challenged me, but every challenge was also an invitation.

Because somehow, Christian West knew exactly what I

needed. He was the answer to the questions I'd asked about love for years. And of course I loved him for it. I loved him for exactly who he was.

And what an idiot I'd been that I hadn't told him that when he was standing right in front of me.

I clasped his beloved silver chain in my hand and squeezed so hard the metal pierced my skin. I ran to the door, looked outside and called his name. He didn't answer. I waited so long that I was shivering violently by the time I closed the door.

I returned to the couch and waited for him anxiously, ready to apologize as soon as he came back.

About five minutes later, I heard the sound of a car engine.

My parents were home.

I walked to the window, hoping their headlights would illuminate Christian through the falling snow.

Instead, I saw tail lights. Driving away.

Familiar tail lights that I recognized as belonging to a fancy black SUV.

Christian West was leaving. Without a word.

My resolutions crumbled and I crumbled along with them, ending up on a heap on the floor.

Because this was my fault, it really was. I pushed him away. Pushed away the one person who knew me better than anyone.

What on earth had I done?

37

CHRISTIAN

What if you had to choose between me and your music?

JJ's words echoed in my head as I drove down the driveway.

I had to admit that I was triggered. I had flashbacks of conversations I'd had with Josh or the reps at Crown House. For years, they'd told me that I had to spend my time prioritizing certain things over others. Even songwriting, creating music, fell to the wayside in favor of doing another music video, another talk show, another tour.

I was used to people presenting these choices to me, forcing me to choose A or B. Putting me in a box to be sold commercially. It was part of the reason I'd stopped caring, because at the end of the day, I couldn't find it within myself to care.

I never thought JJ would be the one forcing me to choose. But of course, my answer was simple: I'd choose her. I'd already decided and told her that.

The problem now was that I already knew she wouldn't

believe me. I'd told her more than a few times that I wanted to be with her, but my words were falling on deaf ears.

As I stared at her in the Barn, watched her face fall as she registered her own words, I knew I had to go. Blow off steam. Because no matter what I said, she wouldn't believe me.

So I left. Walked around in the falling snow and thought about how to get through to her.

That was when I remembered my conversation with Austin and Nicholas.

They'd told me that Ted had let JJ down. I had a feeling that he'd made promises he didn't keep, promises that JJ had relied on. Maybe my words alone weren't enough. Maybe I really did have to prove it to her. SHOW her that I meant it.

As I circled the Barn, wracking my brain, I suddenly had an idea. I checked my phone and knew that I didn't have much time. I debated running into the Barn, telling JJ I'd be back, but I had to get a move on if I was going to make it.

Now, I was speeding down the driveway in the falling snow. I crossed my fingers that I wasn't too late.

I grabbed my phone again, started dialing JJ's number. But then, I took a turn too fast.

My front tires hit a patch of ice and I skidded sideways across the road.

My phone flew across the cab, falling between the passenger seat and the door.

Adrenaline slammed through my veins and I gripped the wheel, got the car back under control.

"Drat." I used JJ's favorite curse word, along with a few choice ones of my own, as I glared towards where my phone was now lost. I'd have to text her when I got there. Tell her that I'd be back.

I could only hope that I was doing the right thing.

38

JJ

I stared out the window long after the tail lights had disappeared down the driveway and around the corner.

My phone was clenched tight in my hand. I wanted to call him, wanted to apologize a million times. But would he answer? Did he want to hear from me? Or was he—understandably—furious?

The man was quite literally running away. In a four-wheel-drive SUV.

I was standing by the window, debating what to do, when I saw the headlights.

My heart raced as I grasped the sill. He was coming back?

As the car approached, it became clear that it wasn't Christian. I watched as my parents got out of their car, smiling and laughing and radiating festive cheer. Apparently, the last planning committee meeting for the Christmas Carol had gone well. Daddy wore a light-up reindeer button on his chest and he laced his arm around Ma's waist as they walked up the porch steps.

The snow was falling heavily now, and with the tender way Daddy kissed Ma on the head before they entered the house, they were the perfect picture of Christmas love.

Something large and wet dropped onto my hand. I swiped at the tears on my cheeks furiously.

Christian wasn't coming back. He was gone.

My deepest, most paralyzing fear was coming true. And I only had myself to blame.

I collapsed onto the couch numbly, waves of hot and cold rolling over my skin. I fidgeted with my fingers, the nail of my index pressing into the skin of my palm. I could barely feel the pain over the frantic, anxious beating of my heart.

What was I thinking? I knew how Christian felt about his life in LA, knew that he hated when people forced his hand. And what I said to him sounded like I'd done precisely that. It was the stupidest thing I could've possibly said.

I shouldn't be allowed to speak to humans. I put my foot in my mouth enough times over the years, hurt the people closest to me when they did nothing to deserve it.

Just like I'd done with Christian.

What a mess I'd made. Hurting him was the last thing I ever wanted to do. I wanted to make Christian smile, make him laugh, be the one to hold him when he was down. If I called him now and tried to explain myself, would I just make things worse? I officially had no trust in myself or my motor mouth.

I chewed my nail and stared at my phone for a long, long time. But I knew what I had to do, knew what the fairest course of action was for him.

I took off his cozy gray pull-over—the one that smelled

just like him—folded it, and left it on the couch. Then, I opened my phone screen.

"I'm so sorry, I didn't mean it," I texted him. Turned off my phone.

Because it wasn't right to talk to him when I was like this. I'd already said enough and the man didn't deserve any of it.

I'd call him when I had myself together. I owed him that much at least.

39

JJ

"JJ, come on," Ella said, her tone all too reasonable for this hour of the morning. I heard a scuffle as she moved her cell phone to her other ear, quickly followed by an offended squawk as she picked up Gia. Or maybe that was Kali. "You've been hiding in your room for, like, three days. You need to come out sometime. Experience the world, breathe fresh air, all that good stuff."

I rolled over in bed. Patted Georgie. She exhaled loudly and laid her head down. Clearly, she wasn't impressed with our new routine. I didn't blame her—I was pretty boring these days.

Actually, forget boring. I'd barely left my room since Christian and I had our fight in the Barn.

"Els, you do realize it's been blizzarding all weekend."

"It's no excuse."

I snorted. "An extreme weather event isn't a valid excuse to stay inside?"

"Not today," she chastised. "The blizzard passed yesterday and you're going to miss all the Christmas festivities if you're not careful. You *know* how much you love the Hot Chocolate Festival."

Drat. She was right. The Hot Chocolate Festival was a glorious, much-too-short event that took place the Thursday before Christmas. I waited all year for it, and Ella knew it.

"I don't feel like it today," I mumbled, even as my mind traitorously flitted to daydreams of bobbing, colorful marshmallows and Belgian chocolates.

"Yeah, right." I could almost hear Ella shaking her head. "You are fooling precisely no one, J. Get your butt in some jeans and meet us downtown. Nicholas, Gracie and Dal will be there too."

"But—"

"I'm not taking no for an answer."

"I just—"

"I will march over there and get you. Don't think I won't."

The stern note in Ella's voice still caught me by surprise. In high school, she'd been so mild-mannered and quiet, but since marrying Austin and becoming a mom, she'd really come into her own. Empowered.

"Fine," I said darkly. "Meet you there in half an hour."

"Good. Don't be late."

With that final warning, Ella hung up.

I stared at the house phone for a few moments, debating whether I wanted to roll over and continue watching *A Cinderella Story*—the latest in my list of heartache-appropriate fairytale-inspired movies. Though why Chad Michael Murray couldn't recognize Hilary Duff in a gorgeous dress and tiny mask was beyond me.

With a sigh, I whipped off the covers and got out of bed. Which made George practically jump for joy. She darted towards the door and I let her out before getting ready to go into town. Alone.

Immediately, a pang of emotion ricocheted through my body and I braced myself against the desk.

It had been 78 hours since I'd seen Christian, and I felt each hour vividly. It was like every single part of me missed him. Even now, the memories of driving into town together made me feel physically weak. The amount of times I'd wanted to turn on my phone and call him was overwhelming. But it didn't matter what I wanted. I knew I shouldn't call him, for his sake.

It was part of the reason I'd avoided my friends too—it felt like every word out of my mouth would be another thing I'd regret.

I still had no idea how to begin to make amends.

My anxieties were all the more heightened when he didn't come back to the farm the night the blizzard hit. I was a mess of nerves and fears for hours, until I checked my computer and noticed a photo some tabloid had posted of Christian landing in LA.

So he was in LA. Of course he went back to LA.

Any sadness I felt, though, was completely tampered by the relief of knowing he was safe.

And with this in mind, I forced myself to change my clothes—my blue jeans and a vest. I ran a brush through my hair and applied some mascara and concealer.

I stepped back and checked the finished product. I'd always gone to the Hot Chocolate Festival with Ted, dressed to the nines in prim Christmas clothing. This year was the first that I was going as me. And even though I was a mess of regret and sadness about missing Christian, I had to give him credit. It was because of him and our relationship that I had found strength in being myself. Not the JJ that belonged to anyone. Just me.

Until I went and ruined it all.

Christian's silver chain dangled around my neck and I ran my fingers over it. It meant the world that he'd given it to me, trusted me to be his home. He was mine too. And right now, in a weird way, it felt like he was here with me.

I wrapped my fingers around the chain, squeezed my eyes shut.

Please forgive me. Please come back soon.

Twenty-three minutes later, I was standing outside of Morning Bell Cafe. Though the morning sky was gray, Center Street was ablaze with Christmas lights, all leading to the huge tree at the far end of the road. The festival was just beginning and families were crowding onto the street, filling the air with the sounds of conversations and laughter.

I held out my hand to grasp the doorknob. Then, I paused.

Through the windows, I saw my friends. Austin and Ella each holding a twin, big smiles on their faces. Nicholas and Grace crowded around Dallas in his bouncer. They all looked so happy, so completely at ease, and I was happy for them. They'd made all the right decisions in their lives, where I apparently couldn't stop making the wrong ones in mine.

Maybe I couldn't do this.

"JJ!" Grace had spotted me lingering outside the cafe, and she was waving at me.

I forced a smile back. I couldn't exactly turn away now.

So with some reluctance, I stepped into Morning Bell. "Hey guys. Sorry, hope I'm not too early."

"Don't apologize," Grace sang. "There's no such thing as too early or too late when it comes to family."

I gestured around the cafe, which had apparently been decorated using everything Santa had in his workshop. "Looks good in here."

"Thanks." Grace smiled lovingly at her husband. "Nicholas brought in the youngest of his King's Kids to decorate."

A pair of arms clasped around my waist and I felt rather than heard Ella's squeal. "You came!"

"I came."

"I knew you couldn't say no to hot cocoa."

"I considered it."

"Sure you did," Grace said.

I shook my head to hide my smile. "Should we get going?"

After bundling Dallas and the twins into their warmest clothes, our little group of families left Morning Bell and began to venture down Center Street. The smell of chocolate was mouth-watering as we strolled from booth to booth.

I looked around for the Morning Bell booth. Austin and Grace's dad always ran it with the help of Kris, one of Morning Bell's employees. Their hot cocoa recipe was a "family secret"—one that neither Grace nor Austin had been shared into yet.

While we strolled along Center Street, I tried to forget about my sadness and focus on the cheerful Christmas spirit and the delicious taste of chocolate. But I was distracted and quiet. Even after five tastings, I hadn't managed to get Christian out of my head. I wished that he was here. Though we'd never spent Christmas together, I somehow knew he'd love this. His presence really did enhance and enrich my life in ways I never could have imagined.

"JJ?"

I fingered an adorable Holiday-themed keychain at one of the booths. The Christmas tree animation looked almost identical to the yellow music note one Christian had bought from Sweets n' Sundaes years ago.

"JJ!"

I startled out of my thoughts. "Huh?"

Ella was standing next to me, hands on her hips. Grace was just behind her, an eyebrow raised. Nicholas, Austin and the babies had disappeared.

"Did you hear anything I just said?" Ella asked.

I shook my head apologetically. "Sorry, wasn't paying attention."

"Space cadet," she joked, then threw an arm around my shoulders. "The boys just took the babies to see Santa. I was asking whether you're excited for the Christmas Carol tomorrow."

"Oh." I frowned. "Right. I dropped out."

Both Grace and Ella raised their eyebrows. "Why?"

"Well, after what happened with Christian the other day—"

I cut myself off.

Whoops.

"I KNEW IT!" Ella pumped her fist as she expertly guided me towards a couple of benches beneath the huge Christmas tree. It was a little quieter here—the perfect location for an interrogation. "I told Austin! I told him something had happened between you two. He thought you were holing up because you missed Christian ever since he left town."

Grace leaned in. "So what happened? Did you talk to him about what happened with Ted?"

My chest squeezed. "No, I didn't. We had a fight. He left."

"Oh, JJ." Grace threw her arms around me, gave me a tight squeeze.

"It's all my fault. I... I said something that sounded like an ultimatum."

"An ultimatum?" Ella looked bewildered. "Why?!"

"I basically asked him what he'd do if he had to choose between me or his music." I shook my head. "And yes, I know it was completely stupid and idiotic. Guys, I'm all backwards these days."

A tear slid down my face and I collapsed back onto the bench.

Ella and Grace both placed their arms around me.

"Yeah, that probably wasn't the best move," Grace acquiesced.

"I wanted to take it back the second I said it. But you know me..."

"Foot in mouth syndrome," Ella said gravely, shaking her head.

"Foot in mouth," I repeated with a nod.

"Christian's coming back, though, isn't he? He's still doing the Christmas Carol?"

"As far as I know. Mrs. A didn't say anything about it when I told her I couldn't do it a couple days ago. And you KNOW she would've had something to say if both Christian and I dropped out at the last minute."

"Did you get a chance to tell him what happened with Ted?" Ella asked.

"What would I say? That the man I thought I'd spend forever with essentially told me he could leave me at the drop of a hat?"

"He did *what*?" The deep, masculine voice boomed from directly next to us and I nearly jumped out of my skin. Both Ella and Grace squealed.

Ella whirled around to whack her husband on the leg. "Aus! Announce your presence."

"Sorry, guys." Nicholas chuckled as he sat next to Grace. "We were calling you from across the street. We thought you heard us. Gia wants her teddy bear."

Ella rifled through the diaper bag for the missing bear as Austin turned to me. "What were you saying?"

I froze up for a moment. I didn't want to bore my happily-married friends with sob stories about my very non-blissful love life. But Ella shot me a glance and Grace smiled at me encouragingly. "Go on, J," Grace said.

I took a deep breath and, with some hesitation, launched into the story, giving Austin and Nicholas a rundown of what Ted had said to me the night we broke up.

Their expressions jumped from shock to anger. By the end of it, Nicholas was cracking his knuckles and peering around the street, like he might go find Ted. Not that Ted would be much of a match for the ex-pro football player.

Meanwhile, Austin's expression went lax. Without a word, he stood and whipped out his phone.

"I have to make a call," he said brusquely. Before he walked off, he shook his head, sympathy crossing his face. "I had no idea that's what happened, JJ. I'm so sorry."

I shrugged. What else was I supposed to do? "It's okay."

"It's not okay," Ella said passionately. "He was meant to be your partner, the love of your life."

"But he wasn't," I said, and for the first time, I realized that I didn't feel any pain or doubt or regret in these words. They were just... the truth. "Ted wasn't the love of my life. And I wasn't the love of his."

I sat still for a moment. When I considered the "love of my life," there was only one person who came to mind. Someone who, for months, I'd believed so steadfastly to be the enemy, when really, he was the exact opposite.

"Then what's the problem, J?" Ella asked gently.

"I just... I thought I did everything right with Ted." My breath caught. "And it all fell apart anyway."

"Oh, sweetie. There's no such thing as 'doing everything right' when it comes to love. You just try to be the best you can be."

"And if that's not enough?" I whispered.

"Well then, the person isn't right for you. But trust me, Christian is right for you. I see it whenever you talk about him. Whenever he talks about you. That's your love story right there."

"The real question you need to ask right now, J," Grace added, "is do you want to be with Christian?"

I remembered what he'd said to me so passionately in the Barn. He'd asked me the very same question, but I'd answered out of fear. Now, I spoke from the heart, without letting my mind get in the way. "I do," I said quietly. "Of course I do. And I want to sing. But how? How could I do that? What if I let the Applebaums down by leaving Sweets n' Sundaes?"

"The Applebaums love you, but you know they'll be able to find someone else to work for them. They would never, ever hold it against you if you wanted to chase your dreams."

"Besides." Ella smiled. "Could you imagine how thrilled Mrs. A would be if you became famous?"

My heart was beating a million miles a minute but I had to laugh. My friends' words of wisdom circled through my mind, and all of a sudden, I knew.

They were right. So right. I couldn't run from what I wanted anymore. This was a matter of the heart, and I couldn't logic myself out of it. And the truth was that I missed Christian, missed him more than I could bear it.

I took out my phone and turned it on. Watched as the texts and voicemails came through.

My heart ached. I assumed he wouldn't have contacted me.

And all at once, it hit me. Hard.

The problem was never Christian. Or even Ted.

The problem was that I didn't believe in myself. Not at all.

At that moment, it was like all of the doubts and anxieties I'd had over the years, all of the frustrations and fears and all the excuses I'd used came to a head. I wasn't fighting at all—I was the one holding myself back.

It was the very thing Christian had told me over and over again. The thing my friends had tried to show me.

Maybe it was time I took a risk, jumped off the cliff, believed in myself.

And I knew exactly how to do it.

40

CHRISTIAN

What was taking them so long?

I sat stiffly on the uncomfortable red leather sofa—a statement piece if I ever saw one. Looked kinda tacky, I thought, compared to the rest of the decor in the reception area. My leg was bouncing and I ran my fingers through my hair for probably the hundred and thirtieth time in the half hour I'd been here.

In my other hand, I clasped the music note keychain. In the past, when I was this agitated, my silver chain was usually the first thing I reached for. But knowing that it was with JJ felt right somehow.

I'm coming for you, JJ.

Every thought about her made me miss her all the more. It was unbelievable the way my mind always skated back to her. I imagined that she was with me every step of this journey, even though I knew how much she would've hated the back-to-back-to-back meetings I'd been in over the past three days. Every night, I fell into bed way too late, exhausted to the bone from the hours upon hours of discussions and negotiating.

But I was doing it for her. She was at the forefront of my mind, and it was the thought of her that made every drawn-out, tedious meeting somewhat bearable.

Late last night, after hours of picking at nitty-gritty details, me and my lawyers finally had a breakthrough.

I was just waiting for the final paperwork now. Then, I would be on my way back to Aston Falls.

Headed back home.

At that moment, my phone buzzed. My heart leapt as I checked the screen, hoping it was JJ.

I hadn't talked to her since I left. After our fight in the Barn, I saw that the blizzard was coming in and knew that I had a very, very slim window to get back to LA and get this done before everyone went on Christmas vacation. When I got to the tiny regional airport that night to catch my flight, I called her over and over, but she never picked up. I sent her a lengthy text explaining that I'd be back as soon as I could, then hopped on the private jet I'd chartered to get back to LA. Judging by the force of the blizzard that hit Aston Falls over the last few days, I left in the nick of time.

Whenever I had the chance, I'd call her, but I always got her voicemail. I'd sent her a few texts, but she never responded. Not a call, not a text, not a word. I was itching to get back to Aston Falls so we could talk in person.

As I checked my phone now, I fell back on the sofa.

"Hey Aus," I said, too exhausted and emotionally strung-out to disguise the disappointment in my voice.

"Nice to talk to you too." Austin chuckled, then his voice went serious. "Are you still in LA?"

"Yeah." I glared at the closed door. "Hopefully not for much longer."

"Well you better get back here. Fast."

The concern in his voice made my heart lurch violently

and I shot up straight. "Something's wrong. What is it? Is it JJ?"

"It is, but—"

"I'll be right there." I dropped my phone with shaking hands and grabbed my jacket. My chest tightened with panic, and my stomach was in a knot. If something happened to JJ, if she was hurt while I was gone, I swear—

"CHRISTIAN!" Austin was bellowing through the phone.

I picked it up as I got ready to fly out the door. "What?"

"JJ's fine." Austin sounded out of breath. "JJ's safe and healthy. Everything's fine."

My head felt light and I almost collapsed. "Why'd you say that then?!"

"Sorry, that was my bad," Austin muttered. "Don't always know when to shut off the doctor voice."

"You almost gave me a heart attack."

"My bad, man. But you really do need to get back. Like now."

I pressed my lips together. Glared at the door again. "I'm just waiting on something. It shouldn't be much longer. Can this wait until later?"

"No, Christian, you don't understand. JJ just told us something and I think you need to hear it."

I froze. Sat down again. "Hear what?"

"Do you know why Ted and JJ broke up?"

I frowned. "I know that JJ broke up with Ted. But I don't know why."

Over the next couple of minutes, Austin explained what had happened between Ted and JJ, what Ted had said to her. The puzzle pieces fell horribly into place—why JJ always seemed surprised when I kept my word. Why she didn't believe me when I told her that I wanted to be with her. Why she would ask me such a question in the first place.

I also knew that Austin was right. I had to get back to Aston Falls. Now.

"I'll be right there, Aus," I said, heart racing.

"Sounds good. And Christian?"

"Yeah?"

"Don't let her go. JJ's good for you, you're good for her."

I shook my head adamantly, though Austin couldn't see it. "I'd never let her go."

I hung up the phone, looked at the closed office door one more time. I couldn't wait any longer. I'd have to figure out another way to get the contract through my lawyers.

My duffel in hand, I turned to leave the reception when the door finally opened.

"Christian? We're ready for you."

41

CHRISTIAN

The first thing I did when I stepped off the jet was drive to Sweets n' Sundaes.

The meeting to review and sign the final contract ended up taking longer than expected and the jet wouldn't fly to Aston Falls until early this morning. So here I was, wearing my frumpled jeans, my scruff overgrown, my hair everywhere from the bad sleep I'd had. And I was determined to find JJ.

When I got to town, groups of friends and families were meandering the streets. It was less busy than usual, but that wasn't surprising. Tomorrow was Christmas Day so people were likely spending Christmas Eve doing fun activities with their loved ones.

Including attending the Christmas Carol and party later tonight. The party where JJ and I would be singing together. But I couldn't focus on that right now.

I managed to get through town fairly quickly and I parked by Sweets n' Sundaes. But the ice cream parlor was closed for the day.

I swore under my breath, then raced back to my car.

As I sped towards the Suttons' farm, my heartbeat was in my ears. The entire flight back to Aston Falls, I was agitated and stressed. Every time I thought about what had happened between JJ and I in the Barn, I felt worse and worse. How must it have looked to her—that I left right after our fight. Did she think that I was leaving her for good?

I prayed to God that she read my texts and listened to my voicemails.

The gravel road leading to the farm was covered with a couple feet of new snow, setting the world in high-contrast. Which was why, even from a ways down the road, I could see the hive of activity on the grounds of the Suttons' farm.

My jaw dropped and all my nervous energy was temporarily put on pause. People were buzzing around left and right, carrying Christmas ornaments, random furnishings, and steaming silver trays. Behind the house, a huge piece of cream fabric was billowing in the wind, rising slowly. An extremely large bouncy castle?

I parked and hopped out of my car, scanning people as they ran by. Finally, I spotted Mrs. S, carrying a home-made wreath. "Mrs. S, what's going on?"

"Oh, Christian, you're back!" she smiled, relieved as I took the wreath and hoisted it towards the front door for her. "You'll never believe what happened. The—"

"Mary!" Mrs. Applebaum's bark echoed across the front yard. I whirled around to see her marching towards us— military-commander style. "Have you seen Earl? We need help getting the tent into—Christian! Hello!"

"Hi, Mrs. Applebaum." I frowned. "What's happening?"

"My dear, it's all been a *complete* disaster." Mrs. Applebaum placed a hand to her forehead like she might faint at any moment. "Come, come. I need a strong, strapping man to help me with something. Do you mind if I steal him?"

"He's all yours, Sue." Mrs. S was already running back towards the garage where she came from.

"Wonderful." Mrs. Applebaum turned to me. "Follow me. I'll tell you as we walk."

With that, Mrs. Applebaum swished off through the snow without even a glance back. I hurried after her, trudging through the new snow. Snow that she apparently didn't notice or feel given how she floated across it.

It took me a couple of moments to get my bearings—I'd never walked through this much snow before, even on vacations to Aspen or Vail. Soon enough, I caught up with her.

While we circled around to the back of the property, in the direction of the cream bouncy tent thing, Mrs. Applebaum gave me the rundown on what had happened. Last night, the ballroom at the Aston Glow Inn had a massive leak and was now flooded. Obviously, this caused a huge panic and the town was about to collapse into chaos (her words, not mine). Mrs. S then suggested that the Suttons host the Christmas party on their farm.

"Which means that we have exactly..." Mrs. A checked her wristwatch. "Ten hours and 55 minutes to get everything set up." She wrung her hands, anxious. "It's going to be an absolute disaster, Christian. We'll need a Christmas miracle to get everything ready in time."

I pressed my lips together—so much for putting the Carol on the backburner. Given Mrs. A's distraught expression, I couldn't leave her hanging. I shook my head, my voice more confident than I felt. "It'll be fine, Mrs. A. It'll all come together."

"How can you know that?" she whined.

"Because this is the Aston Falls Christmas Carol. The show must always go on."

At this, Mrs. Applebaum broke into a wide smile and

shimmied her shoulders. "Right you are, my boy. Now, here's what I need you to do…"

Mrs. Applebaum's to-do list ended up taking me all day. From stringing up fairy lights in the massive party tent—which wasn't a bouncy castle after all—to reviving a broken space heater, to scrounging around the Suttons' cluttered attic for spare carpets. I even spent a couple of hours in the kitchen with the caterers, helping fix one of the stovetops. Delicious, mouth-watering smells made my stomach grumble, but I barely had time for a snack.

Evidently, the sparkle of my celebrity had worn off—Mrs. Applebaum, Ms. Rodriguez and Mrs. S had no problems bossing me around. Not that I minded. It made me feel like one of the family.

The one thing I hadn't managed to do was find JJ. I tried to escape whenever I could, look around the farm for her, but she was nowhere to be found. And Mrs. Applebaum was quick getting me back in line anyway.

I resigned myself to seeing her tonight at the Christmas Carol. It wasn't ideal that we'd be performing together when things were so rocky between us, but I hoped we could talk afterwards.

Finally, after hours of hard work, and thanks to some insane coordination—and, okay, maybe a "Christmas miracle" or two—Mrs. Applebaum's to-do list was complete.

Colorful, twinkling lights covered the Barn, house and stable. A light display had been set up by the house featuring smiling reindeer pulling an illuminated Santa's sleigh. The party tent was filled with fairy lights, heaters, a dance floor, and tastefully decorated tables and chairs. A huge tree was taking up most of the living room, and the soft sounds of holiday music filled the air.

In short, it was anyone's Christmas dream. Complete

with the smell of peppermint, chocolate, and freshly-baked cookies.

Ms. Rodriguez was the one to dismiss me. And by that, I meant that she shooed me back to the Barn with just enough time to get ready for the Christmas Carol. Guests had already started arriving, walking up the Suttons' driveway with long coats, gloves and boots. Some of them carried trays full of homemade treats, despite the catered food.

I took a quick shower, got changed, and grabbed my guitar before launching out of the Barn. Maybe I could catch JJ before our performance. I followed a group into the house, wishing them Merry Christmas as I went.

"There you are, Christian." Mrs. Applebaum appeared out of nowhere. At some point in the last hour, she'd found time to get changed. She wore a festive red dress, her hair pinned up with a reindeer clip, and two Christmas trees flashed on her ears. "How're you feeling about the Carol? Are you excited?"

"I think so." I smiled, pleasantly surprised to find that it was true. Over the past years, I'd grown used to doing big concerts, filling stadiums and amphitheaters. But my favorite venues would always be small, intimate gatherings just like this one. "Is JJ ready?"

At this, Mrs. Applebaum's smile dropped. "My dear, you don't know? JJ dropped out. She's not singing tonight."

My eyebrows shot up. "She's not?"

"I assumed you knew." Worry lines creased her forehead. "This just won't do! I thought you'd be prepared to perform solo, but if you're not..." she trailed off, a panic-stricken look on her face. "I suppose we could get Mr. Bell's nephew on short notice. Though he only plays the flute, and not well. And then, there's—"

I got over my shock enough to shake my head. "That's okay, Mrs. A. I'll do this alone. I'm... used to it."

Mrs. Applebaum's face broke into a relieved smile. "Wonderful. Thank you, Christian. My sister Delia is coming all the way from the Inn she runs near Edendale, and I know she's eager to see you play live." Then, she—somewhat forcefully—turned me around and pushed me towards the small staging area. "Why don't you get set up and we'll start in a few minutes."

I walked stiffly, my legs slow like I was moving through molasses. JJ dropped out? Things were worse than I thought.

My mind raced as I tuned my guitar and got ready to go out on the small stage in the tent. It sounded like the tent was already packed full.

It occurred to me that I'd done this alone so many times over the years—sang up on stage by myself. But this was different. I knew I shouldn't be up there alone, and I didn't want to sing without JJ.

I peeked into the main tent and spotted Nicholas standing with Grace. Behind them stood Austin and Ella. They were all smiles and laughs, but JJ wasn't with them.

Austin looked around and met my eyes. I mouthed to him, "JJ?"

He frowned, shrugged, then said something to Ella. She shook her head, then grabbed Grace and they went into the house. I crossed my fingers that they'd come back with JJ.

They didn't.

Eventually, it was time. The tent was chock-full and Mrs. Applebaum was shooting me the thumbs-up. I smiled at her feebly as she made her way towards the stage.

I shot a final look towards the entry of the tent, but I already knew she wasn't there.

JJ wasn't coming.

"Good evening, everyone!" Mrs. Applebaum's voice boomed through the speakers as she took to the stage with a uniquely sparkling mic in her hands. Everyone went quiet.

"We are so excited to welcome you all to the annual Aston Falls Christmas Carol! As many of you know, we had a couple of issues with the Inn, and the planning committee is eternally grateful to the Suttons for hosting our Christmas party at the last minute. Let's give a hand to the Suttons."

All of the attention went to the edge of the tent nearest the house, where Mr. and Mrs. Sutton stood. Mrs. S waved enthusiastically, while Mr. S simply nodded with a gracious smile on his face.

"To kick off this wonderful evening, we're going to get started with our Christmas Carol. Although this year, we have something very, very special lined up..." she paused dramatically and the entire room seemed to hold its breath. Then, she held out a hand in my direction. "Please welcome the incredibly talented CHRISTIAN WEST!"

At once, the audience broke into thunderous applause and cheers.

Showtime.

I ran my fingers through my hair, forced a smile and ran on-stage. I grabbed the second microphone and faced Mrs. Applebaum. "Thanks for having me. Happy to be here."

Her eyes glowed as she stepped off-stage. I scanned the excited, cheering crowd once more, but I didn't see my favorite fiery mane of strawberry blonde hair.

"Hey everyone, thanks for coming tonight," I said and everyone immediately quieted down. A hundred eager, curious eyes were gazing at me and I felt the weight of it.

JJ and I had prepared a little speech before our first song —all about the magic of the holidays and the joy of being with friends and family. But now that I was doing this alone, it didn't feel right to do our speech.

I decided to improvise. Speak from the heart. "It's been a long time since I had a proper Christmas," I said to the room. "Growing up, I never did anything special for it. It was usually just me and my mom, and we'd watch Christmas movies, eat way too much food, and then play music on her ancient guitar. It wasn't much, but it was our thing, until she passed away."

Soft murmurs of sympathy rippled through the crowd. I took a breath, closed my eyes for a moment.

"After she died, I stopped celebrating. Christmas was a time to be home with loved ones, and without her, well... it wasn't the same." I smiled briefly and scanned the crowd once more, but this time, it was automatic. I already knew that JJ wasn't here, no matter how much I wished she was. "But this year's different. I spent the past few weeks in this sweet little town, and I have to hand it to all of you, you've made me feel at home. This is a really special, wonderful place."

Through the dimmed lights, I saw the light of hundreds of smiles. I cleared my throat, held up my guitar. "I was meant to sing this song with someone else tonight, but she couldn't make it, so bear with me. This is an original song, a brand new single. It's called 'Where I Belong'."

With that, I turned my gaze away from the entrance to the tent for good. I strummed on my guitar. I'd try to make this the best performance it could be without her.

I played the first few chords, and the melody filled the cavernous space. I lost myself in it, allowed myself to fall into the emotions I'd suppressed for so long. Let them fuel my performance.

I leaned towards the mic, opened my mouth...

"First time I saw you, your eyes drew me in like sweet honey."

I froze for a second.

That gorgeous velvet voice wasn't mine.

"Next thing I knew, your lips were calling my name."

My fingers continued to strum the guitar on auto-pilot, but I couldn't speak, couldn't sing, even if I wanted to. I followed the trail of gazes all leading to the back of the tent.

Where JJ Sutton had finally appeared.

Her eyes locked on mine as she sang the opening verse to "Where I Belong" into that uniquely sparkling mic. And my heart managed to slam and skip a beat all at once.

She was wearing a beautiful black velvet dress that cascaded down her body, and her hair was curled around her face. She was breathtaking. But in all honesty, it wasn't about how she looked. I was entranced by her, by the set of her jaw, the confidence in her gaze.

"I've never believed in love, but isn't it funny?
I was far from a fairytale, then along you came."

Now, she started walking towards me through the crowd. People parted around her like she was a goddess—untouchable, unbreakable. She approached, step by step, and I was filled with pride for her. She was so natural, so in her element, so *her*.

The woman I'd fallen in love with in the river all those years ago.

42

JJ

My legs felt numb as I walked through the crowd, step by step.

It had been a very long time since I'd performed in front of people. Especially in front of a crowd like this. The fact that I was singing a song that felt so close to my heart, a song that I'd helped create, made my heart race.

But, strangely, the performance wasn't the biggest reason that a coil of nerves was wrapped around my stomach. Because I'd already decided to be brave. I *wanted* to be brave.

I wanted to believe in myself.

What made me nervous was Christian's reaction. He had every right to be angry with me. As terrified as I was to be putting myself out there like this, I had to do it. I wanted to do it. For him.

Because he had given me the best gift I could've imagined—he'd believed in me, every step of the way. And all he'd ever asked was that I believed in myself too.

I had to hope I wasn't too late.

I summoned my courage and met his eyes. His

gorgeous whirlpool eyes. And in them, I saw everything I needed to see. I found strength and happiness flooded my body.

Then, he began to sing with me, and our voices joined in perfect harmony. I knew immediately that this was right. This was meant to be.

"And when you spoke those first few words to me
All I could think was 'Man she hates me'
Then you walked over at sunset
Hair wild, eyes wide, and if I haven't said it yet
The world melts away whenever our eyes meet
Every breath is a promise of something to come
Your smile, your smile, will always be the key
To bring my heart back from where it went numb."

Our gazes were locked as Christian stood from the stool and stepped off-stage. My heart was thumping so hard, I thought it might be heard over the song.

Christian walked towards me slowly, slowly. There was an incredible, anticipatory silence from the audience as we met in the middle, on the dance floor. The crowd formed a circle around us.

"For better and for worse, I was yours from the start
Like two shooting stars colliding makes sparks
Because with you, with you,
I'm finally where I belong."

I threw myself into the song, into the words. And I meant each and every one of them.

When the song came to an end, our voices and the guitar faded into silence. Then, the audience burst into applause. But I could barely hear it because I was looking at Christian and he was looking at me, and it was like we'd only been singing to each other. Like it was just the two of us.

He took my hand and we faced the crowd, and I laughed as those familiar sparks raced up my arm.

Because the song Christian had written—the one we'd perfected together—told the story of us.

A story I wanted to live forever.

I glanced at the people surrounding us—my closest friends and family, my community. Ella, Austin, Grace and Nicholas were closest, their eyes shining. My parents stood off to the side with beaming smiles. The Applebaums were clapping and cheering alongside Ms. Rodriguez. Pastor McLean was gazing at us knowingly, and I even spotted Mayor Davis with a tear in his eye. I saw Ella's parents, and Austin and Grace's dad, and the girls who worked at Morning Bell and at Austin's Medical Center—Kris and Becca.

And while everyone clapped and cheered, Christian stepped forward and took me in his arms.

"That was a surprise." His gorgeous gravel voice rolled over the words, low enough just for me to hear.

"I am a little proud that I was the one surprising you this time." I winked.

"I'm just glad you're here, JJ," he said this so sincerely, so genuinely, that my heart ached. His eyes darkened as he moved towards me. Then, in front of everyone we knew, his lips met mine in a sweet, heartfelt kiss. A kiss that told me everything I needed to know.

Another kiss for the books.

We stepped away from each other and I blushed furiously as everyone clamored around us. All at once, Christian and I were engulfed in the crowd of people congratulating us and telling us how amazing the performance was.

Through it all, Christian didn't leave my side. And I

didn't leave his. Our hands were clasped tightly together, just like they were meant to be.

"Okay, everyone, let's settle down." Mrs. Applebaum stepped onto the stage. She didn't have a mic—she'd graciously lent me hers for my surprise entrance. But she didn't need one anyway, her booming voice did the trick.

The crowd faced the stage and Mrs. Applebaum shot Christian and me a glower like we'd been bad. I hid my smile behind my hand. "We'll move onto the next performance of the evening, but don't worry, Christian West and JJ Sutton will sing again at the end of the show. So without further ado, I'd like to introduce... Mr. Taylor's Team of Tots!"

A line of kindergartners dressed as elves took to the stage and everyone cheered. But all I was aware of was Christian's hand, warm around mine. I snuck a couple glances up at him, and he caught my eye.

He leaned towards me, and his whisper sent shivers across my skin. "Want to go for a walk?"

I nodded.

We made our way through the crowd, passing by Ella and Grace. They winked at me and I blushed, tucking a strand of hair behind my ear.

Christian and I burst outside, where snowflakes were falling gently. It wasn't too cold, but Christian took off his gray pull-over—the one he'd let me steal—and handed it to me. I slid into it happily, relishing the warmth and the smell of his spicy cologne.

"Thanks," I said shyly.

He wrapped his arms around me, pulled me close, and I clasped my hands behind his neck. Standing here with him, locked together, felt so indescribably perfect. Like we were two puzzle pieces that had fallen magically into place.

He kissed the inside of my wrist. "So, how did it feel?"

"Amazing." I breathed. "Like... destiny or something. Sorry if that's cheesy."

"Not at all." He shook his head. "You did it, J."

"You showed me how." I took a deep breath. "I didn't know what it felt like to believe in myself until I met you. How do you do it?"

He smiled that heart-stopping lopsided grin. "Do what?"

"Trust. Have so much faith in people."

"It isn't hard to have faith when people show you who they truly are. Remember the first time we met?"

"Of course I do. I hated you," I joked.

"You were honest about it." Christian laughed. "But there was something about you, J. The fire in your eyes, the spark in your words. You care a lot—about the people around you, about what you do, about everything. It's one of my favorite things about you."

My heart squeezed at his words and I felt breathless. "I'm so sorry, Christian. I know how that sounded and I want you to know that I would never, ever ask you to choose between me and your music. I regretted my words as soon as I said them. It was so stupid..."

Christian tucked a strand of hair behind my ear. "It's okay."

"No, it's not. You mean the world to me, and the fact that I said that..." I grimaced in disgust, shook my head. "Look, I can't promise that I'll never say something stupid, I can't promise that I won't put my foot in my mouth again. But I want to pledge to you that I will do my best, every single day, to love you the best way I can. Christian, if you'll have me, I'll always, always be yours."

I heard my heartbeat in my ears and I was lightheaded with worry about what he'd say. Instead, he ran a hand gently down my arm, lighting a fire beneath his fingers as his eyes smouldered into mine. All at once, the world seemed to calm down a little.

"J, when we fought in the Barn, I didn't understand where it was all coming from." He took my hand and pressed it to his chest so I could feel his heartbeat beneath his shirt. "You're right—we're two flawed, imperfect people. But I do believe that we're perfect for each other. You're my home, the person I'm meant to be with, and I know that we'll find our way. For better and for worse. Together."

He dipped his head to press a tender kiss on my lips. Just one. But I wanted to lean in, pull him closer, tangle my fingers in his hair. My entire body felt weightless with happiness, like I was floating.

But Christian wasn't done.

He stepped away from me, still holding my hands. "I owe you an explanation too. I'm sorry I ran off to LA like that. I shouldn't have gone without saying goodbye. But I want you to know that I didn't go to LA for me, I went for you."

I blinked. "For me?"

He bit his lip, then stuck his hand into the back pocket of his jeans and pulled out a stack of papers. Held them towards me.

"What're those?"

"It's a contract."

"Contract for what?"

His eyes sparkled. "Your record deal."

My jaw dropped. "Excuse me?"

"That's why I went to LA. I brought our demo to Crown House," he said. "I played them your song and 'Where I Belong,' and they loved it. They loved you. They want to sign you."

I could hardly believe what I was hearing. Was this real?

"That's why I was gone these past few days." He shook his head. "I was in meetings with my lawyers and Crown House's lawyers to get you the fairest deal possible. It's all in the contract, if you want to look at it."

I was beyond floored. "Why?"

"Because this is your dream. And I meant it when I said that I want to help you achieve it." He brought the papers back to his chest, misunderstanding my shocked silence. "And don't feel like you have to do this either. If you don't want to be signed, or you want to be signed with a different label, that's fine. I just want you to know that I want to be with you. No matter where you go or what you want to do. Whether that's staying here in Aston Falls, or moving to LA, or New York, or Paris. I'll do everything I can to make you happy, J."

I cleared my throat. Licked my lips. "I don't know what to say."

"You don't have to say anything. These are just options."

"No, it's not that." My voice cracked. I was completely overcome. "This is beyond anything, Christian..." I trailed off, truly unable to find the words. Because not only did Christian West come back for me, he'd given me something immeasurably precious and valuable.

He'd given me the choice, and the encouragement, to do whatever I wanted—pursue my dreams or leave it all behind.

"Thank you," I said sincerely, from the bottom of my heart. "Thank you so much." I threw my arms around him and held him tight. When I stepped back, a tear rolled down my face. "I never thought I'd get here..."

He wiped the tear tenderly. "Get where?"

"Here. I love you so much, Christian, and I never thought I'd experience this kind of love." I shook my head.

"I always thought love was something that came at the end of a to-do list. Like I had to jump certain hurdles. But you showed me that love isn't about checking boxes. It's not about being perfect or appearing a certain way. It's not even about making someone else happy. Love exists in success and in failure, through weakness and hardship and doubt. It's subconscious and unconditional. Love just *is*."

I placed my hand on Christian's cheek, traced the scruff along his jawline as my eyes scanned his face. I wanted to remember every part of this moment.

He pulled me even closer. "I love you too, Jessica Jade Sutton."

I giggled. "Don't make me throw a snowball at you."

Christian laughed. "For the rest of our lives, JJ. If that's what you want."

I pressed my forehead to his. "It's definitely what I want. I want you. Always."

"Always."

As Christian and I stood together in the falling snow, the sounds of Christmas coming from the party tent, I knew that I was exactly where I belonged, with the person I loved more than anything.

In the end, it turned out that Christian more than my nemesis, more than a country star heartthrob. Christian was my rock when I needed it most, the calm in the eye of a snowstorm. I was his and he was mine. And when he said "always," I had absolutely no doubts, because I'd fight for our always too.

This was in no way our fairytale ending. It was our fairytale beginning.

43

JJ

Four Years Later…

There was nothing quite like Christmas in Aston Falls.

As I looked out the window of our car as we drove through town, I felt a bittersweet pang of longing mixed with pure happiness. Bright, colorful lights danced across Center Street, and crowds of people were milling about, talking and laughing. Snowflakes were falling, landing on pink noses and rosy cheeks. At the far end of the street, the massive Christmas tree stood tall.

I could imagine the smell of chocolate and baked goods, the smoky heat from the fire pits at the riverfront park.

Man, it was good to be home.

A large, warm hand clasped around mine and electricity traveled through my body. Even after four years, those sparks had never faded.

"What're you thinking about, J?" Christian's familiar gravel voice sent shivers across my skin.

"Nothing." I smiled. "I'm just happy we're back."

Christian shot me that beautiful grin and leaned over, planted a kiss on my temple. "It has been awhile."

Precisely seven months and eighteen days. But I wasn't complaining... not really.

Things had been nonstop for Christian and I since we released our second album last year. We'd reached new heights, our songs topping country charts around the world. We were constantly whisked away here and there to do live shows or chat with fans.

In all honesty, I loved it. I loved every minute of our lives together. No less because, at the end of each day, I came home to Christian. We checked in with each other often, took breaks when we needed it. We had a steady flow of work coming in, which made it easier to turn down gigs in favor of more important things.

Like hosting the Aston Falls Christmas Carol, as we'd been doing for the past three years.

After Christian and I purchased some land near my parents' and built our dream house, Ms. Rodriguez seemed happy enough to pass on the baton. Our house was cozy and warm, and built to resemble the Barn—the place both Christian and I had called home for a time.

The best part? There was a big backyard for Georgie.

Who I absolutely could not wait to see. My parents always watched her when Christian and I were in LA or New Orleans or Nashville. They loved George as much as I did, but she would always be my baby.

I snuck a glance at Christian, who smiled back at me. I touched the ring on my finger, the one I'd never taken off. Never even considered taking off.

We finally pulled up in front of our adorable log house with the red slanting roof, and I exhaled a sigh of happiness.

I loved being home for Christmas. Though the lights were on through the house. And smoke was billowing from the chimney. Was someone home?

At that moment, the front door flew open and Ella burst out, Grace hot on her heels.

"JJ!" They jumped on me and we collapsed into the snow, laughing.

"What are you guys doing here?" I asked, thrilled to see my best friends.

"Christian wanted to surprise you," Ella said.

I snuck a peek at the love of my life, who winked, and I bit my lip. This was probably one of my favorite parts of our relationship—Christian kept me on my toes at every turn. "Mission accomplished."

"Come on!" Grace exclaimed. "Let's get you inside. Austin and Nicholas can get the bags, Christian."

My husband smiled easily as he continued to unload our bags. "That's okay. Maybe send them out to help?"

"Done," Grace said, then linked her arm with mine. Ella joined on the other side and our little group walked along the sidewalk to the front door.

"Where are the kids?" I asked as we walked through the hallways of our house, which smelled like a heavenly mix of cinnamon and nutmeg. "Are you guys baking?"

"Thought I'd test out a new Christmas bun recipe for Morning Bell," Grace said. "You have to tell me what you think. Be brutally honest. If it does well in Seattle, we might try it out in the rest of our shops."

"I'll be your guinea pig anytime, Gracie," I said seriously.

Over the past few years, Morning Bell had seen so much success that Grace and Nicholas decided to franchise the cafe. They'd opened coffee shops in Seattle, Bozeman and Portland, and they were planning on expanding into California next. Nicholas had even stepped down as CEO of the national King's Kids programs so that he could focus on Morning Bell. But as chairman, he was still very involved.

Between all of that and their two adorable children, Grace and Nicholas were the happiest and most fulfilled I'd ever seen them.

"To answer your other question, the kids are in here," Ella said as we walked into the living room. Austin and Nicholas were sitting with the kids, who were playing on the carpet in front of the fireplace.

"JJ!" Nicholas said warmly as he gave me a hug. "So good to see you. Christian's outside?"

"He's unloading the bags."

"We'll give him a hand." Austin gave me a quick hug, then he and Nicholas went out to help.

Meanwhile, Gia toddled over and lifted her arms towards Ella, who swooped her onto her hip like her four-year-old child was no lighter than a feather. Baby Isla—Dallas' younger sister who was actually two and no longer a baby—was bouncing around in her playpark, giggling. Grace went over to her and tickled her belly. In the corner, Dallas and Kali were playing together—Kali wearing a crown and bossing around a grumpy Dallas.

Now where had I seen that before?

"Sit, take a load off," Ella said. "It sounds like you and Christian have been busy. How's it all going?"

My friends and I caught up for a while, gathered around the fire with cups of hot cocoa that Grace had brought from the kitchen. It was her family recipe—her dad had finally given it up two Christmases ago and I was beyond thrilled about it.

Ella told us all about her new business venture. She'd recently left *The Weekly Best* and started her own news site.

With her focus on delivering hard-hitting but positive, meaningful news, her site was taking off. And Austin's Medical Center? It was fast becoming a leader in state-of-the-art medical care across the country.

All that to say that there was a lot to celebrate this Christmas.

And I hadn't even shared our biggest news yet. I'd wait for Christian to do that.

"Guess what. Construction on the roadway finally started in October." Grace rolled her eyes. "Imagine how happy Mayor Davis was... only to have it blizzard the next day."

I shook my head. "Poor Mayor Davis. But at least it's coming together."

"Finally." Ella sipped at her hot cocoa. "You and Christian ready for the Christmas party tomorrow?"

"Not to mention your anniversary?" Grace asked with a shimmy.

I blushed, tucked my hair behind my ear. Yes, Christian and I got married on Christmas Eve two years ago. There was more than one reason that I loved Christmas. "Absolutely. I'd marry that man again in a heartbeat."

"Now that's what I like to hear." Christian's warm voice was quickly followed by his sitting next to me on our cozy couch. He kissed my temple. "For the record, I guess I'd marry you again too."

"Oh yeah?" I asked, gazing at my husband. "Because you have to, right?"

"No." Christian laughed. "Because I'd want to. Any day. Every day."

"Okay, okay, we get it." Ella laughed. "You two are living your happily-ever-after."

Christian's eyes didn't leave mine. "Just about."

I took a deep breath. It was time.

"Guys, we have some news," I said quietly as Christian and I faced our friends. "We're going to be staying in Aston Falls a little longer this time around."

"You're staying?" Ella leaned forward eagerly. "For how long?"

"A while." I shot Christian a glance and he nodded. "I'm pregnant."

Ella almost fell off the couch. "You what?! I thought you guys didn't want kids right away. Wanted to focus on your careers and all that."

"We did." Christian smiled at me. "But we both realized that we wanted to start our family too."

Tears of happiness stung my eyes as I looked at our friends. We'd told my parents last week, sworn them not to tell anyone. But now that my friends knew the news, it felt all the more real. Ella, Grace, Austin and Nicholas jumped into action, hugging me and Christian in turn. Dallas, Kali and Gia wanted to be part of the fun, and we hugged them too.

As I sat and laughed with my friends on the evening before another Christmas, I knew that this was the happiest I'd ever been. And I could almost laugh at the fact that I'd finally attained all of the things on that old checklist of mine. But it was better than I could've ever imagined, because the checklist included everything I'd dreamed of. I had the house I'd always wanted, a career I thought was too good to be true, and I would finally be a mom. Finally have a family of my own.

Not to mention the fact that I had the love of my life, my perfect prince, by my side.

Our story had more than a few twists and turns. More than a few surprises. But if I'd learned anything, it was that love just is. It couldn't be controlled, couldn't be managed. For better and for worse.

I was meant to come to Aston Falls in freshman year and become friends with Ella and Grace. I was meant to experience heartbreak. I was meant to meet Christian West in the river and to fall in love with him. And whatever happened next, I knew that Christian and I were solid. We would always find our way. Together.

Thank you for reading!

If you enjoyed the story, I'd appreciate if you were able to leave a review! As a new author, reviews mean everything to me, and I'm so grateful for each and every one of them.

Made in the USA
Las Vegas, NV
14 December 2022